The Touch of Ghosts

By the Same Author

Winter's End

The Touch of Ghosts

JOHN RICKARDS

MICHAEL JOSEPH
an imprint of
PENGUIN BOOKS

MICHAEL JOSEPH

Published by the Penguin Group
Penguin Books Ltd, 80 Strand, London WC2R ORL, England
Penguin Group (USA) Inc., 375 Hudson Street, New York, New York 10014, USA
Penguin Books Australia Ltd, 250 Camberwell Road, Camberwell, Victoria 3124, Australia
Penguin Books Canada Ltd, 10 Alcorn Avenue, Toronto, Ontario, Canada M4V 3B2
Penguin Books India (P) Ltd, 11 Community Centre, Panchsheel Park, New Delhi – 110 017, India
Penguin Books (NZ) Ltd, Cnr Rosedale and Airborne Roads, Albany, Auckland, New Zealand
Penguin Books (South Africa) (Pty) Ltd, 24 Sturdee Avenue, Rosebank 2196, South Africa

Penguin Books Ltd, Registered Offices: 80 Strand, London WC2R ORL, England

www.penguin.com

First published 2004
1

Set in 13.5/16 pt Monotype Garamond
Typeset by Rowland Phototypesetting Ltd,
Bury St Edmunds, Suffolk
Printed in Great Britain by Clays Ltd, St Ives plc

A CIP catalogue record for this book is available from the British Library

ISBN 0-718-14649-2

'I sit beside my lonely fire and pray for wisdom yet:
for calmness to remember or courage to forget.'

– Charles Hamilton Aide

Acknowledgements

Many thanks to my editor, Beverley Cousins, whose mammoth efforts here definitely deserve some kind of award. Thanks also to Louise Moore, Clare Pollock, Rob Williams, Grainne Ashton, Lucy Upton and everyone else at Penguin for all their support with everything; to Luigi Bonomi and everyone at Sheil Land for all the tireless work they continue to do on my behalf; to the Mystery Writers' Forum, again, for all the help and suggestions; and to all the guys back home.

Lastly, thanks once more to Kate for putting up with all this madness.

Prologue

A jewel-clear summer's day. The kind they photograph and sell to tourists on postcards for fifty cents apiece. The late morning sun is a burning ember, a relentless, blazing diamond pinned against empty blue. Acetylene-white light washes over weathered mountain crags that pierce a vast rumpled blanket of forest. It glitters like frost from dozens of lakes and rivers.

Closer, the same light flashes from the glistening plumage of a bird diving for fish in one of these lakes and from its struggling rainbow-scaled catch. It dances from the wings of dozens of insects flitting through the trees surrounding the water. It sparkles in the hair of a running woman.

She sprints across an open stretch of wild grass, a narrow break in the tangled forest, carving a swathe of darker green bent and broken stalks in her wake. Her heart pounds against her ribcage, threatening to punch through it with every beat. Her breath burns her throat as she gulps for air. She can feel her backpack slamming into her spine with each stride, flattening her shirt against her sweat-soaked skin. She ignores it all, waiting instead for the sound she dreads.

Running footsteps, behind her. Sneakers smashing through the grass. The man has followed her downstairs and out through the doors, no shouting, no calls – silent all the way. She knows he's no cop – they shout 'Freeze!' or 'Hold it!' don't they? They *pursue*, they don't *chase*.

More than anything, she wishes she'd never taken a look at the old building with the sagging roof, wishes that her will alone was enough to rewrite the past. Wishes she could wake up from what *has* to be a dream.

Thin, spidery branches rattle against her jeans and whip her face and arms, tracing needle-thin lines of fire on her skin. The air changes, becoming cooler and carrying the acid scent of leaf mulch. The ground beneath the canopy is rough and uneven. Roots and tough, wiry vines lurk in the plant litter that covers the floor, ready to snag her feet as she pounds past.

She could have run for the dirt track, but she saw the man had a car parked outside. She could have made for the lake-shore, hoping that someone from town would see her from the opposite bank, but she knows how far away it is. She can feel the distance, the open gulf between her and safety, tugging at her soul and threatening to swallow her entirely. Her only hope is the highway, north through the woods.

She thinks of the look on her pursuer's face when she turned a corner in the ramshackle structure and nearly walked into him. Panic. Suspicion that mirrored hers. Eyes glittering in the musty gloom. The faint sheen coming from his open jacket, dim light sliding off the gun nestled by his shoulder. How his expression changed when he realized she'd seen it. 'I'm a cop.' His accent not local, voice getting higher, betraying the lie. Didn't offer to show her a badge. Feeling his eyes on her as she walked slowly and deliberately towards the stairs, trying to look like she believed him. Hearing him gasp as her nerve broke and she started running, uncomfortably aware of how alone she was.

Muscles burning as her legs pump up a gentle incline, eyes concentrating on the ground in front of her. Breath increasingly ragged, hacking and blowing. Trying to maintain her pace, to ignore her tiring body. Can't even hear the man's footsteps over the roaring of blood in her ears.

A flash of blackness explodes from her jaw and suddenly she can taste dirt, feel dry, dead leaves against her cheek, head swimming. Her mouth feels warm and coppery, one of her teeth shakes and pulls sickeningly as she squirms, trying to drag herself to her feet again. Weight, heavy against the small of her back, stops her and her limbs feel awkward and rubbery.

As she opens her mouth and the first notes of her scream erupt from within, a hand snatches at her hair, hauling her head back by a thousand tiny points of white-hot pain. Metal, cold, thin and sharp touches the skin of her neck.

In the microseconds it takes for the knife to draw a line of liquid ice across her throat she thinks about her parents, waving as she pulled away in the taxi bound for the airport. She thinks about her two-year-old cousin Charlie, playing with his birthday presents. She pictures her friends from college and how she won't be able to enjoy graduation with them. She tries to remember them all, one last time.

Her ravaged arteries pump and sputter blood across the forest floor, leaving a clear path for her soul to follow after.

Crying bundle of newborn joy.

Photo in a yearbook.

Face on a milk carton.

Name on a grave.

I

A lecture theatre much like any other. Rows of padded benches spread up towards the low, wide windows at the back of the room, surrounding the dais at the bottom like the seats of a Roman amphitheatre. Forty, maybe fifty men and women are scattered around the auditorium – concentrated, I note with an inward smile, in the first five or six rows. If I'd been holding this presentation at college, the back couple of rows would be packed and only half the students would actually be listening. Here I can't see anyone whose eyes aren't on the man speaking next to me or on the notepaper in front of them. Times change.

'Your instructors at the Academy may have told you that there are two broad types of suspect,' Robin Garrett, the man by my side, is saying. My boss; a friend I just happen to work with. 'There's those who just want to get their guilt off their chest. Even if it takes you a while to get the whole story out of them, you'll get your confession, because they want to confide in someone. And there are those who will clam up and won't give you a damn thing.'

The people who've shown up here on a dreary Thursday evening at the start of November to hear our words of wisdom are mostly trainees from Boston's Police Academy. The rest are newly graduated police officers willing to sacrifice an hour or two of their spare time on the chance it'll boost their conviction rates and help them make detective.

'The ones who eventually break down and give you everything they've got aren't a problem,' Rob continues. 'It's the second kind, whether they're experienced criminals or just plain stubborn, that'll make you work for every ounce of truth you can get.'

If I listen hard every time Rob pauses for breath, I can hear hail smashing like handfuls of pebbles against the windows at the back, even over the electrical hum of the projector illuminating the screen behind us. Every gust of wind brings a fresh batch. Rhythmic, like a heartbeat or the sound of a hundred hourglasses being turned over at once.

'Alex will speak in a little while about interrogation techniques and matching your approach to the individual suspect. That's his field. Mine is the proper preparation beforehand to maximize your chances of success, whether you're after a confession or just information.'

Every once in a while we do this. Boston PD pays us a small but reasonable amount to give evening lectures to rookie recruits and patrol division newbies desperate to get their shield. We pass on our experience – Rob as an ex-FBI field agent, myself as a one-time specialist in the Bureau's NCAVC violent crimes division. In return, we maintain our good relationship with Boston PD, and they get cops with a slightly broader degree of training. Everyone's happy.

'If you make sure you have as much relevant evidence and information to hand as possible before you even open your mouth, you'll have more chance of cutting through any bullshit and lies they try to feed you. You may even be able to make them think you know more than you do and trick them into giving themselves up.' He pauses for effect. 'Just make sure you get it right.'

Rob taps a key on the laptop in front of him and the glow from the screen behind me changes colour. I know without turning around that he's showing them a picture of twenty-three-year-old Bernard Leon, charged with murder in

Phoenix two years previously. This is Rob's part of the show. Now that the introduction is out of the way, he'll run the audience through two examples where police have had to rely on confession evidence to make their case, one failure and one success. After the story of the botched Leon investigation, he'll tell them about Dan Rothman, a career criminal suspected of holding up a Detroit jewellery store. The detective who eventually wrung a confession out of Rothman, along with the subsequent successful prosecution, was given a promotion as a result.

I glance down at my watch, trying to hide the motion from the people listening to Rob. Like the rest of Boston, it's a non-smoking building. I'll have to wait until the lecture's finished and we've gone through all the usual questions and chat at the end before I can light up. My girlfriend recently began trying to persuade me to cut my thirty-a-day habit, so far without success. I just don't have the willpower, although the inclination is growing as it becomes harder to smoke anywhere but at home.

Look back up at the windows. Three feet high, six across. Black mail-slot gaps gazing out into darkness. Tiny silver lights twinkle and flicker across them as though there's a clear starlit night out there, not specks of sleet reflecting the lights of the city as they dribble down the glass. My mind wanders as I watch countless drops of icy water trickle and die. I think about groceries I've got to buy, laundry I've got to do. I think about the weekend.

'And now Alex Rourke will discuss the different interrogation techniques themselves,' Rob says, bringing me back to the present. 'They're all yours, Alex.'

I stand up and quickly run my part of the lecture over in my head. A hundred-odd eyes blink and glitter at me as I begin.

*

An hour and a half later, the last of the newest additions to Boston's police force have filtered away, leaving the two of us to pack up and head for home. I've just dropped the laptop back in its holdall when the door at the side of the room opens again to admit Lieutenant Aidan Silva, a man who always reminds me of a bear given human form. A mop of chestnut hair matched by a bristling beard flecked grey by the advancing years, and between them a round, heavy nose and a pair of dark, sunken eyes. How and when he and Rob became friends, I don't know. They shake hands before Silva leans over and offers me a paw.

'I don't know what your people have been putting in their food, Aidan,' Rob says as he stuffs our notes into a bag, 'but we actually had some intelligent questions at the end. Caught me by surprise.'

Silva grins, baring his teeth. 'I hear there's a couple of them can walk and chew gum at the same time, too,' he responds. 'Better hope it's not the start of a trend, otherwise I'll be obsolete in a couple of years.'

'You and me both. We'll end up in a retirement home together. Alex can come look after us and make sure our copies of *Sports Illustrated* are kept up to date. What's on your mind?'

'Jolene's decided to invite some people round for dinner and drinks on Saturday night,' the lieutenant says. 'I figured I'd see if the two of you were free. She doesn't want it to be an all-Department gathering, so I need as many non-cop friends there as I can lay my hands on. Otherwise, I'll have to make small talk with the neighbours.' He shudders.

'Sounds good to me,' Rob says. 'How about you, Alex?'

I shrug. 'I'll have to check. Gemma's coming down tomorrow night so it'll be up to her whether we're there or not.'

'Well, if she fancies a drink Saturday, my place at eight,' Silva says. 'I'll see you guys then, or not.'

I give him a wave as he ambles out through the doors, then go back to making sure we've not forgotten anything. Rob and I head out to the parking lot, instinctively hunching once we've left the shelter of the building and face the full fury of the elements.

'You got anything else planned for this evening?' Rob asks as though we don't both have cold water seeping rapidly past our collars and under our shirts.

'Tidying,' I say, sweeping back my hair where it's become plastered to my forehead. 'I've got to get the apartment neat before Gemma gets here.'

'Don't wear yourself out. You've got to meet a client first thing tomorrow.'

I grimace in mock pain as he drops into his car, then hurry over to mine, trying not to drown. Even in the downpour, my pale blue 1969 Stingray Corvette – a gas-guzzling piece of history that I hardly ever use in Boston – cuts a sleek form, its almost aquatic lines making it seem totally at home in the wet. I dive into its welcoming interior and sit for a moment, wiping water out of my eyes and trying to think warm thoughts. Run-off from the roof sluices down the windshield in front of me, laced with ice crystals that melt and vanish as I watch. Rob's tail lights blur red as his car pulls out of the lot, then disappear altogether.

Only then do I snap out of my trance and fumble in my well-worn tan leather jacket for a pack of smokes.

At two minutes to nine the following morning I reach the door of the building that houses our company. A five-storey red-brick edifice that, though not hugely inspiring, is smart enough to look good on the brochures Rob occasionally throws together for potential clients. There are a couple of copies of that very same promotional literature in the lobby, alongside similar efforts belonging to the other five firms renting space here.

Robin Garrett Associates, the copperplate text on the cover reads. *Licensed private investigators, process servers, business security and criminal consultants.* Most of these end up in the nervous hands of small corporate outfits with problem employees, suspected low-level fraudsters or other sources of the white-collar work which is one of our two main money-spinners. The second field we specialize in – again, something the police would in theory handle if they didn't usually have more pressing problems – is missing persons. Being a college town, Boston has its fair share of students who drop out and, when their parents make their feelings on the matter clear, stop keeping in touch with their families back home. Once things have cooled down, people sometimes need help locating their errant offspring, which is where we come in.

Then there are non-student missing persons cases, which are much more difficult and which have a much smaller clear-up rate. I'm pretty sure this morning's is going to be one of those, if the preliminary information our secretary Jean gathered over the phone is correct.

Jean herself has just settled into her seat when I step out of the elevator and head for the office. I doubt that Rob or any of our three junior staff are in yet. She smiles at me and says, 'Morning, Alex.'

'It is, and I'm certainly feeling it,' I reply. 'My body clock keeps telling me I should still be dozing.'

'Rough night? How did the lecture go?'

'Okay, same as usual. But then I had to spend three hours tidying my apartment. It was midnight before I got to sleep.'

She shakes her head. 'Next time a client calls I'll tell them we can't make any early appointments because none of the staff crawls out of bed before noon. I hate depriving you of your beauty sleep.'

'Thanks, Jean. That sounds like a great idea. I'll mention it to Rob.'

She laughs as I walk past her, into our airy squad-room-style office. Relatively uncluttered, but still with all the furnishings any self-respecting small business should have. I'm a little disappointed to see that Kathryn, one of our junior staff – 'the kids' – has beaten me in. The feeling quickly fades when I realize it's given her time to get the coffee machine on and ready. I help myself to a cup before I've even sat down. There's barely time to find a place to put it amongst the drifts of paper covering my desk when the phone rings on its internal circuit. The client is here.

I look up as the door at the far end of the room opens and a woman somewhere in her forties steps hesitantly over the threshold. Dark hair now going grey, neatly tied back out of her eyes. Steel-rimmed glasses on a lined, tired-looking face. Emerald green wool coat, charcoal sweater and matching pants. Sensible shoes. All of it looks fairly new. Over her shoulder is a brown leather bag.

On the desk in front of me is a short list of Jean's handwritten preliminary notes, based on what the client said when she called us.

Colleen Webb.
Son Adam (25) last heard of nearly two months ago – Burlington, VT.
Husband dead – car wreck – six months ago.
Moving out of old neighbourhood – insurance money.
Can't find son to tell him/discuss with him.
And, in Rob's handwriting:
Don't think she's a time-waster. See what you can do.

At the bottom is her phone number and address in Roxbury. I slide the note underneath a stack of old paperwork and stand to greet her. When she shakes my hand, her palm feels damp and papery but her grip is firm. I give her my best professional smile and offer her a seat.

'Mrs Webb, I'm Alex Rourke. How can we help?'

She sits very straight, with her bag clasped on her lap. Hazel eyes dart quickly over my desk, me, the rest of the office, as she replies. 'It's about my son Adam. He hasn't been in touch in months and I haven't been able to get hold of him.'

'Where was he last time you spoke to him?'

'A place called Burlington in Vermont. I don't know if he was living there or not. He travelled around.'

'Did he have a regular job?'

Mrs Webb shakes her head. 'I don't think so. He used to pick up work now and then, but he never said anything to me about settling down. When we spoke last, he said he was a tour guide. But that was back in August, and I don't know if it would have been for much longer.'

'Did he ever mention a girlfriend or anyone else he knew up there?' I manage to knock back a couple of mouthfuls of coffee while I wait for her answer. In the end, she shakes her head.

'No. At least, I don't think so.'

'Does your family have any relatives in the north-east outside Boston? Anywhere he might have gone?'

'There's just me now. My husband Billy died six months ago. Him and Adam never got on; I think that's mostly why he left, and never came to see us. I thought, now Billy's gone and everything, he might like to come and stay with me for a while. I'm moving to a proper house with the insurance, so there'd have been no problem putting him up.' She looks down at her lap and trails off into silence.

'Okay, Mrs Webb. I've got some standard questions that I have to ask. Don't take offence at any of them.'

She nods.

'Have you told the authorities, filed a missing persons report with the police, things like that? If not, you should.'

'I spoke to the Vermont State Police. That was a month ago. They haven't done anything.'

I grab a pen. 'Do you remember who you spoke to? I'll give them a call and see if they've turned anything up.'

'I've got his name somewhere,' she says, reaching into her bag. After a couple of moments' search, she emerges with a crumpled piece of paper. 'His name was Detective Sergeant Karl Flint. I told him everything I knew.'

'Okay. Has your son ever had any trouble with the law, been involved with drugs, anything like that?'

'Not since he left Boston. Not as far as I know. He grew up in a rough neighbourhood, Mr Rourke. Things happen.'

'And how regularly did he normally keep in touch with you?'

She frowns and her lips pinch together. 'You think I'm panicking over nothing? You think I'm just a stupid woman who can't bear to let her boy out of her sight?'

'No, I don't,' I say, trying to placate her. 'But I've got to ask. I've got to know whether or not this is unusual for him, or if he's ever dropped out of view before.'

'He'd call at least every couple of weeks. And always when he was moving anyplace new.'

Without prompting, she reaches into the bag again and pulls out a couple of slightly grainy photographs. 'That's Adam,' she says, passing them to me. 'They're the most recent ones I could find, but they're still a couple of years old. Sorry.'

The pictures show a young man with short, windblown

black hair and narrow, gaunt features, but the photos were taken from too far away and are too poor quality to get more than a general idea of his face. No distinguishing marks. Even eye colour is difficult, though I'd guess his are the same as his mother's. In both shots he's wearing a cream-coloured jacket with red flashes at the collar, pockets and cuffs. I can't make out any jewellery, a watch or anything else distinctive enough to stand out. Background is an interchangeable town skyline, different in both.

'Does he have any tattoos, piercings, scars, anything that might help identify him?' I ask.

'I don't know what else he's got now, but he used to have a tattoo of a wolf on his right arm.'

Nod and make a note. 'If it's okay with you, I'll need to keep these photos for now. If you've got any letters, cards, anything he's sent you in the past year or so, I'd like to see those too. Also the names of any friends here in Boston or anywhere else he might still be in touch with.'

'I'll see what I can do.' Mrs Webb accepts one of my business cards. She glances behind her as Keith, the second of the three 'kids', precedes Rob into the office. Rob nods to me as he takes off his coat and heads for his desk, which sits opposite mine. 'Do you think you'll be able to find him, Mr Rourke?'

I shrug. 'Honestly, I don't know, Mrs Webb. It all depends on why he disappeared. If he's just switched jobs and forgot to call, yeah, I don't think it'll be too difficult. Same if he's taken ill or been in some kind of accident.' I sigh and look directly into her eyes. 'But if he's on the run from some kind of trouble, or if anything worse has happened to him, it could well be that we never find him. The overall odds of tracing someone who's been gone for more than a couple of weeks aren't good at all, which is why most missing persons cases have a low priority with the police. It's not nice to hear, but it's the truth.'

She nods and seems to relax a little. 'Were you ever a cop?' she asks. 'You sound like you were in the police.'

'I was in the FBI, so was Rob Garrett.' I gesture at his desk. 'I left four, nearly five years ago.'

'Why? If you don't mind me asking,' she adds.

'Health reasons,' I say. 'Then Rob offered me a job in the private sector.' I don't elaborate. I don't tell her about my parents being killed, about the stress at work, psychotic episodes, hallucinations, my breakdown, spending time in an institution. I don't tell her I burnt out at thirty-two. I don't tell her that there have been times since when I've worried I might be losing it again. I don't tell her that I couldn't handle the pressure of working violent crimes which is why I ended up looking for runaway kids and office workers who steal petty nickel-and-dime amounts from their employers. I don't tell her that until I met Gemma a year and a half ago, I used to go home every night to an empty apartment, an empty life, because I couldn't see myself doing anything else, didn't want the responsibility.

I don't tell her because it doesn't pay to dent a client's confidence. Not before they've paid the bill.

She smiles. 'I'll call you if I find something that might help. Is there anything else you need?'

'When you spoke to Jean over the phone did she explain how our charges work and how much you can expect to pay?'

'She did, and it's no problem, Mr Rourke.'

'In that case, that's all for now. We'll keep you posted.'

We shake hands again, then I show her to the door. When I return to my desk, Rob says, 'So, what do you think?'

'This is either going to be pretty straightforward, or he's vanished for good. No middle way. It'll depend what the

State Police have found, if anything, and whether he's got any easy-to-contact friends.'

'I figured it'd be simple for you to check out the Vermont locals next time you're up in the wilds. If Gemma'll put up with you for an extra couple of days, that is.'

I smile half-mockingly, partly in response to his comment about Gemma, partly because of his insistence that any place that doesn't have its own international airport is dangerously rural and therefore an alien environment. Rob is from Chicago and as much of an urbanite as I've ever found, even if most of what he says is just part of his witty repertoire, not genuine prejudice.

'It'll be quite a drive down to Burlington from where she lives,' I say. 'But it'll be easier than doing it from here. I'll see if she can put me up next weekend and into the week after. Meantime, I'll give Detective Flint from the VSP a call, see how things stand from the police end.'

'Sure. Can Gemma tell you whether the kid's been brought in dead at all?'

'If the Office of the Chief Medical Examiner's had anything to do with it, yeah, she should be able to find out. Certainly if it came through Gemma's particular region. But we'd probably have to look for John Does since if he was identified, they should have contacted his family.'

My girlfriend, the pathologist. Regional Medical Examiner for a chunk of northern Vermont, when she's not dealing with day-to-day deaths in the small town of Newport, where she works. We don't normally talk shop, but I make a mental note to ask about Adam Webb when I see her this evening.

'If Mrs Webb doesn't come back with anything today and you don't get anything spectacular from Flint, there's not likely to be anything else to do on her son's case for the time being,' Rob says.

'In which case, once I've got what I can out of the way, I'll do that report for Barnes & Ziccarelli, then I'll head for home.'

'You taking her out to dinner?'

I shake my head, smiling. 'I'm cooking.'

'I never thought I'd see the day. Microwave chicken, is it?'

I eventually reach Detective Sergeant Karl Flint through the Vermont State Police switchboard on the third attempt; he's spent most of the morning at the scene of a hit-and-run, away from his desk. When I explain my reasons for calling, he sighs.

'Look, Mr Rourke, you know how it is with these cases,' he says. His voice is light and quite high, but with an edge to it. 'When the guy's mother spoke to us, we got what we could out of her. I made a couple of phone calls, checked with Burlington PD, asked them to have a look anywhere that kind of transient might hang out. I had his photo sent to Amtrak, Burlington airport, taxi firms, just to see if anyone remembered him. We've had nothing back, no one's seen him, and I've got higher priorities than one guy who's most likely moved out of state.'

'Yeah, I know, and I explained it to her when she came to see us. Did you run him through the system?'

'He's got a record, but nothing other than juveniles. Nothing on his driver's licence. Nothing on tax he might be paying as an employee, but he's not on welfare. He doesn't have any credit cards, and the last time he used an ATM was back before he was reported missing. Unless this guy gets arrested or shows his face somewhere someone knows him, my guess is he'll stay vanished.' Flint pauses, then says, 'I wish you the best of luck, Mr Rourke, but I don't think I can be much help.'

'Could you fax down whatever you've got on his movements? It might not be much, but it could help. It'll also mean I won't have to go over the same ground as you.'

He thinks for a moment. 'Sure, I don't see any harm in that. You'll have to fax me something in writing first, just to confirm who you are and that whatever confidential information we've got stays confidential. Otherwise, be my guest.'

We exchange numbers, then I say goodbye to the detective and hang up. By noon, I have copies of all the information the VSP has on Adam Webb, and it doesn't amount to much. It'll save me the bother of having to go down several investigative dead-ends, but that's about it, and that's all I can do for now. I throw together a missing persons sheet on Webb anyway and print off a batch of copies in case they'll be useful.

By four in the afternoon, I've done some grocery shopping and gone home to await the only person in this world that I love.

2

I met Dr Gemma Larson while helping out Aroostook County Sheriff's Department on a murder case in the far north of Maine. At the time, she was the county's part-time medical examiner. I didn't exactly sweep her off her feet – I was too nervous and afraid of screwing up to dive right in – but we clicked straight away once we'd taken the plunge and embarked on our first date. No secret, no memory was too private or too deeply held to share. None of it seemed to matter, so long as we were together. After my breakdown I hadn't believed any woman would want to trust herself with a burned-out failure. Gemma therefore represented something I hadn't believed possible – a normal family life, something I could anchor myself to beyond the confines of my own existence. Someone I could love without worrying about what I was leading her into, without worrying whether she really knew me. And I've been in love with her for the eighteen-odd months that have passed since.

In April she managed to land a post at Kingdom Hospital in Newport, Vermont, and with it the role of one of the state's Regional Medical Examiners, just so she could be closer to me. It's still a three-hour drive to where she lives from Boston, but it was six to Houlton in Maine. We spend every weekend together, and I've been known to drive up to hers after work sometimes, just because a few hours with her is better than an evening home alone.

Ours is a relationship conducted at some distance, but it works. It makes every moment we have together that much more important, and every feeling that much more intense. I thought I was happy enough before I met her, but all I had was a pale imitation of a life.

I hear Gemma's car pull up outside, giving me a few seconds before she walks in through the door. Enough time to check my hair in the mirror over the mantel – a mess, but nothing unusually bad – and quickly look over the lounge to make sure everything is tidy. I grab a bunch of flowers from where they've been sitting in a vase on the coffee table with one hand and the package next to them with the other as I hear her key scrape in the lock.

Gemma comes through the door with her face hidden in a haze of shoulder-length gold, swamped in a woollen coat and fighting to keep a holdall and her purse under control. She drops both on the carpet and sweeps back her spider-silk fine hair. Only then does she see me, hovering by the sofa, and smile. The expression isn't as quick as it used to be, it's broader and longer lasting, but it's as delicate as the rest of her. Elfin, fragile-looking features, brilliant green eyes, a figure to match the face. At thirty-three, nearly four years younger than me. When she's happy I can almost see the feeling radiate from her. It's how I like to think of her whenever we're apart.

When I bring out the flowers from behind my back she laughs and says, 'Oh, Alex. You didn't need to get me those.'

'What can I say? I'm a born romantic. Plus there's this.' I hand her the long, narrow gift-wrapped box.

She tears off the paper, opens the gift and her eyes widen, soften, when she sees the necklace inside. Delicate silver chain, pendant that's either a flower, a bird or a pair of linked hands, depending on how you look at it, set with a single small stone.

She holds it up to the light and watches it dance for a moment, then says, 'It's lovely.'

We kiss long and deeply, holding each other tight. I run my hands down her sides, feeling the shape of her body beneath the coat, the curves of her figure as it tapers towards her waist and then out over her hips. I can feel every breath she takes, every tiny movement as she presses against me.

Eventually, we break away. She gives me a playful half-smile and says, 'So where's my chocolates to go with them? Don't tell me you forgot.'

I grin. 'The store sold out, so I figured I'd have to do you an entire dinner instead. Three courses, wine, the whole nine yards.'

'Three?'

'Well, you can help yourself to cookies while I'm working on the main event. Think of them as an appetizer.'

Gemma slaps me playfully on the shoulder and immediately wraps her arms around me again. 'So what are we having? I can't smell anything cooking.'

'I didn't know what time you'd be here, so I haven't started yet. Eventually, it'll be salmon in a mushroomy sauce with banoffee pie afterwards. The pie's not my own work; I bought frozen.'

'No one's perfect.' She starts to shrug out of her coat. 'Since you're going to be slaving away over a hot stove, I think I'll ditch this and then have a quick shower, if you don't mind.'

I slip my hands around her waist, underneath her sweater and shirt. 'Depends if I'm allowed to join you or not.'

'You keep your hands to yourself,' she scolds, laughing and shooing me away. 'I expect to be fed on my return.'

I salute and bow my head. 'Yes, ma'am. Whatever you say, ma'am.'

Gemma smiles, quick and sharp, and squeezes my hand. 'I'm all yours once dinner's out of the way, though.'

'Looking forward to it, ma'am.' I give her a quick kiss on the cheek and smile. 'Get out of here, you. I've got a recipe to decipher.'

When Gemma talks about her week over dinner, I take the opportunity to bring up Adam Webb. I show her the photos of him and ask if she can check whether he's turned up in any of the state's morgues.

'Who is he?' she asks.

'A drifter, I think. Grew up here in the city but moved away. His mom's looking for him. Those photos are old; he's about twenty-five now.'

'Can I take one of them back with me? I'll show it around.'

'Sure. If it's no problem.'

She smiles and shakes her head. 'It'll do me good, looking so diligent. There's talk that Dr Kirkland could retire in a few months, which would leave the Deputy Chief ME's post open.'

'You've only been there seven months and you're already looking for promotion? I never knew I was going out with such a career-minded girl.'

'Hey, it can't do any harm, making a name for myself. The higher up you are, the more interesting jobs you get.'

'Fair enough,' I say. 'You're not getting anything interesting at the moment then?'

She sips her wine and I offer her a refill. She nods, blonde hair shimmering in the soft light. 'I'm busy, in a way. I might have to do an autopsy on a kid killed in a hit-and-run when I go back on Monday. The State Police think it may have been something to do with the heroin trade, and the impact might have been a way of covering up some other damage. Blood screens, forensics, everything.'

'Is that kind of thing common?'

'Not the killing.' She spears the last remaining piece of

fish with her fork. 'But heroin's huge all over Vermont. Well, as huge as anything can be in such a quiet place.'

The conversation moves on to other things, stopping altogether once we've eaten dessert and drunk the last of the wine. Then Gemma takes me in her arms once again and reminds me of one more reason why I love her.

The following evening we go to Aidan Silva's gathering at his home in Cambridge, known mostly for being Boston's university hub. Aidan's wife Jolene is in full hostess mode, taking coats, thrusting drinks under the noses of newcomers and merrily performing any necessary introductions in her Houston twang. A few of Aidan's friends from the force have turned up. Rob has brought his wife Teresa, a round, jovial woman whom I know from experience is more than a match for her husband's wit. Then there are some of the Silvas' neighbours – faces and names quickly merging into one interchangeable set – and a half-dozen or so friends of Jolene's, who cluck and fuss over every couple as they arrive; I guess it's part of their usual routine for meeting strangers. Oh, she's ever so nice. Oh, I hope you're making sure he treats you like a princess. Oh, aren't you just lovely together. Just as I'm thinking we'll never escape our turn in the spotlight, they see that one of the neighbours is pregnant and descend on her en masse, leaving Gemma and me to hide somewhere out of the way.

Drinks flow and the details blur. Expectant faces, waiting for the punchline to a joke. The same faces open in laughter. Change the joke, change the comedian, a dozen times or more. Reel out the guys from the department and a handful of amusing anecdotes from recent memory. Get briefly trapped with complete strangers and all anyone seems able to ask is,

'What business're you in?' and, 'What do you drive?' Score points with my answers on both counts, but move on before our reserves of small talk are depleted. Stand in circles with the guys I know best, the same guys I always end up standing with at parties, telling the same stories and reminiscences as every other time we're together.

At midnight, Gemma slips her arm around my waist and whispers, 'Let's go home.' We make our excuses and walk the three-quarters of a mile back, across the Charles River, to my apartment near Kenmore Square.

We've barely got through the front door before I lose myself in Gemma. The scent of honey in her hair, still detectable even after an evening out, the warmth and the feel of her body where it presses against mine. My heartbeat or ours, I can't tell. The soft cries that escape her lips. The peace, a contended tiredness, as we lie together afterwards, holding each other.

Sunday passes quickly, despite my efforts to make it last. When we eventually get up, I take Gemma to lunch at a Greek restaurant near the city centre. We stroll home through the Back Bay Fens, enjoying the quiet. All too soon, night falls and Gemma has to leave me for another week. Parting is tough, and even as her car disappears down the road I feel a terrible sense of loss, missing her in advance for the days that will pass before I see her again.

I'm kept busy when I get into work on Monday. As well as fresh updates on a couple of other cases, Mrs Webb comes through with what little her son has sent her over the past year, as well as the names of some of his old friends in Boston. I'm not surprised to see that Adam didn't write too often – 'He mostly called me on the phone,' his mother says – but I am surprised by the level of affection he plainly had for her. It's certainly not something I'd expect to see from someone who'd willingly disappear unannounced.

There are two letters and a couple of cards, one for his mom's birthday and one for her, but not her husband, from last Christmas. The cards both contain short messages along the lines of: 'I'm okay. Hope all's well with you.' They don't go into much detail. The letters are both from New York State: one from Buffalo and one from Albany.

In the first he writes, 'I've got a job for a guy called Tommy who does credit and property and stuff.' Then he moves quickly on to other things, without going into any further details. From that, and the way he talks about some of the people he works with, it sounds like he was in the repo business, and not the legit end of it, either. I can't tell whether he enjoyed it or not, but since he'd moved on five months later, I doubt it was anything he'd want to run back to. In Albany the only work he could apparently get was working as a burger chef, and he hated it. 'The pay sucks, my manager's a prick and I want to quit the job as soon as I can get something else,' he says. There's no mention of girlfriends or acquaintances in either letter.

For the time being at least, the list of his friends in Boston is mostly a dead end. Of those whose phone numbers I'm able to find, some are out – probably at work – and the others remember Adam but haven't heard from him in years. I make a note to try the rest later in case they can tell me anything, but I doubt I'll get much.

I ring Buffalo Police Department and after three different people ask me to explain who I am and why I'm calling, I'm put through at last to Detective Nicolette Wakefield in their robbery division.

'How exactly can I help you, Mr Rourke?' she asks.

'I'm looking for a guy called Adam Webb who worked in

Buffalo nearly a year ago. He's vanished and his family's worried. I think he was in the repo trade in Eggertsville and his boss was called Tommy. Not a lot of information, I know, but it's all I've got. I don't know how easy it'll be for you to narrow things down.'

'You're right, it's not a lot,' she says with a trace of irony. I can hear typing in the background. 'Why are you interested in this Tommy guy?'

'It might be that he's gone back to work for him, or that they were involved in something together that made Adam want to vanish.'

'You can't have many leads if you're willing to try such a long shot.' From the tone, I know she's smiling when she says it.

'You got that right. Proverbial needle in a haystack.'

There's a brief silence, then Detective Wakefield says, 'Here we are: Tommy Gray. I don't think your boy will have gone back to work for him. He was arrested six months ago for extortion. Currently serving time.'

'Any chance he was ever involved in anything more serious, even if he wasn't charged?'

'Sorry,' she says, sighing. 'He's strictly small-time. Most important thing his kind does is take a piss when they get up in the morning. No mention of an Adam Webb anywhere, either.'

'Nuts. Oh well, thanks for your help, Detective Wakefield. I appreciate it.'

'No problem.' She gives me a number. 'That's my direct line. If there's anything else you need, just give me a ring.'

I try Albany PD with even less information, just Adam's name. They've never heard of him either, and I'm left with nothing much I can do from here except for speaking to the rest of his childhood buddies. That will have to wait until the evening when they're likely to be home.

At four o'clock the phone rings. When I answer, my mood is lifted as I hear Gemma say, 'Hi, it's me. How's your day been?'

'Not brilliant.' I briefly outline my lack of progress. 'How's yours?'

'Okay. I sent copies of the photo you gave me to Burlington, as well as every regional and assistant ME and hospital I could think of. With a bit of luck, I'll hear back from most of them in a day or two.'

'Thanks.'

'That's one of the perks of going out with a pathologist.'

'And such a gorgeous one, too.'

I smile as she laughs, the sound slightly distorted by the connection. 'Very smooth. When do you want to come up to look for this guy?'

'Well, I'll be seeing you at the weekend, so why don't I stay on for the first few days of next week as well? If it's okay with you.'

She laughs again. 'Of course it is. The more time I get to spend with you, the better. I can thank you properly for all those compliments you keep paying me. I doubt you'll have the ideal weather for wandering around Burlington – it's been snowing on and off since the end of last week. Are you sure Rob trusts you to get any work done while you're here?'

'I think he suspects I'll be too distracted to go trawling around town.' I glance across the office, where my partner is shaking his head.

'Tell her I'll have you fired if she keeps you from doing your job,' he calls out, grinning.

I relay the message. Gemma says, 'I'll be at work myself, so he needn't worry. I'd better go now. Duty calls.'

'I'll ring you later, then. Looking forward to the weekend.'

'Love you.'

'I love you too,' I say, then hang up.

Rob rolls his eyes. 'It's enough to make you hurl.'

The evening's phone calls to Adam's friends aren't a total success. There are still a couple of people on the list who aren't answering, for whatever reason. Those who do echo the responses I received earlier in the day – they've not heard from him, and they have no idea where he is or what he's doing.

Late the following afternoon, having spent the morning on other matters, I drive to the houses of the final two friends in the company car – I don't fancy the idea of parking my 'Vette in the rough neighbourhoods where they both live. The first house on my list is a run-down brick duplex in an equally run-down street. The box-like front yard is overgrown with yellowing grass and creeping weeds, most of them dying off as winter sets in. Posted on the front door is a notice that says the property is being repossessed and its occupants evicted. The place is empty.

The second is an apartment in a dingy building at the end of a row of stores. A 7-Eleven, a video rental place, a couple of liquor stores. The stairwell reeks of piss. My knock is answered by a scrawny guy I guess around Adam's age. He's wearing a Metallica T-shirt from a good five or six years ago, stained jeans and has bare feet. A mop of blond hair tops a pale, tired-looking face.

'Yeah?' the kid says.

'Justin?'

'Yeah,' he repeats. 'What you want?'

'I'm trying to find Adam Webb – his mom wants to get in touch but she doesn't know where he is. Have you heard from him recently?'

He stays still, thinking, or so I hope. Then he nods once

and says, 'I got a call from him maybe two, three months ago. I think. Said he had the two hundred bucks he owed me. Is that recent enough? He in any trouble?'

My brain kick-starts into life. This is the only confirmation I have that Adam even existed two months ago, apart from what his mom told me. 'It's recent enough, and he's not in any trouble. What else did he say?'

'We talked a bit, y'know. Asked how he was doin'. I mean, he borrowed the money years ago when he first took off. I'd forgotten, but I guess he hadn't. He sounded like he was doing pretty good for himself, up north.'

'Did he say what he was doing?'

The kid shrugs. 'Not really. Got the impression it might not have been totally on the level, but I didn't ask. He said he was working with some chick called Jessie, sounded like he maybe had a thing for her. At least, they were friends n'all.'

'Did he say anything else about her?'

'Nah, not to me. Sent me the two hundred, though. I hope he's okay.'

I look at the kid. 'Why wouldn't he be?'

'I dunno.' He sniffs. 'Just that when people need to come asking about someone, they usually end up on the six o'clock news, y'know?'

'I hope he doesn't. Look, if he gets in touch again, or if you remember anything else, give me a call. He's not in any trouble, and I'm not a cop.' I hand the kid a business card wrapped in a fifty.

'Sure, man. No problem.'

I make my way back to the foot of the stairs, scribbling down what the kid told me. Then I ring Adam's mom and ask her if she ever heard him mention a girl called Jessie.

'No,' she says, 'I don't think so. You think he could be with her?'

I can't give her anything much to be hopeful about. 'Maybe, but all I've got is a first name and a guess that maybe she was in Burlington with Adam. Unless I can find anything else out, it's going to be nearly impossible to trace him or the girl based on just that.'

'But you'll try to get something else?'

'Of course. I'll be going up to Vermont next week to see what I can find out. I've already managed to eliminate some possibilities, but there's still plenty to do. I'll keep you posted if I come across anything.'

I say goodbye and hang up. I slightly regret sounding quite so optimistic about Adam's case, but I figure it'll help keep his mother's mind at ease for the time being.

After work I walk home, thoughts wandering ahead to the weekend. I know I'll have to make a list of the places I should look for Adam, maybe phone around Burlington first to find out where he might have stayed or worked. The more I can get done before I go, the more time I can spend with Gemma, taking advantage of the extra days together. The idea of huddling with her in front of the fire with a bottle of wine stays with me all the way back to my apartment. I think about calling her to make plans, but I know how stupid I'd sound.

At half past eight that evening, the phone rings and I listen stone-eyed as the voice of a total stranger tells me that Gemma is dead.

3

I can taste spruce bark in the air – dry, earthy, bitter. The scent is strong but not overpowering, mingling with those of a hundred other plants, trees and flowers without destroying them. The mixture reminds me of old wine casks, though I have no clear idea why. Grass stalks rattle next to my head where it rests on the unyielding turf. Sunlight flushes warmly against my skin, relaxing. The hum of insects going about their daily lives makes up the chorus-line behind the sound taking centre stage – laughter. I know that if I open my eyes now, I'll be in time to see a pair of red-brown butterflies skipping through the air above me in a complex, whirling mating dance. I'll shade my eyes against the glare and watch until they're past my field of vision. And then I'll hear –

'Mr Rourke.'

But I won't. I won't hear a thing except the sound of my own thoughts beating against the inside of my head. There are no butterflies and the sun has gone down. I can't go back to that hiking trail near Smuggler's Notch, not without going alone and in the cold. No matter how much I want to.

'Mr Rourke.'

I reluctantly return from that July day, back to the present. I look up at the white-coated figure in front of me. A grey-haired woman in her sixties. Lined face, wide brown eyes with the studied sympathy of a professional. She has blue doctor's coveralls beneath her lab coat.

'Mr Rourke,' she says, 'I'm Dr Kingsley, the Chief Medical

Examiner. I'm pleased to meet you. If you're sure you want to do this, follow me.'

I say nothing, just stare bleakly at her as I climb out of my seat. She leads me down the hallway to a small office. A couple of desks with computers sitting on them. Textbooks, papers. Everything is clinically clean and so tidy you'd think no one ever works here. The air carries the faint ammonia odour of disinfectant. A door in the far corner leads through into what looks like a laboratory, judging by what I can see through the single pane of glass set into it. The adjoining wall has a large window running a good ten or twelve feet along it. There's a surgical screen across it, but bright blue-white light streams around the edges. A set of aluminium double doors leads from the office into the room beyond the window, the mortuary proper.

'I know how hard this must be for you,' Dr Kingsley says. It's an off-the-peg platitude but I'm not paying much attention to her words anyway; I'm too wrapped up in myself, misery and memories combining with the awful knowledge that this isn't some dream I'm about to wake up from.

'It's always terrible when something like this happens,' she continues. 'It's cruel and senseless, and obviously we do what we can to accommodate the wishes of loved ones. Her family haven't contacted us, so if you're not sure you want to do this . . .'

'Her mom and dad are on vacation,' I mutter. 'Weren't going to be back until Friday. I don't know about the others.'

She nods. 'Well okay then. We'll start slowly. We can stop at any time.'

Dr Kingsley opens a file she's holding, pulls out a pair of glossy photos and hands them to me. I glance at them, swallow once and say, 'I'm not interested in pictures, Doc.'

She takes them back and closes the folder. 'You'd still like to see her?'

I nod. 'Yeah.'

She reaches over and pushes a button on one of the desks; presumably some kind of intercom buzzer. Inside the morgue, a technician in blue coveralls draws back the screen that blocks out the window to reveal a gurney draped in white.

'I'd like to go in,' I say.

I follow the doctor as she takes me through the double doors and into the mortuary. The disinfectant smell is even stronger here, and the fluorescent lights in the ceiling seem to throb and hum louder than they should.

Gemma is lying with her eyes closed, skin nearly as pale as the thick, heavy sheet that runs almost up to her chin. Her hair hangs still and flat back from her face, tumbled in drifts around her head. There's a faint bluish tinge to her lips, which have opened the tiniest fraction, just like they used to when she was asleep.

For a long, long time I stare down at her lying there, cold and sterile and dead. My mind stays empty. Blank, fled to some happier place perhaps, leaving me alone without any thoughts of grief or comfort, sorrow or anger, anything at all. I know I should be in tears, or railing in anger against the unfairness of the world, or doing something to express my grief. But my head stays silent and hollow and all I'm left with is a gut-tightening sense of longing that can never be fulfilled.

I turn and trudge out of the mortuary. Dr Kingsley says something to me as we pass through her office, but I can't make out the words. Then I let the door swing shut behind me and I'm alone again.

The corridor seems gloomy after the stark light of the

morgue. Fluorescent tubes scattered along its length spit out a yellow light so dirty I can't tell if the walls are beige or badly lit plain white. Where the glow hits the slightly uneven surface of the polished floor, dark whorls and pools seem to collect like a desert mirage, as if it's casting shadows instead of reflecting the striplights above. I walk up the hall and slump into one of the chipped chairs back where I was waiting before. I rest my face in my hands and gaze mindlessly at the liquid blackness by my feet.

Footsteps, heeled shoes rapping against the floor, echoing from the walls so their speed and distance distort and merge. 'You must be Alex,' a voice says next to me.

I look around and up to see a woman, maybe in her late twenties, wearing a thick coat over a sweater and jeans. Brown hair tied back in a ponytail, thin features and green eyes. Attractive, maybe, though I'm not in the mood to notice. There's a note of genuine sympathy and warmth in her voice which Dr Kingsley – and everyone else I've spoken to since that first phone call, despite their best efforts – hasn't been able to match. The woman drops into the chair next to me.

'I'm Bethany,' she says. 'Gemma was my friend.'

'Oh.' I can't remember if Gemma ever mentioned her or not. 'Did you work together?'

'No, not really. I have a job here with the OCME. I heard that she was . . . y'know. Dr Kingsley said you were coming and that you might like a friend to be here. Have you been in yet?'

I nod, slow and leaden. 'Yeah.' Try to show interest, feign normality, and add, 'How did you two meet? Work the same case?'

'No,' Bethany says. 'There was a meeting for OCME staff here in Burlington a few months ago. We were both new to everything around here, so we got talking. We met up every few weeks after that.' She sighs. 'Do you know what happened to her?'

My throat seems to contract as though I'm having difficulty breathing. I try to force air through it, to make my vocal cords work, but it's hard going. 'The police told me she was driving home. Someone shot her, they think through the windshield. She got hit in the base of her throat. They reckon she died instantly.' Breathe in, breathe out. 'When the Sheriff's Department saw her car, they thought it was just someone gone off the road in the snow. They didn't realize what'd happened until later.'

She stays silent for a while, then asks, 'Do they know who did it?'

An orderly walks past pushing a cart full of cleaning equipment with him. He stares strangely at us for a moment, then sees me looking back and his eyes flick forwards and stay there.

'I don't know,' I say. 'The State Police are handling it. They're going to speak to me tomorrow.'

'They're going to ask you questions?'

'Yeah. Just the usual stuff, I guess. Did she have any enemies, that kind of thing.'

Bethany nods. 'Did she?'

'What? No, of course not. They speak to you at all?'

'Not yet. I don't know if they will. It was a couple of weeks since I last saw her.'

We lapse into silence for a while. Eventually I break it by saying, 'I just hope they catch whoever did it.'

'Gemma said you used to be in the FBI and everything,' Bethany replies. She sounds surprised. 'I thought you'd be helping them investigate.'

'Don't be so fucking stupid. Cops don't let civilians,

especially the victim's loved ones, work like that.' I pause for breath, then rub my eyes and sigh deeply. 'Look, I'm sorry I snapped at you. I'd like to catch whoever killed Gemma, I really would, but it doesn't happen that way. Even when I was in the FBI, when my parents were killed, all I did was answer the standard questions. Cops worked the case, not me.' I laugh once, grimly. 'Much good I'd have been even if I'd tried. You can't stay focused, not that close to things.'

'You can't be sure of that.'

I don't reply. I *am* sure, but I don't want to turn this into an argument. For all that, though, talking with Bethany has helped. Even anger is better than the desolation I felt before. It won't last – rage never does – but I'll settle for a brief burst of emotion over continuous emptiness.

Bethany gets to her feet. 'I've got to go now,' she says. 'I'm supposed to be at work in about eight hours' time and I'd best get some sleep. It was nice meeting you, Alex.'

'Sure.' I look up at her as she adjusts her coat. 'Thanks for talking to me, I needed it. I'm sorry I'm not in the best of moods right now.'

'Catharsis,' she replies, smiling wryly. 'It's good for you. And you've got nothing to apologize for. If you need me, here's my number.' She hands me a slip of paper. 'Take care.'

I nod and listen to her footsteps echo and fade away. I stay in the chair for I don't know how long, still too dazed to do very much, before an internal autopilot suggests I find a motel and try to sleep. My legs feel weak, dangerously so, but I manage to stagger to my feet and shuffle away down the corridor. Forces tug at me, trying to slow my escape; every step I take is one further away from Gemma, but sooner or later I know I'm going to have to leave her behind.

I wander out to the parking lot. Dark, dirty slush and snow blanket the asphalt, but although the sky above is utterly black, cloud cloaking the stars, no fresh snow is falling. I'm too numb to feel the cold.

I drive to the nearest motel, slowly so I don't have to worry about losing the 'Vette on a patch of ice. At half two in the morning, Burlington is quiet. A couple of taxis making late-night pickups, a handful of delivery trucks, some light traffic, but there's little life out on the streets. Even the interstate, visible from the ramp up to the parking lot, is pretty much free of traffic.

The E-Z-Rest Motel isn't right at the bottom end of the accommodation scale but it's close, a prefab rest stop owned by a small chain franchise that seems to be in it for the money, not the guests' comfort. I switch on the light, which flickers and buzzes before finally holding, and slump into the room's sole PVC armchair, which is definitely at least a decade past its prime. I'm tired, but sleep isn't something I want. I flick the TV on and stay in the chair. My only concession to comfort is to empty out my pockets, depositing wallet and keys on the nightstand. As I take out my cell phone, I notice that its display is showing the 'you have voicemail' symbol so I check it.

I almost pass out when I hear the voice on the message. It's Gemma.

4

You have . . . one . . . new message. Message received . . . yesterday at . . . five . . . thirty-three . . . p.m.

'Hi, honey, it's me.'

She's calling from the car; I can hear the vibration of the engine in the background. No steady traffic noise though, so I guess she must be on her way home and the road's not too busy.

Oh, baby, I miss your voice.

'Um, I thought I'd ring to ask you about the weekend. Susan's invited me to a party in St Johnsbury on Saturday and I said I'd see if you wanted to go. It's more of an evening on the town, apparently. Some friends of hers are going to be taking over a bar for the night, so I guess there must be a lot of them. But she said it's like an annual thing. It sounds kind of fun.'

I can hear the high-pitched watery noise of the car's wheels cutting through snow on the road. The whirr of the heater. The squeak in the seat she was going to get fixed.

'But I don't know if you fancy doing that after driving up all this way, even if you're not going back on Sunday. I don't think you've ever met any of the people who are going, though I know I've mentioned them to you before. Again, it's up to you whether you want to or not.'

Gemma's tone changes. She's smiling and I can hear it, almost see it. 'Even though you do owe me for that bash for your police friend. Maybe I'll make you repay me.

'Oh, and what do you want to eat when you're here? I

don't have much in the house right now, but I can make a trip to the store after work on Friday. I thought I might do some kind of Thai thing in the evening, but I haven't decided what, and I'm open to suggestions for the rest of your stay.

'Anyway, I'd better go because it's just started snowing again and I'd better keep my eyes on the road. I love you, honey . . .' – I love you too, I think to myself – 'and I'll—'

Crack.

I can almost feel the bullet hit. The noise itself is enough to make me double up with pain, hugging myself tight as if I've been kicked in the gut. I drop the phone as the tears begin streaming down my face. My girlfriend's dead, dying, fucking *dead* as I listen. It hurts as much as when I got the call to tell me she'd been killed – worse, because this time I don't have the half-hope to cling to that it's a joke, or a dream, and she's really okay. My world has ended and fate has conspired to make the whole event available on instant replay.

If there's anything left on the message, I let it bleed out on the floor where I can't hear it. I don't dare pick up the phone in case I find out that Gemma didn't die in that instant, that she whimpered in pain as her life drained away, or in case I hear her last shuddering breath. I couldn't bear it.

When I finally have enough control, and enough minutes have passed, I pick up my cell and gingerly hold it to my ear.

. . . three. If you would like to hear the message again, press one. If you would like to save the message, press two. To delete the message, press three. If you would like . . .

My first instinct is to wipe it, and never again have to face the agony of Gemma's final moments. I don't know if I'd ever want to relive the grief that would inevitably come from hearing her voice. For a moment my thumb hovers over the '3' button, but then I press '2' instead.

Thank you. Your message will be saved for thirty days.

I can't erase my girlfriend's last words on this earth. Instead, I'll have someone download the message on to a computer so I can keep that recording for as long as I want, just so I can hear her. Perhaps time will dull the hurt that comes from knowing I can listen to her, but can't talk back ever again.

I sit in the armchair until daylight streams through the window behind me. Sleep, unlikely before, would be impossible now, and I don't even try.

The following morning I drive down to State Police headquarters in Waterbury, twenty-five miles or so from Burlington. I turn south from I-89 and swing into the town, which is about as non-touristy as Vermont gets. The VSP is based along with several other government agencies in the Waterbury Complex, the new name for a section of what used to be the State Hospital for the Insane. Trees gone brown and bare with the onset of winter dot the asylum's campus, surrounding each patch of snow-covered open ground. I sense a walled-off, prison feeling from its past use, emphasized by the rounded red-brick buildings that make up most of the complex. Even though the parking lots are full of cars and people are going to and fro between offices where the lights are on in almost every room, I can still imagine how terrible it must have been to be an inmate here, particularly during the harsh winter months.

Once I've found a parking space I light a cigarette and sit in the car, heater running, to collect my thoughts before I visit the police. Last night's lack of sleep has left me drained, but not wholly exhausted. The only place I can tell how much rest I need is in my legs. Calf muscles and ankles stretched and worn, maybe from the drive down, maybe not.

After a slow smoke, I swing out of the car. The cold outside hits me like I've fallen into a river, with every gap and opening in my clothing quickly filling with a biting chill that overwhelms whatever warmth I'd built up. Keeping my hands wedged firmly in my pockets, I do my best to haul my jacket tight around me as I head for the doors.

Inside the air smells stale and a little acidic, overly warmed by a heating system that recycles every cup of bitter coffee and every sour armpit. The woman at the front desk directs me down the hall and tells me I'll be seeing Detective Sergeant Karl Flint, the same man I briefly spoke to about Adam Webb. I walk down a corridor that dully echoes my footfalls, then turn right into a quiet, orderly office. Filing cabinet. Computer. A pale veneer desk bearing a collection of files and papers. Sitting behind it is a guy whose age I'd place somewhere around forty, pale and more or less clean-shaven with close-cut dark hair and wide, watery brown eyes. He wears a dark grey suit and burgundy tie like he was born in them.

'Good morning,' the man says, standing and extending a hand. 'I'm Detective Flint.'

'Alex Rourke,' I reply. 'We spoke on the phone.'

'We did?' A blank look crosses his face.

'Adam Webb.'

'Oh, yeah, right. Small world, isn't it?' He changes the subject, getting back to business. His bedside manner is straight out of a textbook and I get the impression he doesn't use it much. 'Mr Rourke, I know this is a tough time for you, but I need to ask you some questions that might help us figure out what happened to Dr Larson and why, okay?'

'Yeah, I know the drill.'

'Good.' He smiles, pulls out a notebook. 'When did you last speak with Gemma?'

'Monday.'

The detective's pen skitters across the paper in front of him. 'What did you talk about?'

I shrug. 'Nothing much. The usual, just about our days, things like that. Are you married, Detective Flint?'

'No,' he says, shaking his head.

'Well, imagine what married couples talk about when they come home from work. That's what we did.'

'Okay. And that was the last occasion you spoke to her?'

'She called me yesterday, but my phone was engaged so she left a message on my voicemail. We didn't talk.'

The chair creaks as he leans forward. 'What time was this, Mr Rourke?'

'Just gone five-thirty.' I keep my gaze steady, and if he notices a touch of hoarseness in my voice, he doesn't acknowledge it. 'Right up to the point she died.'

Flint's hand hovers over his notes, rolling his pen between his fingers. 'What did she say?'

'She was talking about the weekend – I was coming up to stay with her. Some stuff about a party in St Johnsbury, what she was going to be cooking. Nothing strange. Then she said it had started snowing again so she was going to hang up to concentrate on the road.' I pause, breathe once or twice. 'Then I heard her window splinter.'

'Did you hear a shot?'

I try to think back to the recording on my phone. No, no shot. I shake my head and refocus on the detective. 'No, just the glass breaking.'

He leans back in his chair, breathes out. 'And that was all? Do you still have the message?'

'No,' I tell him, wondering as I do so why I'm lying. Perhaps I want to keep Gemma's last moments private, not something to be shared with the world. Since there's nothing on the message that I'd guess could help the police, I'm not going to lose any sleep over it. 'I erased it,' I say. 'I didn't want to hear it again.'

Eyes widen further in surprise, mouth sets in a line. 'What the fuck did you do that for?'

'Like I said, I didn't want to hear it again.'

Flint shakes his head and makes another mark in his notebook. 'Dammit. There could have been something useful on it.'

'She was driving along and then the bullet hit. That's all.'

He pauses for a moment, breathes steady, then says, 'Moving on. Did Gemma sound upset or agitated in any way when she spoke to you, not just on the last occasion but anytime recent?'

'No, she never said anything to me about being worried. I don't know of anyone who might have wanted to kill her. She hadn't had trouble with anyone lately, or ever, that I can remember. She wasn't the sort.'

'No strange occurrences, at home or at work?'

I shake my head. 'Everything was normal.'

Flint nods and drops his pen on the desk. 'That seems to be the picture we're getting from everyone we've spoken to.'

'Have you got any leads, anything to go on?'

'Nothing much. A Lamoille County Sheriff's Department cruiser found her, but they thought she'd gone off the road in the snow and it wasn't treated as a crime scene until someone from the medical examiner's office got there. We haven't found any witnesses who could tell us what happened – that patch of Route 100 is pretty quiet. Since she didn't seem to have any enemies, we're currently guessing it was either some kind of wandering lunatic or it was a freak hunting accident.'

'An accident?' My eyebrows shoot up at the suggestion.

'A rifle slug can carry a long way. If someone took a shot and missed . . . it's possible.'

'Wouldn't they have come forward? Have you found the bullet?'

'We're out of season for most animals, so it may have been someone poaching, which is why they wouldn't want to tell us what happened. And no, we haven't found the bullet. The state of the ground where she went off the road makes it hard to know where to look.'

Flint leans forward and rests his arms on the desk. 'Look, Mr Rourke. I know it's hard to accept, but shit does happen, and it sometimes happens for no good reason. You've got to leave it to us to figure out the truth.'

'Sure.'

I trudge back to the parking lot feeling frustrated and helpless. I don't like being outside the loop, and it's made worse by the clock that runs on most murders. I've heard different numbers – 24 hours, 48, 72 – from different people, but it's widely accepted that the sooner you can get to a solution, even if you don't yet have a concrete case against the killer, the more likely you are to make the arrest and have a conviction that sticks. But there are other matters that stop me working to that kind of timetable.

Three days later, we bury Gemma in a cemetery near Bangor in northern Maine.

It's a cold, hard morning. A blanket of ice like shattered glass covers the ground, broken here and there by frozen tufts of straggly grass. It snaps and crunches beneath my feet as I move to the front of the small crowd of mourners gathered by the side of a dark casket strewn with red and white flowers. The sky is a brilliant pale blue above, with hardly a wisp of cloud to be seen. The sun is weak, bright but distant. A clean, icy breeze blows in a constant stream across the top of the low hill on which we stand, turning pale faces paler still, clenched hands whitish-purple. Gemma's family are all here as well as several of her closer friends. Some I know, some I don't. Her mom and dad, both nearly sixty, are crying softly as the white-robed priest conducts the burial service. His voice is low and nasal, but I'm not listening to his words. I guess like most of the people here, I'm too busy thinking about Gemma, all we had together and all that could have been. I'm trying my best to burn her face, smile and laughter into my memory, not to let it fade and pass.

The reverend finishes speaking as the coffin vanishes slowly into the earth. The wind almost carries away his final syllables; 'dust to dust' is a mere whisper. I swallow hard and close my eyes.

When I open them again, I can hear movement behind me, footsteps crunching through the ice. People are beginning to filter away in the uncertain manner that always follows a funeral. They're not sure whether they should say anything to the other mourners, or leave them to handle it themselves. Most say a few words to Gemma's parents, then make their way slowly back towards the cars. A couple, including her elder sister Alice, do the same for me too. Her brother and one or two others stay for a while at her graveside, silent.

I turn and walk away, feeling hollow. A figure is standing fifty yards off, among the tombstones. Bethany is waiting near the bottom of the hill, dressed all in black, looking uncertainly up towards Gemma's resting-place.

'I didn't know whether to come or not,' she says as I reach her. Her eyes are raw and her voice trembles a little as she speaks. 'I wasn't invited, not as such, but I heard where it was and so I thought . . .' She trails off.

'I think her parents preferred to keep it small, but I reckon

Gemma would've liked it that you wanted to be here.' My eyes itch, but rubbing at them only makes it worse.

'Are you all right, Alex?' Bethany asks. 'I mean, are you handling this okay? You look terrible.'

She's right. My skin feels like it's hanging off my bones and when I glanced in a mirror earlier on, it was starting to look that way too. Greying flesh, sunken cheeks, eyes deep-set and bloodshot. I haven't shaved, either, which doesn't help.

'I haven't been sleeping well,' I say. 'Five, six hours maybe, maybe less, since we met at the hospital.'

'You should see a doctor. That can't be good for you.'

I smile humourlessly. 'It's not the first time. How are you doing?'

'Okay, I guess. My boyfriend Mike works in Montreal, but he was due to come visit me a couple of days ago anyway. That helped.' She looks down at her feet, examines her hands. 'Gemma was one of the best friends I had in Vermont. It doesn't seem fair.'

'These things rarely do.'

'Have the police come up with anything so far? Have they got any leads?'

'They haven't called me, so I don't know. I guess not. Idiots think it might have been a freak accident anyway.'

She frowns, not at me but over my shoulder, up the hill. 'It doesn't sound like they're getting anywhere.'

'I know what you're thinking. I'd have a look myself, but I don't know if they'd appreciate it. I also don't know if I'd be any good. I'm not much use for anything right now; I can't think properly and I'm just . . .' The sentence slips away from me. I glance down at the grave next to us. At this moment, swapping places with 'William Clayborne, 1923–1985' doesn't seem so bad.

The carpet of ice behind me crackles. Anna and Murray Larson, Gemma's mom and dad, are standing behind me. His arm is around her shoulders. Murray, a normally stocky, tough man now looking wilted and unsure, fixes me with watery eyes and says, 'Hello, Alex.'

'Mr Larson.'

'I don't know how you're doing right now, or what's going on in your head, but I want you to know that my daughter meant everything to me.' Murray's voice cracks as the words jam in his throat. 'Damn you for getting her killed.'

'What?' I can't believe I heard him right. It's too surreal, a sudden sheering in the world. Although we've met on only a couple of occasions, and spoken on just a few more, I always thought Gemma's parents liked me, more or less. I blink twice, three times, waiting for him to explain.

'This is your fault. She wouldn't have been there if you hadn't wanted her to move down south. She was happy in Houlton. Why couldn't you have let her be?'

I say nothing and just stand, looking at him. My stop-start tide of shifting emotions is trying to push me into defending myself, but I don't. Gemma's father is angry, but I know he's also grieving for his daughter, the same woman I loved. I couldn't live with myself if I tried to stop him; he's got the right, the same as me.

'God help you if I find out she died because of something you did,' he says before clasping his wife tighter and moving away. Anna glances briefly at me, a flat gaze devoid of emotion, then buries her face in his shoulder.

I watch them go, not moving. The fire kindled by Murray Larson's misdirected anger burns on, but I don't want to lash out. Bethany's argument is starting to make sense, that I should find out for myself why Gemma died. If it will mean justice for the woman buried on top of the hill, some peace for an old man feeling the pain of outliving his daughter, and maybe some rest for myself, I'll try.

I look around for Bethany, but she's gone, slipped away without a sound, leaving me alone among the frozen graves.

5

After the funeral I don't go back to Boston. Instead I follow US-2 west, out of Maine, across the White Mountains of New Hampshire and into Vermont. From St Johnsbury I switch to smaller local routes all the way to the isolated town of Bleakwater Ridge, Gemma's home for the past six months. Miles of hill country, evergreen-covered ridgelines marching off into the distance. The boughs of the trees that blanket the slopes are nothing but sombre black shapes beneath their dappled coat of snow. The horizon ahead slowly seems to rise to meet me; the advancing wall of the Green Mountains steadily cuts off the sky, lining it with stone. By the time I get close to town in the steadily deepening dusk, the jumbled peaks and sawtooth foothills are barely discernible, looming shadows that seem to overhang and encircle the highway, the forest and the cluster of buildings huddled within.

I crest the top of one slope as the highway loops to the right and the twin beams from my headlights flash across something up in the trees by the road. It could just be a patch of shadow, something half-seen and misinterpreted by my brain, but it's enough to tighten my grip on the wheel. Breath sticks in my throat.

I catch only the briefest glimpse as I drive past, but it looks like the corpse of a large black dog, maybe a German shepherd. Suspended somehow, hung or nailed to the trunk, head upwards. Its back legs hang limply downwards towards my car. The lights sparkle off something shiny, wet, on its coat.

I glance once or twice in my mirror in case I'm able to see

it again, but I don't stop. Either it's someone else's problem, or it wasn't what I thought.

When the town appears up ahead it almost takes me by surprise. Glimmers of yellow, cream and orange light appear like stars through the unseen foliage by the roadside, and then suddenly the trees break and I'm passing houses which ramble up and over the rocky fold that gives Bleakwater Ridge its name. The buildings are large and old-looking with whitewashed walls and pale roofs. Living ghosts of an earlier age. With their small yards and closeness to the road it is impossible to tell just how far the town spreads away from its sole major artery. The uphill climb is only a few hundred yards and the couple of side streets don't give much away; the roofs of the houses lining each junction mask the view to either side until I cross. A brief sense of space, some lights in the darkness, then they're gone.

At the top of the ridge I make a right on to West Road. The intersection with Main is the focal point of the settlement, judging by the cluster of buildings around it: a barn-like town meeting house, a tiny run-down church, a general store with a couple of other shops either side, and the Owl's Head Inn, its only bar. Fifty or sixty yards down West, I pull into the driveway of Gemma's darkened home and kill the engine.

'How'd you afford a place like this?' I ask, climbing out of the car as Gemma trots down the steps to meet me. My eyes take in the two storeys of white boards, the high sash windows, the deck to the side and rear, the upturned V-shape of the dormer roof where it juts out above the attic room casement.

'No one much wants to live this far from the big towns,' she says as she throws her arms around me. 'Besides, it's not in pristine shape.'

Looking again, I can see spots where the wooden siding has warped, twisting and splitting around knots just visible beneath the paint, which is peeling and blackened in places. The window-frames show their age. Minute cracks laced along the grain of the wood. The front door's rusty hinges creak as it swings shut in the breeze.

For all that, though, the place is beautiful. From where we stand on the driveway I can just make out the grey sheen of Silverdale Lake through the trees and houses to the east; the ridge runs steadily downhill all the way to its shore. In the opposite direction the forested, notched face of Windover Mountain punches up into the sky behind the town like a vast ancient rampart, sheer and indomitable. There's more birdsong than traffic noise, and the air that rustles through the leaves is clean and pure.

'You doctors do get all the good things in life.'

'Come on,' Gemma says, 'I'll show you around.'

I clamber out of the car and fetch my bag from the trunk. The street around me is silent, though not entirely dark. A couple of the houses further down the road have lights shining through their windows, perhaps a hint of movement glimpsed as silhouettes behind the curtains. I turn away from them and crunch through the undisturbed snow up to the porch, hunting around in my pocket for the keys.

Inside, the house is cold, though not as bad as outside. I flick the lights on in the hall and drop my bag at the foot of the stairs, then go back outside to retrieve the handful of mail that's built up over the past few days. Junk, most of it. A couple of personal letters I don't open but leave propped up by the mirror.

The living room is much the same as last time I was here. The burgundy felt couch starting to wear thin in patches, the not-quite-matching armchair, the coffee table and its collection of personal clutter – a TV guide, a couple of other magazines, a coffee mug, an open envelope. At the far side of the room near the fireplace is the antique rocking chair I came across when we went to a fair in Burlington. On the mantel is an LCD alarm clock intended for travellers. Next to it is a photo in a cheap wooden frame of the two of us together; apart from that and a few lighter patches on the pale yellow walls to show where the previous owner's pictures once hung, the room is undecorated.

The cavernous kitchen beyond is a little homelier, though it doesn't stop my footsteps ringing from the tiled floor. The table in the centre is spread with a blue and white cloth, half a dozen cookery books sit on top of the fridge and there are a variety of utensils stacked semi-neatly along the worktop. A couple of dishcloths hang from cupboard doors, splashes of colour against the wood, and there's a bunch of wilted flowers – the ones I gave her that last time – in a vase on top of the microwave. I skim my eyes over the notes stuck to the wall by the phone, but nothing grabs my attention. I glance through the back windows at the deck outside, then check the fridge and cupboards. Although I should be all right for breakfast, there's not much food in the house and I hope that the bar on Main does meals as well.

I head back into the hall and collect my bag. Up the groaning stairs, Gemma's bedroom looks like she just left. The covers are crumpled, unmade, and the pillow still holds the shape of her head. There's a shirt and a sweater that never made it to the laundry hamper lying on the floor, a scattered collection of jewellery and the small amount of make-up she used on the table by the mirror. The remote for the TV is on the floor next to the bed, alongside a half-read paperback. I glance both ways, at the smaller spare room – 'the study' – that I know houses her computer and a collection of junk she never got round to unpacking, and at the bathroom at the end of the landing, just to make sure Gemma's not here. It's stupid, but I do it anyway. Then I drop my bag just inside the bedroom and make my way downstairs again, heading for the front door and the outside world.

Keys safely back in my pocket, I light up a cigarette and step off the porch. The glowing tip and the hot smoke do nothing to ward off the cold, and my jacket fares little better. My breath steams in the stiff breeze that blows down off the mountains, rubbing raw against my face, thrumming and whistling through the wires that suspend the stoplights over Main, making them shudder and dance. The Devil's eye-glow of the red light preventing traffic from crossing the larger highway glowers at me as I hurry over the junction towards the Owl's Head Inn. A small, unlit sign beneath its name says: 'Bar – Grill – Rooms'. I finish my Marlboro and shoulder my way through the door.

A roiling cloud of stale warm air and the low murmur of conversation. Somewhere in the background a jukebox is playing Dire Straits' 'Brothers in Arms', so quietly that even the *clink* of bottles and glasses is enough to swallow it. With its dark wood dominating the décor, it's possible to believe the bar has changed little since Revolutionary times. Black wood tables, ceiling, counter, doors and windows. Carpet a red so deep it might just as well be black. Even the walls are no lighter – dark green.

It may be Saturday night but there are still no more than thirty people in here, tops. I'm not surprised to see that none look like tourists, though the locals aren't all the grizzled mountain types you'd associate with backwater towns like this. Maybe a third to a half I'd guess are white-collar workers, like Gemma unable to afford to live anywhere closer to their jobs. The rest are split between farmers and retirees. More than one pair of eyes glances at me as I make my way to the bar, though the conversation doesn't stop. Service is provided by a woman in her forties and a guy of about the same age with greying hair. The former intercepts me as I reach the counter.

'What can I get you?' she asks. Her eyes quickly scan my face, jacket, clothes, trying to work out who I am and what I'm doing in town.

'A Bud, thanks. Is the kitchen still open?'

She checks her watch. 'Yeah, just about. What you fancy?'

'A burger, fries maybe. Whatever's big and won't be too much hassle this time of night.'

'No problem.' The woman smiles briefly at me as she scribbles an order down on a notepad and rips off a page. I pay up before she vanishes out the back, presumably to the kitchen.

I sit at the counter and nurse my beer, absent-mindedly listening to such snatches of conversation as I can make out. Normal nothing-talk for the most part – complaints about work, road repairs, hockey games. Husbands bitching about their wives, wives bitching about their husbands.

I don't know what I was hoping for; a pack of suspicious types in long coats huddled in the corner maybe, talking murder, or a couple of ratty guys covered in jailhouse tattoos bragging about their shooting skills.

The closest I get to that is a pair of old-timers sitting at one of the tables, talking in voices too quiet for me to catch. One of them eyeballs me periodically; I can watch him in the polished surface of the beer tap in front of me. Speculating about the newcomer, I guess.

This continues as I work through my dinner and two more beers. The Owl's Head has filled up a little, with maybe around forty people now gathered in the gloomy bar. Eventually, on one of his occasional trips to the counter, one of the old gossips says, loud enough to catch my attention, 'Cold evening we're having. You from away?'

'Yeah. More or less.'

He nods as if that was expected. 'We do get folk passing through. On your way out again tonight?'

I look across at the old man. On first impressions his question seems like a typical 'get rid of the unwanted outsider' comment; common enough, though not usually so unprovoked. However, his tone makes it less of a threat and more as though he suspects he already knows my answer.

Like he already knows who I am and what my business is.

The guy himself is unassuming, not even looking at me but instead in the direction of the barmaid. He must be in his late sixties at least, with a whitish-grey beard and close-cropped white hair thinned almost to baldness on top. He's wearing a thick cloth jacket and trousers, good warm stuff to keep out the chills.

'No, I'm not,' I say. The man's eyes widen a little, though he does a fair job of covering it. 'I'm probably going to be around for a while.'

'You here for the hiking or somesuch? Same again, Bella,' he adds to the barmaid.

'I'm here because of my girlfriend.'

'She live here? If you don't mind me prying.'

I drain the bottle and gesture for another. 'Not any more. She was killed last week just north of town.'

'I see.' The surprise in his eyes vanishes to be replaced by expectation. Hope, maybe. I guess a second theory as to what I'm doing here has just been confirmed. He holds up a hand to stop me paying for my drink. 'Here, I'll get that. Fair exchange for putting up with an old man's questions.'

'Thanks.'

'Don't mention it. So are you just sorting out everything that needs sorting out, or is there something else on your mind?' The knowing tone is back.

'I thought maybe I could find out why she died, and who killed her.'

'So you're a cop.'

I shake my head. 'No, not these days. Do you know anything about what happened?'

'Only what I heard.' He picks up his beers and nods his head in the direction of his drinking buddy, who's still sitting at their table. I follow him over and find a vacant chair while he places one beer in front of his companion and takes a slow draw from the other. 'Ed Markham,' he says. 'And this here's Charlie Kanin.'

Charlie is almost identical to Ed, except that his beard is much shorter and he's completely bald. Otherwise they could be brothers.

'Alex Rourke,' I say.

'Mr Rourke's looking for whoever killed his ladyfriend, that doctor.'

Charlie nods. 'That sort of thing shouldn't happen, not to decent people.'

'I talked to Sylvia Ehrlich, one of the sheriff's deputies, afterwards,' Ed says, looking back at me. 'She didn't say much, just that there was a woman they found dead in her car, and that when the doctor checked her, they saw she'd been shot. Then it was a murder case, so they had to turn everything over to the State Police.'

'Bad business,' Charlie says.

Now it's Ed's turn to nod. 'I only found out who it was a couple of days ago. You talked to the police?'

'Yes and no,' I say. 'I haven't seen anyone from the Sheriff's Department yet.'

The conversation dies away after that, although I continue to sit there while Ed and Charlie chat slowly about local people I've never heard of. Give it some time, then I bid them both goodnight and make for the door.

Outside, snow is falling again. Tiny specks of ice are caught in the breeze, spiralling into vortices where they pass trees and buildings, pricking my skin like frozen grains of salt and collecting in my hair. I pull up my collar to keep my ears out of the wind and walk back to Gemma's house as quickly as the slippery footing will allow. The old building creaks faintly, stiff beams flexing and groaning. The breeze whistles and pipes through a stray knothole or gap somewhere in one of the corners of the roof. I turn the key in the lock, briefly check behind me, then step inside.

The house has warmed up a little while I've been out, so I guess the heating system's still working. I wipe cold water out of my eyes, drop my jacket over the back of the couch and make a cup of coffee.

There's something about the building that makes it hard to settle for any length of time. I try watching TV, but every few minutes I catch myself looking over my shoulder at the rest of the room, scanning the corners, the space behind the door. Get a glass of water. Take a piss. Think I hear the window rattling in the hall and go check – it's not, and in fact the snow is stopping and the sky looks to be clearing a little outside. Smoke a cigarette. Get a fresh pack from my jacket. Change chairs. Change back again. I don't know whether it's the unaccustomed emptiness of the place, something about the journey up here or the funeral this morning, but I'm jumpy. My eyes pick up every shifting shadow or stray dust particle caught in a draught.

After an hour or so of this, I decide that I might as well unpack my things and try to get some sleep. I make my way upstairs and along the landing to the bedroom door, where I pause. The room beyond is dark, enough so that I can only just make out my bag near the doorway. The bed is a vague silhouette against the far wall. The only illumination is the faint glow from downstairs and the even fainter silver sheen coming through the windows. The room still carries Gemma's scent, and in the gloom it's possible to believe she's asleep in the bed, breathing just too softly to hear. It's like stepping into a memory of one of those nights when I stayed up late to watch a movie and had to creep into the bedroom in the dark, trying not to wake her. If I cross the threshold, pass into this dreamlike bubble of the past, could I stay there? Could I slip under the covers, warmed by her body, and feel her skin gently brush mine?

The answer to both is 'no', and I know it. Still, just imagining the possibility is comforting in a strange way, as though Gemma is still alive in another world, another time, and maybe I'll be able to look through and see her now and then. I'd like that.

I sigh heavily, then break the bubble by walking into the room. As I bend to pick up my bag, I catch a glimmer of what looks like movement outside the window. Peering through the frost-speckled pane, I can see that the snow has indeed stopped. The moon is up, although strips of cloud torn by the wind repeatedly scud across it, making the light rise and fall like a heartbeat. Past the remaining houses on West Road, over the trees at the base of the ridge, the frozen surface of Silverdale Lake glitters like the few stars visible up above, twinkling through the screen of twigs and branches that surround it. As I gaze at the almost hypnotic sheen on the ice, the moon briefly emerges fully from the clouds. The extra luminescence picks out a handful of regular, yet jumbled shapes in the woods on the far bank of the lake, right at the edge of vision.

'What's that?' I ask, pointing through the open window. 'Another town?'

Gemma comes to stand next to me and follows my outstretched arm, peering at the outlines of buildings where they peek out from beneath the distant leafy canopy.

She shakes her head. 'North Bleakwater, according to the realtor. He said it's been abandoned for years, something about a flood in the 1920s. The woman who lives next door called it Echo Springs.'

'Real-life ghost town, huh? Have you been to take a look yet?'

'I went for a walk around the lake on Wednesday evening. There's a dirt track that runs there from the highway, but it's muddy and overgrown, like the buildings. There's only a few that still have more than a couple of walls. Give it another twenty years and it'll probably be nothing but trees and a handful of stones.'

'So I should have brought a spare pair of shoes if I wanted a romantic walk in the woods?' I say with a grin. 'That'll teach me.'

Gemma returns the smile and throws her arms around my waist. 'We'll just have to see what we can do here to make up for it.'

I turn away from the window and collect my bag. Then I grab a blanket from the closet and leave the room, shutting the door behind me. I can't spend the night in there, not now. It just wouldn't feel right.

I lie on the couch, still half-dressed, and try to sleep with the blanket wrapped as tightly around me as possible. It's not easy; the unsettling atmosphere remains. With my eyes closed I'm not bothered by glimpses of movement in my peripheral vision, but stray noises sound louder and their sources are more uncertain. A floorboard that shrieks as the house sways and settles, a *drip*, *drip* which I guess is water trickling down somewhere, even though there's none in the room with me. My ears strain towards every new interruption, a primal defence mechanism with associated spikes of adrenalin that make it impossible to relax long enough to fall asleep. It seems as though every time I'm about to doze off, something shifts in the darkness and *bang* – I'm wide awake again. The shape of the couch doesn't help; it's just a little too short to accommodate me in a comfortable position and its bulky arms wedge into my face and force my jaws together at an angle.

Insomnia is an old friend, something I've suffered from, on and off, for years. It's a frequent and serious enough problem that I have a bottle of sleeping pills in my jacket, my emergency supply on prescription from home. They work, but after a couple of bad experiences with them, I'm less inclined to rely on them than I once was.

I open my eyes and strain to make out the LCD display of the clock on the mantel.

02:47

I clamber out of my nest and stumble to the stereo through the gloom. I switch it on and flick the selector switch to 'radio'. I hunt around until I find a station that's still transmitting at this late – early – hour.

'. . . SEEN THE SHADOW ON THE MOON . . .'

I hurriedly twist the volume control to change the blast of noise into something more bearable. I don't recognize either the song or the singer, but it falls roughly into the area of blues where my personal preference lies – low, gravelly and guitar-driven. And, most importantly, it's loud enough to drown out most of the night-time sounds the house makes.

I drop back on the couch, close my eyes and let the music carry me slowly off to sleep.

6

The first thing I see on waking is a crimson-brown haze, no burning streak of morning light. I open leaden eyelids a fraction and peer out from the stale wool-smelling blanket that surrounds me. There's a dim greyness bleeding faintly around the edges of the drapes, enough to see by but only just. I sit up, rubbing sore neck muscles, and stretch some life into my stiff back.

Only then do I check my watch to discover it's not even seven o'clock yet.

I groan, consider trying to get back to sleep, then figure it's probably not worth it, not after the effort it took the night before. Instead, I lumber over to where the radio is playing softly to itself in the corner and turn it off, then go in search of a cup of coffee.

Through the kitchen window, the back yard is a featureless mass of white that rapidly slopes down away from the deck. The sun has yet to break over the horizon to the left, though the sky has started to turn a kind of inky blue like deep ocean water. Patchy cloud, dark in the half-light, lurks in clumps, the remains of yesterday's snow flurries.

After coffee and what passes for breakfast, I leave the house wearing an extra sweater under my jacket and carrying a bag over one shoulder. The street outside is deserted this early on a winter Sunday morning, and the icy crust has been disturbed only by animal tracks and a couple of slushy tyre marks in the road. The church looks unoccupied, hardly what I'd expect. Even an hour or two before today's service,

I'd have thought someone would come in and turn the heating on. But God's house is empty.

I follow Main north, downhill. This side of town is almost a mirror image of the other, what I can see of it. Towards the bottom of the slope, though, things are different. Houses change suddenly from Victorian-era clapboard to rust-brown weathered brick; newer, but I'd guess still well over fifty years old. This dark band of homes is centred around the quick, shallow flow of Bleakwater River and the bridge that carries Route 100 across it. The smooth charcoal-coloured stones that form the bed of this glorified creek make the water seem black and poisoned, which I assume is what gave the river its name. From the bridge I can see up to the forest covering the lower slopes of Windover Mountain, where the sombre, shadowy river has its headwaters, and down to where it vanishes in the mist-shrouded trees that surround the lake.

Standing on the bridge, watching the stream pouring down the hill, I feel a chill pass through me as though last night's breeze has returned. But the air is still and milder than yesterday evening. Nevertheless, my extra layers suddenly seem unable to retain any heat and I start shivering. With the cold comes the feeling – the paranoid certainty – that someone is close by, maybe in the bushes by the river or in one of the houses nearest the bridge, and they're staring at me. An unseen pair of eyes is burning through me, baleful and laced with hatred. I remember the corpse of the dog I thought I saw the night before and shudder.

The bridge now seems an empty, lonely place to be standing and even though there's no logical reason for it, I hurry off and up the road. The cold and the sense of evil fall away as I pass the last two rows of houses – the only homes built on the north bank of the river – and leave Bleakwater Ridge behind.

I hike up the highway for half an hour or so. Traffic is

sparse; only half a dozen vehicles pass me as I hug the shoulder, trying not to get caught in the dirty ice-water slop kicked up by their tyres. A couple of the cars slow down as they pass – perhaps wondering whether I'm a motorist who's broken down, or whether I'm a stray hitchhiker going from nowhere to nowhere much. None of them stop.

A couple of miles outside town the road takes a sharp right-hand curve before plunging down into a particularly long and deep furrow between ridges. The trees on either side are tough, ragged evergreens. Just before I reach the bottom of the dip, I come across a gap torn in the wiry undergrowth to the right, leading away downhill. The shredded ends of twigs, branches and old, dead bushes look fresh and the gap itself is more or less vehicle width. It might be the site of nothing more than a traffic accident caused by the ice, but I know it isn't.

This is where Gemma died.

Before I follow the trail carved by her car as it rolled off the road, I take out my digital camera and photograph the gap left in the trees and the roadside around it. Then I walk out into the middle of the highway and start taking pictures of the view up, down and around the area where she was shot. Barring the long-distance hunting-accident theory, the bullet would have travelled in a flat arc from the shooter's position, so I know the place he fired from should be visible from the road. I've finished with the southbound pictures and I'm almost through their northbound counterparts when a horn blares behind me and I have to scurry out of the road to avoid a close encounter with a red pickup. The driver slows as he passes, waving a hand and shouting incoherently at me. Then he speeds up and disappears. Job done, I let the camera hang around my neck, collect my bag from the bushes and step off the road into the trees.

The air under the canopy seems to be colder than that outside, ice-cloaked needles shielding the world beneath them from the weak heat of the winter sun. Undergrowth is sparse, the forest floor dry and brown. The trail of snapped twigs and shallow ruts in the earth left by what I'm assuming is Gemma's car runs for maybe thirty feet down the slope – a drop of eight or nine feet from the level of the road – before coming to an end in front of a solid-looking pine. The bark of the tree has been mashed and battered a couple of feet off the ground, though not seriously. I guess the car wasn't travelling very fast by this point. I photograph the damage, along with the rest of the tracks, before checking the tree itself. There are chips of dark blue paint in the mangled bark, the same colour as Gemma's Malibu.

I examine the ground at the base of the tree, digging my fingers into the frost to determine the position of the wheels, and from that, the area that would constitute the crime scene surrounding the car. I have to fight the impulse to ignore it and check the road since that's where she was shot. I keep telling myself that the cops haven't found the bullet, that there's a slim chance it was lodged in her sedan, only to be thrown clear once it came to a stop.

It only takes a minute or so of moving my fingers through the crust and over the surface of the frozen dirt beneath to ascertain the final position of the tyres. I can guess the angle of the car from the path between here and the gap leading to the road, but the disturbances caused when it was winched out make it impossible to be more exact. I find a couple of stubby sticks a foot or so long and wedge them into the earth to mark the outer edge of the wheels. It takes a fair amount of effort to dig them into place and I've just stood up to admire my handiwork and rub my chafed hands when I hear a woman's voice from behind me, up the hill.

'Are you okay down there, sir? Is there anything I can help you with?'

I know even before looking that the voice belongs to a cop. And she doesn't sound particularly pleased to see me. I guess I've been mistaken for either a souvenir hunter with a freakish taste for death, a journalist running a story behind the police's back, or a meddling amateur trying to solve the case. Maybe that's all I am.

I turn around. Framed in the gap at the top of the slope is a woman somewhere in her mid to late twenties with dark hair barely visible beneath her cap. She's wearing the dark uniform and puffy winter jacket of the Lamoille County Sheriff's Department – I can make out the badge with its five-pointed star even from here.

Up to the highway, to where the woman stands by her cruiser. As I get closer I can see that her face has flushed pink in the cold – the difference between the heated interior of the red-and-white Impala by the roadside and the outdoor air, I guess. She's attractive in a boyish kind of way.

'I'm fine, thanks,' I say when I reach her.

'We had a report that there was someone wandering the highway in this area,' she says. Her uncertain tone suggests she's not sure how to phrase the 'what the hell are you doing here?' question that is undoubtedly on her mind. 'Are you out here hiking, sir? Are you living or staying somewhere local?'

I think for a moment, trying to work out who might have told the LCSD about me. 'Was the guy who gave you the report driving a red pickup?'

'I couldn't say.'

'I was taking a photo from the road over there –' I gesture a few yards down the blacktop – 'and was late seeing him coming. That's all. I'm not hiking and I am staying somewhere local.'

The officer nods. I realize I must look a little ragged and this won't help shake her suspicions. 'And what exactly are you doing out here, sir?' she asks.

I glance behind me at the trees, then over at the road. When I answer, it's almost as though I'm speaking to myself. 'This is where she died.'

'That's a police matter, sir.' The officer's tone is curt and distinctly unfriendly. 'I'd appreciate it if you left it for the authorities to handle and don't go disturbing things. Let us do our jobs and let the victim rest in peace.'

'My name's Alex Rourke. She was my girlfriend.'

My reply forces her to reconsider her attitude towards me and her response to the whole situation. I watch as her expression changes, hard-nosed authority fading to the soft, dead-eyed smile of pity reserved for overwrought relatives. I've seen it plenty of times before. When she speaks, though, there's real warmth and compassion in her voice.

'Look,' she says, 'I'm sorry for what happened to her, I really am, and I do know what you're going through isn't easy. But you've got to let the professionals work through this.'

'What makes you think I'm not here just to pay my respects?'

'People who do that don't normally take photos,' she replies. 'And I saw you digging around down there. A crime scene team from the State Police already went over the ground where we found her. If there was anything there to find, they'd have got it already. They're trained for exactly that sort of thing.'

Something kicks at the back of my head. Fatigue-addlement keeps it blurred for the moment, though, so I say, 'I used to be an FBI agent. I was trained for that sort of thing as well, and I've done it plenty of times. I know you're giving me the "distraught loved ones getting in the way" speech, and I understand why. But I'm not some grief-stricken accountant who's watched too much *CSI* and got it in his head that he's the best hope there is for cracking the case.'

She smiles and sighs, shaking her head. 'Maybe so, but if you start hunting around on your own you're liable to end up being arrested for interfering with an investigation.'

'I spoke to Detective Flint. The State Police are working on the theory that either it was a hunting accident, or that there was some nut wandering out here with a rifle and that she was just the first person he saw. Both of those are a crock of shit. Who hunts at night around here, this time of year? Why hasn't anyone noticed there's a lunatic living in town? I won't interfere with their investigation because I don't believe they've got much of one.'

I look at the woods behind me, as much to get my breath back and try to maintain my calm as anything else. 'Besides,' I say, 'the scene's been released. I'm not breaking the law coming out here.' The thought that kicked earlier comes into focus. 'You said "where *we* found her". I spoke to a guy called Ed Markham in the bar last night and he said he knew what had happened to Gemma because he'd talked to Sylvia . . . Sylvia Ehrlich in the Sheriff's Department.'

'That's me,' she says, plainly surprised that I know her name.

'You found her?'

'I was on patrol shift that evening. I saw that someone had ploughed into the trees. It wasn't much of a gap, but the bare ends of the branches where the wood had snapped were enough to make it stand out. I took a look, then radioed in.'

'And you went down to check out the car.'

Sylvia nods. 'It looked like she'd gone off the road in the ice. You could see where it'd rolled into the woods. She looked bad, and when I checked for a pulse there was nothing. Wayne – Officer Cevik – arrived a couple of minutes after I called it in – he'd just finished with a breakdown south of Bleakwater. We waited for the ME and the ambulance to show up. We only realized what had actually happened after they came.'

'How bad did it look?'

'Mr Rourke, I don't think I should be going into details with you.'

'Yeah, I know this is awkward for you,' I say, frowning. 'But it's more awkward for me. I'm trying to get a picture of how the woman I loved died, and if you can't help me then I'm going to have to go on guessing and imagining and never knowing for sure. Let me tell you what I believe so far, and you can fill in anything you want to.'

I take a breath, fixing the details in my mind, before continuing. 'It had just started snowing again. She was somewhere right about here on the highway, probably not going very fast because of the weather, when she got shot. The car swerved off the road and into the trees. If it had gone off the other side, it'd have rolled to a stop straight away. But it went downhill, so it still had a little speed when it hit the tree. Not much, or there'd be more damage to the bark. So I'm guessing the car wasn't too badly smashed when you found it.'

Sylvia searches my face for something. 'How do you know it had started snowing?'

'She was speaking to my voicemail when she died. I got the message later.'

'Oh boy, that must've been so awful,' she says and from her tone, she really means it. 'You've got more guts than me to go through this after hearing . . . well, after hearing it all.'

I try a smile. Not great, probably out of place on my weary

features, but it's the best I can manage and it's a way to avoid thinking about Gemma's last words.

'So how'd it look?' I ask again.

'The windshield was a mess, the front end was all bent out of shape and the radiator had gone,' she says. 'It was still steaming when we found it. The back window was all smashed and there were still bits of glass on top of the trunk.'

I'm impressed by her memory for details. A good cop trait. 'And Gemma?'

'You sure you want to hear it?'

'Yeah.' I nod, swallowing hard.

'She was forward, face down over the wheel. I could see blood on the front of her coat, but nothing else. The driver's side door had popped open a fraction from the impact, but the glass was intact. I opened the door so I could lean in and find out if she was alive or not.'

'Was there any sign that anyone else had been near the car – footprints, things like that?' I ask, unwilling to dwell long on the image of Gemma slumped, dead in the wreckage. 'Did you check the road at all?'

'I don't remember seeing any tracks in the snow, but it was dark and I was looking at a car wreck, not a murder. I think the State Police examined the road when they took over the scene, but I'm not sure. By that time, there'd been me, Wayne, the doctor and a couple of paramedics around the place.'

'So at least two cruisers, a car and an ambulance, plus whatever the VSP turned up with. How much other traffic was there?'

'Not a lot – mostly folk either coming back from work or heading into Bleakwater or Johnson for the evening.'

The radio in the Impala crackles into life with the indistinct voice of a dispatcher. Sylvia leans into the car and has a short conversation with the disembodied soul on the other end of the connection, then turns to me and says, 'Sorry. Duty calls.'

'No problem. Before you go, is there any way you could get hold of a copy of the crime scene report that I could look at? You could tell Detective Flint or whoever's in charge that, I don't know, your department wants to see if you could have been more careful or something.'

She purses her lips and frowns. 'I don't know about that, Mr Rourke. I mean, telling you what we found is one thing, letting you have the report's another.' She sighs. 'I'll ask my sergeant, Ken Radford, and see what he says. But don't get your hopes up.'

'Thanks, I really appreciate that.'

'Have you got a number I can reach you at?'

I give her my cell before adding, 'Just in case I find anything, is there some way I can get in touch with you?'

'Well, you can get me through the department.' She thinks for a moment, then reads off a number. 'That's my cell phone. But don't go calling it unless it's important, okay? Christ knows what my husband would think.'

I thank her and she waves goodbye, drops into her Impala and slips it into gear.

7

Once her cruiser has vanished down the road, my eyes wander beyond the blacktop and up the wooded mountain spur to the south. The point where Gemma died sits at the bottom of a trough of land, and it occurs to me that if I were to choose a spot to shoot someone, this would be it. There's more than enough cover, her car would have had to slow to handle the icy road and, with the bend in the highway on top of the southern ridge, it's possible to look all the way along this section from hiding. Not far from the road the slope steepens considerably, with jumbled boulders interspersed through the forest.

In my mind's eye I try to envisage a line between the rocks and Gemma's position when the bullet hit. It's easy to get a rough idea, but the human brain isn't built for accurately estimating height and perspective. In the end I walk out to the middle of the southbound carriageway and sight along an outstretched arm, then try and follow the resulting angle back behind me.

As far as I can tell, if there'd been no car there, the bullet should have smacked into the asphalt where the road begins to rise again. But there doesn't seem to be any obvious damage to the surface, aside from normal wear. I check the edges of the woods to either side of the highway, just in case the shooter wasn't aiming directly in line with the blacktop. I've found nothing after half an hour and as my toes are going numb and I continue to draw strange looks from everyone who passes, I give up on that line of enquiry. Since there's a chance the bullet lodged in the car and then fell out as it went off the road, I go back to the gap in the trees and start combing through the snow, looking for anything metallic.

For nearly two hours I follow the path left by the Malibu down, up and down again. Every once in a while I have to stop to breathe some life back into my fingers; I can't wear gloves for grubbing in the snow because I need my sense of touch, even though the cold does a pretty good job of robbing me of it regardless. And it's not just my hands that suffer the effects – my knees become stiff, my back is increasingly sore and my face feels like it's been replaced with a loose rubber mask.

But I can't give up. The reason I'm here is too overpowering, and it's only possible for me to think about Gemma's death because I'm here trying to figure it out. With each new pass over the ground I become a little more desperate. More than once I catch myself muttering like a madman as I feverishly run my hands through the ice, pine needles and frozen mulch that cover the ground.

Then I see that the snow is starting to melt and stain red.

Every sweep I make with my hands adds to the streaks of crimson. Blood flows slowly but steadily from my left index finger. A short, clean cut has opened in the flesh, running parallel to the side of the nail.

I follow the trail back to what seems to be its beginning. The thin band of scarlet starts about a foot away from where I'd guess the back of the car to have been. There, invisible in the snow, I find a shard of glass maybe a quarter of an inch square. I hold it carefully and gaze thoughtfully at it as if hoping it will reveal some great truth to me, all the while sucking on my injured finger until it's warmed up enough to sting with pain.

Checking around, this time alert for stray reflections, I find eight or nine more shards hidden in the ice. All of them are near the back of the car. I'm too cold, too tired and too relieved to have found anything at all – even broken glass makes me feel less like an idiot for being here – to try and work out if it means anything. I photograph the scene a few more times, probably not very well, then creakily straighten up and return to the road. When I get there, I'm hit by a sudden nicotine craving and realize I haven't smoked in hours; I guess old habits of not contaminating crime scenes die hard. I light up, hoping just once that the glowing stick will warm me or give me enough of a rush to lift my fatigue.

It does neither but I finish it. I pick up my feet to start the walk home, but where the road crosses the ridge to the south, I make a detour up to the rocky section of slope overlooking the highway.

The woods thin out over the difficult ground, and this in turn has opened up the space underneath for thorns and tough, scrubby weeds. I'm not much of a woodsman but I grew up surrounded by enough greenery in the far north of Maine to know a little, and I know someone has been this way before. Here and there are broken and crushed stems leading in what seems to be a coherent trail uphill. They're not close enough together to give a continuous set of tracks – the woods are too packed for the wiry plant growth to have spread far – but what there is has been perfectly frozen in place, as though the land itself has been waiting for me to find it.

Forty feet or so above the level of the highway, I come to a weathered outcrop of rock which looks directly down the road as it runs across the dip between ridges. I brush away the snow that coats the stones and the dirt of the forest next to them, hoping for something that will confirm my theory

– a cigarette butt, footprints, even the spent shell casing from the bullet. Nothing but small scrapes in the lichen on the rocks, and I'm not sure I didn't cause them myself. All I can do is photograph the view and the maybe-marks, then head back down to the road and hike home.

'What do you want?' The voice is guarded rather than unfriendly. Expectations of insurance sales pitches, new windows, informational pamphlets. I don't blame him – it's only natural when a complete stranger shows up on your doorstep on a Sunday afternoon.

'I'm calling about the woman who lived across the street. Did you notice anything strange in her behaviour, or people hanging around the neighbourhood? Anything at all that was out of the ordinary over the past couple of weeks.'

The guy regards me suspiciously, an unspoken *No, but I sure am now* running through his mind. A little podgy around the midriff, receding hairline, very ordinary red sweater. There's a newish-looking SUV on the driveway, and I'd guess that he has a white-collar job in Waterbury or somewhere similar. I can hear some sort of classical music playing in the house behind him. No idea which composer; it's not my genre.

'I already spoke to the police when they called round,' he says after a moment's thought. 'Who the hell are you?'

'My name's Alex Rourke. I'm a private detective and I am – was – the woman's boyfriend.'

He doesn't tell me to get lost, but I have the impression he'd like to politely bid me goodbye nonetheless. He's just trying to think of a way of doing it that won't seem insensitive. In the end, he settles on saying, 'I didn't see nothing, like I told them.'

'Nothing at all? You didn't see anyone you don't know in the street, no one called on her?'

'Not that I saw, not in the last couple of days before . . . y'know.'

I frown. 'Did you see anyone before then?'

He folds his arms and sighs. 'Last time I saw anyone call on her must've been a week or so before it happened. She spoke to some guy on the porch. Looked like she knew him. They chatted away for a couple of minutes, she might even have invited him in, but he'd left his car engine running and didn't stop by. Gave her a cardboard file folder, she waved goodbye. Like I said, he looked like a friend. Apart from that, the last person I remember seeing there was you, or at least someone with the same car as you. If you're looking for any more than that then I'm sorry, I can't help you.'

I've spent most of the afternoon going to every house on the street within sight of Gemma's. Until now, it's been the same story at every single one: we saw nothing, we told the police, we still don't remember seeing anything. 'What did the man she spoke to look like?'

'I don't know.' He shrugs. 'Regular guy. Middle-aged. Wore a tie and a long coat, one of those expensive wool ones. Might have had a suit as well. His car was silver, new looking. I don't remember the model. That's all I know.'

His eyes dart in the direction of the door, which closes an inch as he does it. I guess my time is up. 'Yeah, well thanks for the information,' I say, then leave.

I'm tired and I'm cold again. Tomorrow I'll speak to the people who worked with Gemma; I'd guess from his description that whoever called by the house was one of her colleagues. If not, it could be something worth following up.

For now the only thing I can do is to go through the house and see if there's anything to suggest she'd made any enemies, and also to see if I can find the file the guy left with Gemma. I don't know if the police have already done this, but since the place seemed pretty much undisturbed when I arrived, I doubt it.

The first thing I check is the unopened mail, the personal letters I left alone when I arrived the day before. One has a handwritten address, the other is printed. I open the former first; a couple of pages of tight, neat script folded around a photograph. It's from her parents, letting her know how their vacation in San Francisco was going. It's postmarked last Wednesday. Gemma was already dead by the time it was sent.

I don't dare dwell on the letter or its contents, but move on instead to the second envelope. It contains a bill, nothing more. I drop it back by the mirror and head into the kitchen to properly check the notes by the phone. There doesn't seem to be anything of any great importance among them. Aside from a couple of scribbled phone numbers with 'Bob K', 'Celia' and other cryptic names next to them, there are what look like times and a couple of numbers for the St Johnsbury party. The remaining two pieces of paper seem to be responses – both negative – to enquiries she made for me about Adam Webb: 'Brattleboro – don't recognize' and 'Chief – not as far as she knows'.

Upstairs, I try Gemma's computer. Her most recently accessed files look to be notes from work she was typing up at home and the results of some email correspondence she was having with a couple of other pathologists. I can't see anything of importance there, though most of what they talk about goes over my head. The rest of her old email contains nothing threatening, just the usual mix of personal messages and, in the 'trash' mailbox, deleted junk. I download what messages are waiting for her. There are two more responses from other regional medical examiners saying they've not seen anyone resembling Webb. There are also a couple of messages from her sister Alice. The first asks what Gemma and I want for Christmas this year. The second arrived on Tuesday evening at about the time I was driving up the interstate to see her body.

Gem,

I tried to call you earlier but I guess you must be out. You doctors, always partying! Let me know what you and Alex want for Xmas so I can get my shopping done. Maybe he'll have popped the question by then, you never know. Have you got any plans for Thanksgiving yet?

Talk soon, sis. – Alice

I reread the last couple of sentences, then close down the program and move on, keeping my mind carefully blank. To let it slip would loose too many collected thoughts, feelings, about a future we'll never have. I have to lock down those parts of my soul. There are some papers and file folders in her study, but all of them relate to her job. If whatever the guy left with her was one of these, he must work at the hospital or for the ME's office. Once I've finished with the computer I go through the rest of the house, checking the drawers, closets and even the trash. I make the climb up into the attic room to see if Gemma moved any of her things into what used to be empty space; she didn't. Having finished with the interior, I step out into the back yard just in case anything's been disturbed.

The sun has vanished and although the sky above is still slowly-fading blue – the parts of it that aren't obscured by another advancing bank of tumbled cloud – the outside world seems gloomy and dark, more than I'd expect even with the advance of evening. The mountains to the west have already turned a deep grey, and I realize that it's the shadow of these vast granite buttresses that is deepening the twilight, shortening the day. The monolithic crags rise in a wall behind the town like a vast stone tidal wave that could, at any moment, engulf the tiny settlement in a shattering deluge of rock and earth, burying it for ever. I turn away from the looming, sinister presence and head back indoors.

Eight o'clock, the Owl's Head. The Sunday night crowd is thin, down a dozen or so heads on yesterday. Ed and Charlie are both in again, sitting at the same table as before. Once I've ordered dinner, Charlie gives me a little wave and I head over.

'Evening, Mr Rourke,' Ed says as I reach them. 'Pull up a chair.'

'Thanks. You guys come in here every night?'

Charlie glances at Ed, who doesn't seem to notice him or my question because he says, 'I hear you've been out and about asking folk about what happened. How's your investigation going?'

'So far, so nothing. How did you know I've been talking to people?' I wonder how well Ed knows Sylvia Ehrlich. It could be real useful if they're good friends.

'May Tyler saw you calling at houses on West. I guess no one could help you, huh?'

Bang goes the link to Ehrlich. 'No,' I say. 'They didn't see anything suspicious. I take it you guys haven't seen anyone strange around town? You seem pretty keyed-in to everything that goes on.'

Charlie's eyes flick towards Ed again, then he says, 'No one like that. There's not many out-of-towners stop here.'

'We'll keep our eyes open, though,' Ed adds. Like last night, there's a hint in his tone that suggests either he knows more than he's saying, or that there's something else going on.

The barmaid, Bella, slides a plate of beef stew in front of me. The conversation dies away somewhat to accommodate my meal. The quiet is broken, however, when Ed goes to take a leak. Charlie leans across to me and drops his voice to a conspiratorial whisper.

'You can trust us to keep our eyes open,' he says.

I'm not sure if it's a genuine, if rather odd, sentiment, or if he reckons I think they're a couple of old nuts ripe for a retirement home.

'We're in here every night, looking for anyone strange.'

'Why?' I ask. 'You get a lot of trouble in town?'

'No. It's Ed's idea. For two years now, he's been –' Charlie clams up as his companion emerges from the men's room. I get the impression that he doesn't want Ed to know that he's spilling some shared secret, so I don't ask what's going on. From the little hints and glances I'm getting from him, I'm hoping Ed will tell me himself once he feels he can trust me.

'I spoke to Sylvia Ehrlich from the Sheriff's Department,' I tell him after I've finished eating.

'Uh-huh.'

'She might be able to help me out. Maybe get hold of some files from the State Police for me.'

Ed sighs and shakes his head. 'Good luck to her. She's a good girl, Sylvia, but I doubt she has much chance of getting anything. Don't hold your breath.'

Not long after that, I make my excuses and leave. Snow is falling again, chalk dust blowing down from the mountains, and I hurry back. The town remains deserted. The stoplights at the intersection with West continue to shine like the pitiful strobes at a 1970s high school disco, but they do so to an empty dancefloor. I'm alone as I cross and vanish into the shadows.

I've had a little time to get used to its emptiness but the

house is no easier to settle in than last night, creaking and groaning. I try to prepare for the following day's tasks – which doesn't involve much more than making sure I know how to get to the hospital where Gemma worked – and then stretch out on the couch in front of a movie.

This is the first time today when I've properly relaxed, and fatigue slams into me almost immediately. I still don't – can't – feel tired, not in the sleepy sense of the word. By the time I'm halfway through the film, my raw, itchy eyes are picking up blurred spots of dark, shadowy movement at the edge of vision. Eventually, I decide I've had enough of this and crawl off the sofa on a tour of the house, checking all the doors and windows, just to be sure everything's locked down for the night.

The house is fairly warm; despite draughts blowing through some of the chinks in its armour, the heating system is a good, sturdy one. My first thought when I walk along the landing to Gemma's bedroom is therefore that the window inside must have blown open somehow. The air immediately in front of her door is cold, and as soon as I hit it my breath begins tracing fine spiderwebs of steam. The change from the ordinary warmth of the house to this pocket of winter is so sudden that a breeze coming from under the door seems like the only possible culprit. When I touch the handle the metal is ice cold and numbs my fingers, just like when I open the 'Vette on a frosty morning. I step inside and flick the light on, expecting to see the casement wide open and snow dancing on the bedcovers, collecting by Gemma's closet door.

The window is firmly shut and locked and the air is the same temperature as the rest of the house. I run my gaze around the uncomfortably deserted room just in case, but nothing seems out of place.

Puzzled, I turn off the light and close the door behind me. I pass back through the narrow band of cold and finish checking the last two rooms on this floor, still with no sign of where the mystery draught could be coming from.

The last place I look is the attic. Its bare floorboards seem solid enough, and there doesn't seem to be anything much wrong with the windows. From here I can hear the rattling and scraping of wood on wood. The breeze is tugging at the bare branches of the trees that mass by the lakeshore. Their gnarled limbs twist and sway, stark black shadows against the ice beyond, like fevered dancers at a religious ceremony. I watch for a while before breaking away and retreating towards the glow rising from the landing.

8

Driving north to Newport along the border between the mountains and the rolling piedmont of the state's Northeast Kingdom the following morning, my cell phone rings. I pull over before picking up.

'Mr Rourke?' A woman's voice.

'Good morning, Officer Ehrlich,' I say, hoping I'm right.

'How're you holding up?'

'Okay, thanks.' I don't tell her that I've only managed about ten hours' sleep in the past four or five days and that if I move my head too fast, brown-blue blotches surface briefly in my field of vision. 'What can I do for you?'

'I spoke to Sergeant Radford about getting hold of that scene report, if you're still interested.'

'Shoot.'

'Good news. He's asked the State Police for a copy and he's willing to let you look at it.'

I offer up a silent prayer. 'That's great, really. I appreciate that more than you know.'

'Don't get carried away yet. It might take a day or two to get hold of it, if the VSP agree in the first place. Ken doesn't want you coming into the office; he says if you do it'll be obvious to anyone with half a brain why he really pulled the report and he doesn't want word reaching Those On High.'

'Sure, I understand. You want to drop it off, or me to pick it up?'

At the other end of the phone I'm sure she's shrugging. 'Whatever's easy,' she says after a moment. 'Let's cross that bridge when we come to it. I just thought I'd let you know where we stand.'

'Thanks. What does your sergeant drink?'

'Um, hold on.' There's the clatter of the receiver being laid on a desk, then the *thump, thump* of Sylvia's footsteps fading. I hear a door open and some muffled conversation. Then she returns. 'Scotch,' she says. 'Usually as good as he can get, but he's not too fussy.'

I smile. 'I'll see what I can do.'

'Just don't go telling the newspapers.' From her tone, I guess she's joking. 'If they found out you were able to bribe two cops with sympathy and a bottle of whisky we'll all end up out of a job.'

'Your secret's safe.'

Newport would be nothing more than a small town in most other places. In this corner of Vermont, though, it's about as close to urban as it's possible to get. The city is neat and well kept, although there's nothing much in particular here. Sure, the lake's nice when it's not frozen – tree-lined and hilly right across the border into Quebec – but that's not exactly unusual in New England. Just now the town looks almost monochrome – black highway, spindly leafless trees, white snow; even the red-brown of most of the buildings looks dark from a distance.

I find Kingdom Hospital without any difficulty and park in the lot outside. I don't have any official reason for being here, no badge to show, no authority to back me up. I'd like some; it'd be a lot easier to ask someone the way to the morgue instead of wandering around without directions.

As it is, I wait until I see someone else heading for the entrance, then tag along a few yards behind. I let the old woman negotiate the doors first, dogging her footsteps, then head purposefully in the direction indicated by the 'elevators' signs while she's occupying the receptionist. No one gives me a second glance as I push the button for the basement and vanish behind the sliding steel doors.

Downstairs, it turns out my problem is going to be finding the mortuary. I wish I'd visited Gemma at work. I've been walking aimlessly along empty corridors for what seems like hours – probably more like fifteen minutes – when I start to hear a whirring hum that echoes and bounces from the walls. Rounding the next corner I come across a young guy in a blue uniform pushing some kind of combined floor polisher–cleaner system; it's this barrel-like contraption that's making the noise.

'Mind how you go,' he half-yells as I reach him. 'Tiles might be a little slippery.'

'Thanks.' He doesn't seem to be regarding me with any suspicion, so I say, 'I'm looking for the morgue, but I'm kinda lost. Which way is it?'

'Morgue, huh? Back the way you came, two turns to the right.'

I thank him and I'm turning round when he adds, 'Figured it. You got the look.'

I stop and look back at him. 'What do you mean?'

'She was nice. I liked her. We talked some times.'

'Who? Gemma?'

The janitor nods, but I'm not sure whether it's in answer to my question or part of some unfathomable interior monologue. 'I see it.'

'What?'

'In your eyes, in your face. I liked her. It's a real shame what happened, and now you've got the Angel of Death riding inside you. I can see it, looking out. She's killing you, eating you up from inside.'

I blink in confusion, unsure whether he's referring to

Gemma or the 'Angel of Death', but I don't ask. I just wait to see if he continues.

'It burns, and it's burning you up. You'd best finish it before the Angel kills you. I see it.' He smiles, eyes turned upward in fond recollection. 'She was nice. I liked her.'

'Sure.' It's about all I can think of to say. Since it seems a little impolite, I add, 'Thanks.'

'I see it,' the guy calls after me as I head for the morgue. 'Black wings, all around you, man. Darkness. Hounds to the hunters. Hounds to the hunters!'

I hurry around the corner and out of sight.

The hospital's morgue is small but well equipped. There's a cosy laboratory-cum-office to the side; I can see it through the safety-glass windows in the door. The mortuary itself is sealed away from prying eyes. Two people look up from desks in the lab as I knock softly on the door and then step in. A third desk is conspicuously empty, blank. Gemma's, I guess, her personal items now cleared away. The first lab worker is a man somewhere deep into middle age, with thick glasses and a kind of studious puppy-dog look to him. The second is a woman around Gemma's age, tall and thin without appearing hawkish. She speaks first.

'What do you want?' she says with an exasperated sigh. 'Visitors aren't allowed down here.'

'My name's Alex Rourke. Gemma's boyfriend.'

Her expression changes immediately, a reaction I'm well used to by now. 'Come in, come in,' she says. 'She used to talk about you all the time. This past week must've been hell for you. I'm still not used to working here without seeing her. I keep expecting to find her in the morgue or at her computer. I'm Ashley, Ashley Lynch.'

'Clyde Turner,' says the guy, extending his hand. 'We all miss Gemma.'

'Thanks. She's talked about you both quite a lot too. Nice to meet you in person. But this isn't exactly a social call. I'm trying to find out what happened to her and why.'

Ashley nods. 'She said you were a detective or a cop, something like that.'

'Something like that.' I nod. 'You two worked with her all the time, right? Were you here the day she died?'

They nod almost in unison.

'Can you think of anything that might have made anyone want to kill her? Did she mention that she'd seen anyone strange at all, had she been in any arguments, anything like that? Doesn't matter how small.'

'Not that I can think of,' Clyde says. 'She didn't mention anything to me. Seemed normal. Nothing strange at all about the day she died.' He says it quite flatly, a subconscious reminder that, like Gemma, these two spend every day around death.

Ashley nods. 'Same here. She never had any trouble with anyone that I can think of. The closest she got to that was Frank – Dr Altmann from Physical Therapy, but that wasn't trouble so much. Kinda sweet, in a silly sort of way.'

'What do you mean?'

'He had a bit of a crush on her, I think – *everyone* knows about it. He never did anything about it, though. I mean, if he knew of any parties or anything he'd make sure she got invited, and he'd always talk with her whenever he saw her, but he's too shy and polite to have ever tried going further.'

'What do you mean?' I repeat.

She frowns, thinking. 'Well, like, if the two of you had ever broken up, I don't think it would have been long before he asked her out. But while she was spoken for, he wouldn't do anything to make her unhappy, if you see what I mean.'

'Unrequited,' Clyde chips in. 'Gunther from *Friends* but without the creepy stalker vibe.'

'Yeah,' says Ashley, smiling at this description. 'He's nice. He was real hurt when he found out what happened. We went for a drink that evening, talked everything over.'

Clyde flashes a quick grin. 'Now who's being quick to move in once things don't work out?' He blinks and looks at me, apology written all over his face. 'Sorry,' he says. 'That was in poor taste.'

Mortician humour. I shrug. 'Don't worry about it.'

'I think I'm going for coffee before I put my foot in it any more, just the same,' he says. 'I'll keep an eye out for any of the management heading this way. They don't often come down here – I think they're scared of seeing a dead person in the flesh – but it'd be best if they don't know you're here.'

He slips out into the corridor. The distant whirr of the floor polisher briefly overlays the lab's background electrical hum before the door shuts again and cuts it off.

'Was Dr Altmann here the day Gemma died?' I say to Ashley.

'No. He had the first half of the week off work. You don't really think he'd have done anything, do you? I doubt he even knows how to fire a gun.'

I shake my head. 'You're probably right. I'll talk to him. What does he look like?'

'Forty, almost as tall as you. He's got dark hair but it's starting to show grey. It makes him look distinguished. He drives a silver Audi.'

'Where does he live?'

'Barton. I can't remember the address; I've only been there once, to a retirement party he threw for one of the doctors. I can find out if he's working today and what time he'll be free if you want.'

‘Thanks. What about recent cases – was there anything Gemma worked on over the week or two before she died that might have had anything to do with it?’

‘Like what? Death’s a tricky business. Everyone takes it differently.’

I shrug. ‘Anything unusual, I guess. Someone killed Gemma for a reason, so maybe that reason was something to do with what she was working on.’

‘You mean homicides?’ she asks.

‘Not necessarily.’

‘I can’t recall any particularly sensitive cases, not recently.’ Ashley moves to the door and quickly checks the corridor outside is clear. ‘I’ll tell you what, I’ll run you off copies of everything we’ve handled over the past couple of weeks or so, and you can look through yourself. But *please* don’t ever tell anyone you got them from me. If word got out, I could kiss my career goodbye. These things are supposed to be confidential.’

I raise my eyebrows in surprise. ‘Don’t take the risk if you don’t want to. I don’t want you to lose your job on my account.’

She smiles and shakes her head. ‘Gemma was a friend and I want to see whoever killed her get caught. Whatever I can do that helps you, it’s yours.’

Half an hour later, I leave the lab with a bundled wad of paper wedged firmly inside my coat. Clyde eyeballs me in either a conspiratorial or suspicious way as we pass in the doorway – I can’t tell which – but he says nothing even though he must know what I’m carrying. The maniacal janitor is nowhere to be found as I head back to the elevator, but I catch sight of him again as I walk through reception towards the parking lot. He’s using a spray bottle and cloth to wipe down some of the seats, but pauses long enough to hold up a hand in what could be a wave or some sort of salute. I give a half-hearted gesture of reply and step out into the cold again.

According to Ashley, Dr Altmann's shift finishes at half past four, so I have some time to kill until I can catch him. I drive the 'Vette down to a spot near the lakeshore and read through the files.

Eric Burns, 20, suspected homicide. Hit-and-run victim, the last post-mortem Gemma carried out. Death caused by blunt trauma consistent with vehicle impact, impossible to tell whether any of the damage was caused beforehand. Preliminary results of blood screening indicate small amounts of heroin or a similar opiate in his bloodstream. This must be the guy Gemma mentioned last time I saw her. She doesn't seem to have turned up anything unexpected, so I don't see anything that might have got her killed. I skip over the final few notations and move on.

Rosemary Saunders, 59, unattended death. Hospital patient in for surgery on one of her knees, died unexpectedly two nights after her operation. Post-mortem needed to determine the cause of death. Coronary thrombosis is the conclusion in Gemma's report.

Lester Hoffman, 34, and Kate Wylie, 32, accidental deaths. Both were killed in a rather messy traffic accident on I-91. The only real work for Gemma to do was to determine whether Lester, the driver, had been drinking or if he'd simply lost control of his car. She concluded the latter. There's no mention of anyone else involved in the accident.

Arthur Styles, 72, unattended death. Had a heart attack in his sleep while at his home in Newport. His post-mortem seems to have been little more than a formality.

Adele Laine, 28, unattended death. Laine seems to have been a habitual drug user, eventually falling prey to an overdose. From Gemma's notes, it seems that if her last hit hadn't killed her, kidney or liver damage would probably have done the job before too long. There's no mention of any suspicious circumstances, and although I can't be sure without the State Police case notes, I doubt there could have been any connection between Laine's death and Gemma's.

After these first half-dozen files, the pattern of normal, inconsequential passings continues. This corner of north-eastern Vermont certainly seems quiet – Eric Burns is the only homicide in the first fifteen cases, and I can't see any more on a quick flick further through.

I root around in the glove compartment for a rubber band to hold the bundle of paper together, then go buy myself a coffee and a sandwich.

'It's been ages since I've done this,' Gemma says. We're ambling along the boardwalk that runs along Newport's lakefront. Late spring sunshine sparkles from the water but there's a chilly breeze blowing down from the north. I'm nursing a cup of coffee and we're both wrapped up in our coats.

'What do you mean?'

'Gone for a walk along the shore like this. I think the last time, I must have been with my dad. My family used to drive down to a beach on Blue Hill Bay sometimes when I was little. We'd walk along by the sea, play around on the beaches. Most times we went you could see out as far as Mount Desert Island. Us kids would have ice cream or doughnuts and Mom and Dad would let us run off so they could have some time to themselves.'

I smile. 'You should have said. We passed a doughnut place five minutes ago. It's a bit cold for ice cream, though.'

'Ice cream is *always* good,' Gemma replies, grinning. 'You should know that by now.'

'How could I have forgotten?'

It's nearly five by the time a guy matching Ashley's description of Dr Altmann steps through the doors of the hospital and hurries across the parking lot. He's wearing a long coat over his suit and he's carrying a briefcase. When he climbs into the silver Audi, I know it's him and I follow out on to the road, keeping the 'Vette at a sensible distance as he heads for the interstate and the fifteen-mile drive to his house. No deviations or stops en route. He keeps to the speed limit and shows no sign that he's noticed me. When we reach Barton I tail him to a street of large houses with even larger yards. I pull up by the junction and watch as he turns into his driveway. Then I park out of sight. No sense letting him see my 'Vette, just in case I have to do this again.

'Yes?' he says when he opens the front door to find me on his porch. He's ditched the jacket and tie, but hasn't finished getting changed for the evening. His voice is soft and quiet.

'Dr Frank Altmann? My name's Alex Rourke. I'm a private detective. I just need a few minutes of your time.'

'I know the name from somewhere . . .'

'Gemma Larson's boyfriend.'

He looks me over, then nods, frowning nervously. 'Come in.'

Altmann's home is spacious and looks like he's always lived in it alone. The only family photos in here are of him and an older couple, presumably his parents. There's also a couple of framed pictures of groups of his hospital colleagues, including one that features Gemma. He doesn't offer me a seat and I don't take one.

'Dr Altmann, you were friends with Gemma, right?'

Mixed emotions cross his face. 'Yes. We met at a staff party not long after she joined the hospital. I don't usually have much to do with the mortuary, but I've known Ashley Lynch, one of the lab technicians, for some time. If we had our breaks at the same time, I'd sometimes have lunch with Gemma or Ashley.'

'You saw each other fairly regularly. Did she act strangely at all before she died? Worried about something or someone? Anything like that.'

'Not that I noticed.'

I nod. 'When was the last time you saw Gemma?'

'The week before she died,' he says. Again, there's something in his eyes, his face, when he replies.

'Have you ever been to her house?'

'What the hell has that got to do with anything?'

I hold up my hands. I'm not trying to be rude; something about him just grates. 'I'm just trying to find out as much as I can about the time leading up to my girlfriend's death, Dr Altmann. Someone was seen calling at her house a week before her murder. He drove a silver car and seemed to be a friend of hers. He left a file folder of some sort with her. I need to know whether that was you or if there was someone else who'd visited her recently.'

'Yes, that was me,' he says. He still doesn't look too happy. 'The hospital administrators are working on some procedural changes and I'd said I'd drop a copy off with her as I had to go to Burlington that day.'

'And you noticed nothing strange?'

'No,' Altmann says, sighing.

'Are you married, Dr Altmann? Regular girlfriend, anything like that?'

He flushes red. 'What the hell does that have to do with you?'

'You said you were friends with Gemma. Did you ever want to take things further than that, y'know, get into a relationship with her?'

For a moment he pauses, unmoving. His eyes narrow slightly and he says, 'I want you to leave, Mr Rourke.'

'I'm just trying to figure out what happened, that's all.'

'It strikes me that's the job of the police!' he snaps. 'I'll happily answer any questions they have, because I cared for Gemma. She was a friend. You are neither a cop nor a friend. So get the hell off my property.'

I can't stop myself pushing. A kick of bile at the back of my throat; anger, grief, jealousy by turns fighting for control even as I lose it. I *want* it to be Altmann who killed Gemma. And I *want* him to give himself away. 'You cared for her. Did you fancy her, Dr Altmann? She was good looking, wasn't she? I know that, you know that. Did you want to get her into bed? You want to fuck her? Must've stung you that she didn't return those feelings, huh?'

'Get the fuck out of here!' the doctor yells. Takes a step towards me, face red, hands clenching.

'You weren't working on the day she died, right?' I say. 'Just so I have as complete a picture as possible, could you tell me where you were between, say, five and six that evening?'

Altmann rushes at me, fury in his eyes, yelling incoherently. Hands scrabbling for grip on my jacket collar, around my shoulders, grab, hold and push. Almost like playing football. There's a surprising amount of strength in his arms and I figure he must work out. I don't resist, though I could, as he barges me backwards before hurling me away from him with all his force, out into his porch. By the time I've caught my balance he's slammed the door shut.

From somewhere inside, I think I hear him sobbing.

9

Night has well and truly settled over the countryside by the time I stop the 'Vette at the side of the road and check my directions for the fifth time. I'm just outside the town of Centerville, a name that must have made sense at the time it was founded but now seems a little ludicrous because it doesn't seem to be the centre of anywhere much. I'm looking for a dirt track that joins the road about half a mile north of town, just past a fallen tree lying in the grass bordering the blacktop.

I've been up and down this stretch of winding, icy asphalt four times without seeing anything. The land on either side of the highway all looks the same to me, and I'm starting to wonder whether you need to live here to know what to look for. Nevertheless, I make a U-turn and give it one more try. At last I see the track, squeezed between two vast clouds of snow-covered bushes that jut out into the roadway and all but cover the opening.

The dirt road runs three hundred yards to a farmhouse with light shining yellow through its windows and a large wooden barn. Parked on the gravel between them are a blue SUV and a well-used pickup.

Sylvia Ehrlich is waiting on the porch, wrapped in a thick sweater and jeans, when I climb out of the 'Vette carrying a bottle of whisky for Sergeant Radford. The air outside is clean and sharply cold, like it's been flash-frozen from some earlier time to preserve its freshness.

'That's quite a car,' Sylvia calls out to me. 'I must've heard it a mile off.'

Now she mentions it, the land around does seem to have been shocked into silence; ordinary night noises have yet to return and fill in the considerable void left by the 'Vette's thunderous engine.

'Well, I figured I'd been driving the standard Bureau sedan for long enough, so when I left I thought I'd try something different – you know, make a clean break and all that. Saw it at an auction not long after.'

'What is it, a '71 Stingray?'

'Sixty-nine – a very good year. Unless you have to buy gas for it, of course. Ten, twelve miles to the gallon makes it an expensive anachronism.' I light a cigarette. 'Beautiful machine, though. Sorry, I should've asked if you minded,' I add, holding up the Marlboro.

'Life wouldn't be easy for me if I did; Bill, my husband, gets through about forty a day. Come on in.'

I follow her through into a house that has clearly been standing for a good hundred years or so. The hallway is long but narrow, the same with the stairs, and the ceiling is higher than I'm used to from my own place in Boston. The place even smells old, a faint hint of oak and a musty gravy-like scent that permeates the air. Although the interior is brightly painted and spotlessly clean – I'd feel safe eating my dinner off the floorboards – the Ehrlichs have kept the farmhouse look, preferring old wood and rough-to-the-touch plaster-work to cleaner, more clinical modern aesthetics.

There's quite a collection of shoes, boots and coats stacked or hanging from hooks just inside the door, but while some of them are a little muddy, none look particularly battered. From that and the lack of machinery, milk storage tanks and other quasi-industrial clutter I'd expect outside, I'm pretty certain this isn't a working farm any more.

Sylvia leads me down the hall to a doorway that opens out

into the living room. The tinny sound of TV laughter pipes from somewhere beyond. There's a rangy, soft-looking guy probably a good seven or eight years younger than me sitting in an armchair, watching whatever's on. He's wearing a blue-checked shirt and jogging pants.

'This is Bill, my husband,' she says, doing the introductions. 'This is Alex Rourke.'

Bill stands and offers me a hand. 'Sorry about what happened,' he says. His skin is rough, but I don't figure him for a manual worker. Then I catch sight of the handful of small wooden figures on the mantel and I guess he's some sort of sculptor or artist; the barn outside would make a good workshop.

'Thanks.'

'I'm glad Syl's helping you out.' I catch a look of intense study in his eyes as he speaks; perhaps trying to judge whether I'm the kind of idiot who's going to tell everyone who it was let me see the scene report. The kind of idiot who could get his wife fired.

'So am I. I appreciate it a lot.'

He releases my hand, nods slightly to himself and sits back down. Sylvia guides me back through the hall.

'We can talk in the kitchen,' she says.

The room into which I follow her looks like it was made to the same design as Gemma's – big, airy and with more space than one or two people on their own can possibly hope to fill. A hefty oak table, couple of chairs. There's a dark blue cardboard file on the work surface near the oven. Sylvia places this in front of me and says, 'Coffee?'

'White, no sugar, thanks. Is this the scene report?'

She nods. 'They dropped it off at the office late this afternoon.'

'That was very quick of them. I was expecting a day or

two of waiting, at least. While I remember, here's the Scotch for Sergeant Radford as promised.'

'Thanks. We told the VSP we wanted it to see if the way we handled the scene could have been improved at all. It looks good for them, doing their bit to ensure police standards are high, all that sort of shit. Plus I know there's a couple of people in the VSP who just love any opportunity to look down on us poor little local departments. Not that they'd ever admit to it, of course.'

'There's always a few, on any force.'

She looks back at me while she waits for the kettle to boil. 'I guess you must know a bit about that, being with the Feds.'

'Sad, but true,' I say, nodding. I've not opened the report yet – I don't want to seem rude – but it's calling to me and my fingers are itching. 'It's human nature to piss on the people you think are beneath you, I guess. You aren't angling for a transfer to the State Police, then?'

'No, not yet. It'd be nice to be a detective, but I'm happy enough where I am right now. Less pressure.'

I smile wryly, but say nothing. Sylvia brings two cups of coffee over and sits down. I take that as my cue to open the file.

'Is this the entire scene report?' I ask as I quickly scan the first few pages. It looks like it's complete.

'Yeah. The photos are printed copies of the originals.'

I start reading, doing my best to assimilate as much of the information contained in the report as possible on the first time through. I'm not even going to bother asking if I can take it away with me. The first couple of pages consist of typed notes describing the scene as it was found – considerably disturbed by the activity of the Sheriff's Department and medical personnel – and the location of Gemma's car.

'How do you know Ed Markham?' I say, mostly to avoid

sitting here in uncomfortable silence while I read. 'The Owl's Head doesn't strike me as the kind of place you'd drive nearly ten miles just to go for a beer. You used to live in Bleakwater Ridge?'

'No, I know him through his granddaughter, Stephanie.'

'Yeah? Friends?'

She shakes her head. 'Work. She went missing two years ago. When Ed called the department, I was the one who dealt with the report and did the initial investigation.'

I look up from the file. 'What happened?'

'She was up here to spend a couple of weeks with Ed during the summer, same as she'd done for a couple of years. She went out hiking – she was a real keen walker – and never came back. She'd said she might camp out for the night, then come home next day, so she could have been anywhere by the time Ed got worried enough to call us.'

'Accident?' I sip my coffee. It's too hot to drink properly, so I put it down again.

'Maybe, but we couldn't find her on any of the marked trails and no one's seen a single trace of her since. If it had been winter then it might have been possible that she had some sort of slip and froze to death, but in summer I don't see it. Officially she's still missing, but I think she was abducted or killed and the body was hidden away.'

'And so does Ed,' I say, thinking back to what Charlie told me in the bar. About Ed coming in every night for the past two years, looking for strangers, keeping a watchful eye on anyone he doesn't recognize. Searching for the man who killed his granddaughter.

Sylvia nods. 'That's one of the reasons I was willing to let you see that report. Kind of.'

'In what way?'

'Stephanie was last seen crossing the bridge over the

Bleakwater River and heading north. Once she was out of the town, we couldn't find anyone who'd seen her or any sign that she'd been anywhere. Orleans County helped search over their side of the county line, but they had no more luck than we did. After those first couple of days, her case became a State Police show. For a few days, they worked on a theory that she might have tried to get on to the Long Trail, up on top of the mountains, and that maybe she got lost or something happened. Then they went back and redid some of the work we'd already put in. Then they printed a few flyers with her face on and gave up.'

'Yeah, missing persons isn't big once they've tried the obvious.'

'Detective Flint, the one who's working your girlfriend's case, he was in charge of looking for Stephanie Markham. From what I've heard, he's got a good record and all, not great but he knows the job, but I wasn't too impressed with the way he handled things. He swept in like God's gift with a couple of pet ideas, then gave up as soon as they didn't work out. I guess I want to make sure every avenue gets explored this time.'

I acknowledge the remark with a nod that I hope looks appreciative and go back to the report. The photos of the scene are harsh – flash photography at night always is – but clear.

'Was the snow and leaf litter around the car churned up at all when you found it?' I ask Sylvia. 'I can see how it was by the time the State Police crime scene tech arrived, but were there any marks at all before, tracks or anything? I know I asked yesterday, but it's important.'

She thinks for a moment before answering, and I hope the memory for detail she's shown previously doesn't let her down. Then she says, 'I honestly don't know. I had my cruiser parked up on the road with its strobes on. I was using a flashlight to see where I was going, and I was more concerned about the driver of the car than I was about the ground. I had to watch my step, but apart from the fact there were tyre tracks leading down from the road, and all the usual crap wheels throw up when they're turning, I don't remember anything else.'

I shrug and go back to reading. After finding the car and checking Gemma for a pulse or signs of breathing, Sylvia and another LCSD cop, Wayne Cevik, waited for Dr Ted Chapman, one of the state's Regional Medical Examiners, same as Gemma, to arrive from Stowe. He duly pronounced her dead at the scene and, since she'd apparently been shot, ordered the investigation to begin. Detectives Karl Flint and Fiona Saric arrived just over an hour later, along with crime scene technicians.

Forensics found very little at the scene. Like me, they noticed the glass fragments from the rear window, but nothing much else. There were no prints on the car except for Gemma's, and there was no residue on the windshield to suggest the gun that killed her had been fired from anywhere other than at a reasonable distance.

I look at the photos again, particularly those showing the inside of the car. I try not to think about the fact that the slumped form behind the wheel with blood over the front of her shirt is Gemma. Instead I concentrate on the spiderweb fracture of the windshield and the ragged tufts of foam thrusting through the hole made in the back of her seat.

'They didn't find anything in the car?' I ask. 'No bullet, bullet fragments, anything at all that could have come from the thing that killed her?'

'No. Why?'

'I don't like it. If the killer was shooting from the ridge

that overlooks the spot she went off the road, the bullet would have come downwards at an angle. Now, I can buy it hitting, penetrating and then lodging in the seat – it was a shot from range, and it could have been a silenced gun since you can't hear a shot on the phone message. I can also buy it hitting, penetrating and going clean through, out the bottom of the car and into the road surface. What I don't like is the idea that it travelled flat in relation to the car; hit, went through, on out the back window and off into God-knows-where. The angle wouldn't make sense.'

'Uh-huh.' She frowns. 'I did hear someone suggest maybe the gunman was at the bottom of the slope, firing up at the car. That'd work. Could even have been a freak ricochet.'

'I found tracks leading up to the place I think he shot from.'

'Did you find any shell casings, signs that a gun had been fired in the area?'

I shake my head. 'No.'

'So you've got no way of knowing who, or what, left the tracks. It could have been anything from an animal to a winter hiker who decided he didn't fancy the ground in that direction after all.'

'I guess.' I fall silent again. Maybe I'm looking too hard for something that doesn't fit, anything to fuel my dreams of justice and revenge. Still, I can feel something forming at the back of my mind, an idea or theory trying to make itself known. Without success.

'Why was there glass on the trunk of the car?' I say to myself.

Sylvia frowns. 'I don't follow.'

'The car wasn't going fast when it hit the tree. So if the rear windshield was broken, presumably it must've been the bullet that did it. But if it *was* the bullet, why—'

'Why were the glass fragments from the hole it made on

the trunk of the car and the ground around where it stopped, and not up on the road where Dr Larson was shot?' she finishes. 'Should the glass even have shattered at all? Why wouldn't it just spiderweb?'

'It's possible that whoever killed Gemma had to knock a hole in the back window to make it look like the bullet had gone clean through her car.'

We both pause, taking stock. Sylvia frowns. 'But why do it? To make the State Police think the shooter fired from the roadside? It hasn't stopped us being suspicious. The only thing I can think of is tool marks. Maybe he didn't want the cops to wonder why we couldn't find the bullet. It could have been something to cover the fact that the guy came down and dug the shell out.'

'If the same rifle had been used for other crimes before, it'd make sense,' I say, nodding. 'If there were other crimes, there must be a motive for them. Whether the guy's a psycho or a pro, they all do it for a reason. Removing the bullet and covering their tracks suggest the killer planned this beforehand, but why?'

'I don't know.'

I run through everything in the report one more time in the hope that doing so will dislodge something, but it doesn't work. I wonder how much my suspicions are due to the need to have something to focus on, so I can avoid dealing with the fact that Gemma's dead. The case steadies me against how much I miss her. In the end, I bundle everything together again and close the file.

'Are you going to be able to keep this at your office for a while? Just in case there's anything more that comes to mind.'

'Yeah, we'll be able to hang on to it for a good while I reckon.' She smiles. 'We'll have to if our explanation for why we've got this report is going to work.'

‘Thanks for letting me see it. You’ve been really helpful.’

‘Any time,’ Sylvia says as she stands to show me to the door. Her tone drops, more serious. ‘There is one way you might be able to say for sure whether or not someone smashed the window afterwards. Do you still have the voicemail recording Dr Larson left for you at the time she died?’

I nod. ‘Yeah.’

‘You could listen to the message again. If the connection stayed open, you might have the killer on tape.’

10

The house is in darkness when I open my eyes. I've been sleeping, not much, but some, since I returned from Sylvia's. I still haven't touched my voicemail, and won't at least until morning. Right now, I'm wondering what woke me up. My breathing sounds loud and ragged in the near-silence. Even the wind outside has stopped rattling the boards. I lie wrapped up in the blanket and listen hard.

Creak.

A floorboard. It didn't sound like normal building noise. There was weight behind this. Something – someone – walking around.

Creak.

From a slightly different position this time? It's hard to say. I swing my legs off the couch as quietly as I can. I'm already pretty much dressed so I slip into my shoes and grab my gun. I leave the lights off and make for the living room door.

The hallway seems to be empty. Looking up to the rail along the edge of the landing, I can't see anyone moving behind it. The angle is against me though, so the only way I can know for certain what's happening is by going up there.

I walk slowly and carefully up the stairs, edging along against the wall, gun down and slightly to the side. My gaze is fixed on the landing. Once I'm high enough to see directly across it at floor level I stop and hunker down, risking only the quickest of looks before ducking back again.

Nothing.

I clear the last few steps. The air at the top of the stairs is cold, as bad as it was outside Gemma's door the previous evening. If this is the same mystery draught as before, it's moved a couple of yards. I quickly check the bathroom behind me for the intruder before sidling back into the frozen patch, eyes on the remaining two doors and the hatch leading up to the attic room.

With every step I take, the cold soaks further through my clothes and begins to seep past my skin, chilling muscle and bone and sending involuntary shudders passing through my numb body. With it comes an overwhelming flood of emotions – fear mostly, tinged with wide-eyed confusion and, running deep beneath it all, anger. I'm the six-year-old who daren't move because the coat hanging on the closet door at the far side of the room looks like the shadow of someone waiting in the dark, watching.

Swallow hard and try to push the feelings down. No sense in freaking out completely before I've checked everything. My hand closes around the bedroom doorknob.

Thud.

Downstairs.

I haul ass back to the ground floor, watching for movement all around me and wondering how the hell whoever made the noise got past me.

The hallway is empty. I sidle along it, ears straining through the silence, into the kitchen. Melting snow shines darkly against the tiles. Footprints, leading from the back door. I follow them to where they fade out as they reach the hallway.

Creak. This time it's almost ear-splitting it's so close. I jump and snap a look behind in the second it takes to realize it was I who trod on an old board this time.

Look back and bring up the pistol as there's a clatter from the living room. A dark figure sprints out, a blur, and wrenches open the front door. I don't bother yelling at them to stop. I just chase, having enough presence of mind to snatch my jacket from inside the lounge door.

Past the front yard on to the slush-covered road, the intruder keeps going. They have a head start on me and they're a little faster. I don't shout anything, I don't even think about using the gun, not on a public street. I just run, heart hammering at my ribs. It's all I can do.

Through a parking lot by the lakeside, into the trees. The ground changes from blacktop to snow-covered leaf litter, darkening as I leave the town behind. Twigs flick tiny chunks of ice at me as I brush through the trees, specks of cold that turn to slush wherever they touch flesh. My face covered by a webwork of drying rivulets like tear tracks.

Muscles burning, my throat blasted raw, I keep running. On adrenalin, maybe, or the thought of someone else invading Gemma's private space, touching her stuff, desecrating her presence. Something pushes me on.

I have no idea how far into the woods we are or where we're going. Every so often I catch a glimpse of the intruder in the darkness ahead, pass branches still swaying from where they pushed through. I've not gained any ground on them, but all I can think about is catching the son of a bitch.

Sensation of space – a break in the trees, moving into clearer ground, maybe. The running figure ahead is gone, no longer in front of me. I realize my mistake, what this means, and start to turn. Hear the intruder's feet crunch through the snow behind me. Something cracks into the back of my skull and I'm falling, falling.

Everything goes white.

11

When I finally come round I'm lying in the snow, looking upwards at a huge, dark shape jutting out against the gloomy sheet of the overcast night. The sky is a little lighter than before. The back of my head is numb from the ice, but still throbbing. My gun is in my hand. Everything is silent and I seem to be alone. When I stand up, my legs feel awkward and rubbery and I realize I'm shivering with cold. I put my jacket on and look down at the snow I lay in. A dark stain, blood, but not too much of it. I gingerly explore the base of my skull – a swollen, split patch, something that would probably hurt if I wasn't so cold because bright spots flash in front of my eyes when I touch it. I don't think anything's broken, though. I feel almost drunk, light-headed and nauseous, and my eyes are having a hard time focusing. I try to work out where I am.

My first thought is that I must have run in a circle and wound up back in town as there are buildings all around me. This idea quickly dies. The structures are tumbledown: two walls, three walls, in one case just a jumble of rubble with a perfectly preserved stone chimney rising from it like a post-apocalyptic copy of the Washington Monument. The ones I can see are brick for the most part, weathered and cracked. Thin, straggly trees have forced their way through the detritus as the forest slowly takes over. Best guess I can take through my probable concussion is that I'm in North Bleakwater. With numb fingers I fumble through my jacket until I find the remains of a pack of Marlboro. As I do so,

I notice the line of footprints weaving away from me. The intruder's trail.

The tracks take me to the middle of the silent, overgrown town, where a treeless space that might once have been a village common, now an expanse of coiled weeds, opens out between buildings. Down its centre, following the slope from east to west towards the lake, runs a gully maybe six feet from side to side crossed by a short stone bridge. Whatever water once flowed through it is long gone; nothing but tangled plant growth and a crust of snow remain inside.

There are tyre ruts running across the bridge. All the way through the town along what would, I suppose, have been its main street. Given the plant life that has spread over the remains of the buildings here, the thoroughfare shouldn't be more than a footpath by now – if visible at all. I walk to the far side of the bridge, off the stonework and back on the frozen dirt of the road surface, and take a closer look at the tracks.

Multiple sets, overlaying each other. Regular visits, I guess. Looks like a couple of different tread marks, too. Reasonably fresh, but I wouldn't like to guess an exact time. I presume that one set, at least, belonged to the intruder's vehicle as his prints vanish here. He's long gone, driven away while I was unconscious. I drop my Colt back into my jacket.

The other ruts could mean nothing – some kind of town official perhaps, or the Sheriff's Department keeping an eye on the place, or a farmer who owns a stretch of land near here. But maybe not.

Forty or fifty yards from the bridge, an edifice of white clapboard looms sullenly out of the woodland bordering the former village common. Unlike most of the rest of North Bleakwater, this building and the couple of low stone structures on the other side of the street still seem mostly intact.

A rotten, mildew sign hanging over the main doors reads: 'E–ho S—i–gs —tel'.

Despite its dilapidated state, the hotel almost looks as though it's open for business. The slatted shutters are drawn back, and most of the glass in the window frames is still intact. The double front doors are chained and padlocked, however, and once I start moving around the T-shaped structure, the decades of abandonment become apparent. The wraparound deck that once paraded along the head end of the hotel's first floor has collapsed halfway along to become a pile of rotten timbers. The paint on the walls has been peeled and blasted by the elements. At the northern tip of the hotel's head, a five-storey tower-like structure rises from the roof; even at the gables the remainder is no more than four floors high. The small wrought-iron balconies beneath some of the upper windows of this blocky, lighthouse-like edifice are mere shells now, their flooring and much of their supports eaten away by rust.

What I guess would once have been a private lawn spreads out at the back of the hotel, now overrun by thin, straggly bushes and saplings from the forest that is slowly devouring the corpse of North Bleakwater.

And *someone* has been here recently, though I don't think it's whoever I was chasing – different prints. There's a narrow line of flattened grass and crushed snow running along the edge of the lawn, close to the hotel wall. It's too dark to see how many people may have been this way. Again, they could mean nothing, kids from town maybe, hiking round the lake so they can check out the ghost town. Or tourists. I go to see where they lead.

The trail of trampled foliage runs for forty yards or so. The weeds growing in what used to be the hotel's gardens are a fair height, even bowed down with the snow. It's impossible to see that anyone has been this way except by looking straight down the gap they made.

I walk along the edge of the once-empty space now filled with the indistinct shapes of plants, trees and God knows what else. Keep catching glimpses of blurred dark movement from the corners of my eyes; nothing more than deeper shadows or folds in the icy blanket that covers the area. No comfort from the hotel – the old structure smells of damp and decay.

After passing half-a-dozen high Victorian windows, all darkened, the tracks stop at the hotel's old back doors. Once glass set in wooden frames, now boarded over. The doors open inwards, so there's no way to tell if they've recently been used. However, there's also no lock on them.

As my fingers touch the cracked wooden surface, there's a whispering, hissing noise. The treeline that borders the hotel lawn comes alive with movement. Shadows emerge from the darkness between the boughs to the periphery of the lighter open ground before fading back or flitting between trees. Hard to make out, but they're a variety of shapes and sizes – some as big as people, others smaller like kids or animals. The black shapes writhe slickly on the edge of the clearing, keeping up a low, sibilant murmur.

I don't run. I slowly take my hand off the door, then back carefully away, heading for the road. I have to grit my teeth to master the impulse to panic and flee, but I do it.

Seeing things after a head injury is not a good sign. I'm familiar with the routine, but if my battered brain wants to amuse itself by playing shadow puppets with the scenery, it's impossible to take anything it says on trust any more. I need to go home, lie down.

But to get home, whichever way I take around the lake I'm going to have to go back through the forest. And hallucinations or not, I still don't like that idea. Give me the red shoes from *The Wizard of Oz*.

In the end I have no choice. I can stay here and catch hypothermia or I can risk the woods in the dark. I can't clearly remember how I got here, so retracing my steps would be mostly guesswork. But I do have a set of tyre prints to follow which seem to know where they're going – hopefully to the highway.

I set off at a brisk march, doing my best to ignore anything not directly in front of me. Before long, as that hissing from the trees dogs me still, this becomes a trot, then a slow jog.

Pain has begun to pound from the back of my head by the time I reach the asphalt of Route 100. Nearby, I recognize a couple of huge, old-growth trees from my hike to the spot Gemma was killed. At the time I didn't notice the narrow track plunging into the forest. I'm less than a mile from home.

I walk, slower this time and more wearily as the final ounces of adrenalin turn sour to leave me hollow and empty. No one sees me trudge across the Bleakwater River and through the silent town that clusters along the ridge above it.

When I reach Gemma's I search the entire house. There's no one there and no sign of what they were after. It doesn't look like anything's been disturbed, but I can't be sure. They broke in through the door to the kitchen; I can see the tracks they left in the back yard. One set, cutting through the snow. The wet prints inside have partially dried and lost all shape so I can't tell any details.

In the warm my head injury is free to kick in properly. I throw up, then bed down on the couch with an icepack for company.

12

Tourist Goes Missing

LAMOILLE COUNTY

Authorities are searching for a tourist reported missing while hiking in the area between Belvidere and Windover mountains. According to a statement from Lamoille County Sheriff's Department, Stephanie Markham, 20, was last seen three days ago heading north on Route 100 near the town of Bleakwater Ridge, where she was staying with relatives. Anyone who may have seen Markham, described as having short brown hair, 5′ 4″ and weighing 100 lbs, should contact the LCSD.

Morning at Fletcher Free Library in Burlington. Running through archived copies of the *Burlington Free Press* from two years ago. The stories I'm interested in start small, becoming larger and more important as time passes. Each details what happened to Ed Markham's granddaughter. I still haven't followed Sylvia's suggestion and listened to Gemma's last voicemail again. I don't feel up to it just yet. Maybe this evening.

Hunt Continues For Missing Hiker

LAMOILLE COUNTY

Police and civilian volunteers are still searching for missing hiker Stephanie Markham, 20, in northern Lamoille County. The search, led by officers of the Lamoille County Sheriff's Department, has so far found no sign of the woman. LCSD spokesman Sergeant Ken Radford said: 'As yet we have been unable to find any trace of Stephanie Markham on the listed trails in the area she was known to be heading for. We will be widening our search area with the assistance of Orleans County Sheriff's Department and volunteers, and we have every hope of finding her. Stephanie was an experienced hiker and knew the area well.'

Searchers were yesterday concentrating on trails near Broken Notch, the site of a number of accidents in the past. Stephanie is described as 5′ 4″, 100 lbs, with short brown hair. She was wearing a red shirt and jeans, and carrying a dark blue backpack.

The next story carries a photo of Stephanie, a picture taken with what look like friends of hers from college. It's grainy, but it's enough to put a slim, pretty face to the name. She seems happy, grinning naturally for the camera. By the time the story ran, it had been five days since anyone had seen her alive.

State Police To Help Hunt For Markham

by Elijah Charman

The State Police have taken over the search for missing hiker Stephanie Markham, last seen near the town of Bleakwater Ridge in Lamoille County. Three days of searching by police and volunteers in Lamoille and neighbouring Orleans counties have failed to find any trace of the missing 20-year-old. Detective Sergeant Karl Flint, in charge of the State Police's efforts, said Stephanie was still being treated as missing, and the possibility of her being abducted or murdered would not be considered while there was still hope of finding her alive.

'I will not speculate on other possible scenarios at the

present time,' he said. 'We owe it to her and her family to keep up the search for her. If she has been in an accident, if she is lying somewhere, unable to move, she would not want us to abandon the hunt or be distracted by wild guesses as to what may have happened.

'As far as I am concerned, Stephanie Markham is still alive, and she's out there somewhere in need of our help,' he concluded.

Detective Flint went on to thank the Lamoille and Orleans county sheriff's departments for their work, and said that since their search of the lowland countryside and mountain trails in the area she was last seen have proved fruitless, the State Police effort would be concentrated further afield.

Sources in the VSP suggest that police search teams are working on the theory that Stephanie may have tried to reach the Long Trail where it passes west of Belvidere Mountain, but became lost or had an accident. They will also be checking the areas around the trail for several miles north and south.

Stephanie had been staying in the town of Bleakwater Ridge with her grandfather, local resident Edward Markham. Mr Markham was unavailable for comment yesterday, but friends said they were helping him cope with his granddaughter's disappearance and that they were praying for her safe return.

Reading the article, I wonder whether anyone else noticed Flint's self-contradiction. He didn't want to follow 'wild guesses' about her whereabouts, yet he jumped straight on the Long Trail theory. It's possible that the State Police had access to information not in the press report, and that's what sent them haring all over the mountains. But maybe Sylvia's opinion of Flint holds good.

Four days after the last article, there's one final piece on the story, further from the front page than before.

VSP Launch Flyer Campaign For Missing Hiker

by Elijah Charman

The State Police are printing flyers of missing hiker Stephanie Markham in the hope of turning up fresh information. Search teams have found no trace of the 20-year-old despite scouring the area in which she was last seen. Detective Sergeant Karl Flint said: 'We'll be distributing flyers with Stephanie's photo and description all over the northern half of the state in the hope of jogging people's memories. We're hoping someone could have seen her after she left the town of Bleakwater Ridge on Route 100 and maybe they can shed light on what happened to her.'

The VSP had been concentrating on a section of the Long Trail until yesterday morning, when the hunt was scaled down. Officials would not comment on the chances of finding Stephanie alive.

I copy down the phone number of the *Burlington Free Press* editorial department and hope that Elijah Charman is still working there. If anyone's going to remember any details that weren't in the stories, it'll be him. Or Flint, I guess, but I'm aiming to see him later anyway.

Stand, rubbing my eyes, and try to ignore the pounding sensation from my skull. I hope the pain will be gone before long, that it's only mild concussion, nothing worse. I can recall only snatches of the drive here from Bleakwater Ridge – the rest I must have done on autopilot – and if asked I couldn't say what the front of the library looked like. Best to see a doctor, I guess.

Fletcher Allen's main hospital campus in central Burlington, not far from the library, is quiet when I arrive and I'm seen almost straight away by a young-looking doctor with dark hair and an unsettlingly flat, empty gaze. When I show him the back of my head he asks, 'How did this happen?'

'I was putting up a light on my porch last night and I fell.' I don't elaborate further. It's a sign of a liar.

'Why didn't you see someone straight away?'

'It's a long way, I didn't feel like driving and it didn't seem serious enough for an ambulance.'

He probes the battered area of skin with his fingers. I guess he's gentle but it still makes me wince. 'And it's just a headache you've got, no problems with your vision, nausea, anything like that?'

'Now it's just the headache. A hefty one.'

'Now?'

'I had a couple of vision things last night,' I tell him. 'Moving shadows, things like that. Nothing too clear.'

He looks me in the eyes. 'And these stopped when?'

'I don't know. I went to sleep and I've been fine since I woke up. I figured it was probably concussion.'

'Well, you were probably right,' the doctor says. 'Still, it would have been best if you'd been checked out last night. Sensory distortion means your brain took a fair-sized knock. There could have been serious damage there and you ignored it.'

'Sorry, doc.'

'Okay,' he says after a couple more prods. 'We'd better have it x-rayed just in case there's any damage to the bone. I doubt it, though. If there's nothing serious there, I'll give you some painkillers for the headache. But if it persists too long, or you start feeling unwell or seeing things again, you come straight back and we'll have another look.'

'Sure.'

Forty-five minutes later I leave the hospital with a small box of pills which I don't intend to take, despite the pain. I have to keep a clear head, so I'm restricted to nothing more than paracetamol. I go hunting for a cup of coffee or two before I phone the newspaper.

As luck would have it, Elijah Charman not only still works at the *Burlington Free Press*, he's also in town and free to meet me at the small, steam-filled coffee shop in which I'm stocking up on caffeine. I'm on my third large espresso and starting to get a little wired when the round figure of the journalist bustles through the door. Swaddled in bright winter clothing, Charman bears a passing resemblance to a beachball topped with a pudgy head that turns out to be completely bald when he removes his woollen hat and sits down. I ask him what he wants to drink.

'Large chocolate with vanilla,' he says, then sneezes. 'Sorry, think I'm going down with a touch of flu.'

'Right time of year for it,' I reply sympathetically once I've ordered the drinks.

'So you're interested in Stephanie Markham, Mr Rourke. What's a private detective from Boston want with a two-year-old missing persons case? I wouldn't have thought your agency did much work up here.' Seeing my raised eyebrows, he adds, 'The internet – great invention. Did a quick check for your name before I came here.'

I reassess the man sitting opposite. He might look slightly comical wrapped up in more layers than an Arctic explorer, but his dark eyes obviously hide a fair amount of resourcefulness.

'I'm a friend of Ed Markham,' I tell him. It's a slight exaggeration, but not an outright lie. 'Someone told me what happened to his granddaughter and I thought there was a chance it was connected to a case I'm working on, so I'm checking it out.'

Elijah's chocolate arrives and he thanks the waitress before getting back to the conversation. 'You're lucky I don't often trash my notes. Without them to push my memory, I wouldn't have much to say that you wouldn't already have read. Not that there's a lot worth adding, I should warn you.'

'So warned.'

He pulls a wad of folded paper out of his coat and starts skimming over the ballpoint scribbles that cover the pages. 'Let's see . . . I don't think there was anything much on the actual disappearance that wasn't in the paper. The last person to see Stephanie alive was a woman called Brenda Ingledow; all she could really give us for a quote was "Yup, I saw a young woman walk up the highway past my house about ten in the morning" so we left her out of the story. I got her name from an officer at the Sheriff's Department. No one around town knew Stephanie, and she didn't have any friends there. There were some who knew the grandfather, though, and that she was staying with him for a couple of weeks.'

He flicks forward, running his finger quickly over the illegible text as he takes an absent-minded sip of his drink. 'Everyone I spoke to reckoned the police had done a fair job of checking all the local trails. There were quite a few of them though she might have fallen from some place called Broken Notch. I've no idea where it is, but it seems to be about the only place people have accidents and such in the area.'

'One of the stories said the LCSD checked it out.'

Elijah nods and momentarily brings his wandering finger to a halt, tapping the digit on one section of notes. 'That's right,' he says, 'but they didn't find anything. I got the impression at the time it was pretty much guesswork, looking there for her.'

'What happened once the State Police took over?'

'About the same, really. They made a big speech about doing things right, then took off on a wild goose chase up in the mountains. By the time they'd finished with that, she'd been gone for a week and almost no one was expecting to see her alive again. Not unless she'd gone somewhere else on her own, like a runaway, but that didn't seem likely. So they packed up the search.'

So I wasn't the only one to notice the contradiction between Flint's words and his actions. 'I'm surprised there wasn't any criticism of the search effort at the time,' I say.

'I was planning to write some, but my editor said he didn't want it, not while the cops had more important things to deal with, so I left it. Then, by the time they'd given up and forgotten her, I'm afraid she just wasn't news any more.' I gesture for another large espresso and Elijah raises his eyebrows. 'You want to go easy on that stuff, man. Looks like you're missing enough sleep as it is.'

'Is it that obvious?'

'You don't just have bags under your eyes, you've got a whole set of matched luggage and a trolley to carry it around on,' he says, smiling.

I return the grin. 'You wouldn't believe some of the nights I've had. Did the police ever say why they thought Stephanie might have gone up to the Long Trail?'

'I spoke to a woman called –' the finger skips to a different piece of paper – 'Detective Saric. She said they'd had a call from someone who thought they might have seen a girl like her heading up that way, and that the description was a fair match. I guess that was as good a lead as they'd got.'

'She was one of the cops in charge?'

'There were two detectives running the show, but most of the work was done by state troopers. The other detective, Flint, told me off the record that the search was mostly public relations. Looking for one person in an area that big and that empty without any clue where to go was impossible, but they had to make it look good for the cameras.'

'Uh-huh.'

Elijah drains the rest of his chocolate and smacks his lips contentedly. Then he brings a second bundle of paper out of his pocket and looks at me. 'You said you thought Stephanie Markham might be related to a case of yours?' he asks.

'That's right.'

'I don't suppose you can tell me what case it is you're talking about?'

I shake my head. 'Sorry.'

'No matter. It's just that I've brought along some other stuff I gathered at the time Stephanie went missing. About a year before, there was a couple from Minnesota on a hiking holiday in foliage season. Last time anyone heard from them, they were just leaving Jay Peak State Forest, heading south to Hazen's Notch and beyond.' He slides across a couple of photocopied photos. It's barely possible to make out their faces, let alone any details, such is the quality of the pictures.

'Will and Althea Haley,' Elijah says. 'At the time, there wasn't much publicity – nothing like Stephanie Markham – and it was a couple of weeks before anyone wondered where they'd got to; a car rental place in Waterbury called their family when they didn't pick up their Volvo. The only reason anyone knew where they'd been last was because they phoned Haley's sister. State Police posted them as missing, but that was about it. I think the cops back in Minnesota had a look to see if there was any reason they might want to disappear, but I don't know what became of that.'

I thumb through the sparse information Elijah's collected on the missing couple. 'Why didn't this get brought up when Stephanie vanished?'

'Technically, they went missing in Orleans County, maybe Franklin, but as far as the way the statistics and everything is organized, definitely *not* from the same area as Stephanie. I thought of writing a piece on them, linking the two together, but I couldn't get nearly enough information to make it worthwhile. You're welcome to keep these copies of what I got, if you're interested.'

'Sure, sure. Thanks, I appreciate the help.'

'No problem,' Elijah says, waving a hand dismissively. 'If you want to know any more about all this, you'd be best off talking to the State Police.'

'I'm planning to. Do you remember who it was who was technically in charge of the Haley case?'

He shakes his head before pulling on his woollen hat once more. 'Afraid not. If there's anything posted about them anywhere, it might say who to contact.'

'Maybe so. Take care.' A thought strikes that since I'm in Burlington anyway, I might as well spend a couple of hours trying to clear the Webb case and leave me totally free to pursue Gemma's killer. I don't want to let Rob down. I also don't plan on spending more than a few hours on it.

'Oh, one last thing,' I say before Elijah leaves. 'You know Burlington much better than I do. Where would I go if I was looking for a cheap bar where I might find out if anyone's offering casual work, or maybe to meet a couple of small-time criminals? Or if I wanted somewhere cheap and anonymous to call home for a while, where would be the best bet?'

'Well,' he answers after a lengthy pause, 'you might try the Mountain Bar on Patrick. Or there's the Hart, and Cavanagh's. There'll all pretty rough places. As for accommodation, there's not much to choose from. Maybe some of the newer developments in South Burlington, but most of those still wouldn't be cheap. There's a couple of low-rent apartment blocks and boarding houses that advertise in the classifieds. The kind of places where you can get a room for thirty bucks a week so long as you don't mind sharing a bathroom with everyone else on your floor and a bedroom with every form of parasite known to man.'

'Classy.'

'I can't remember where they are, but they shouldn't be hard to find. I don't know much about cheap motels. I guess you could try asking around the train station in Essex Junction – there must be plenty of people get into town and need somewhere to stay for a while.'

'Thanks, I might do that.'

'Another story?' Elijah asks. He sounds curious, but there's a definite wry undercurrent to his tone.

'Another missing person. His mom back in Boston is worried about him. All she knows is that last time she spoke to him, he said he was in Burlington. Not much to go on.'

'It sounds like it. Well, happy hunting.'

The two of us shake hands, then Elijah ambles through the coffee shop and back out on to the street. I spend a few minutes skimming through the material he's given me – which confirms most of what he said without seeming to add much to it – then go looking for my missing person.

13

Any one of the satellite suburbs in the orbit of Vermont's only metropolis could be, or could have been, home to Adam Webb, but if he was here for any length of time, I'd guess he'd have stayed central. When he last spoke with his mother, he said he was working as a tour guide, but that doesn't ring true. There are plenty of places to visit around Burlington and in the surrounding countryside, but not so many and so close together that people would need to employ a guide. And the tour companies who might organize group trips aren't likely to hire a guy with few formal qualifications or references who wasn't local to the area. The police would probably have contacted them already anyway.

Itinerant workers like Webb aren't likely to pick up office jobs or become bank tellers. They're mostly limited to places with on-the-spot hiring, zero qualifications and weekly paychecks – bars, diners, nightclubs, bottom-end convenience stores. Failing that, Adam could have fallen back on the kind of petty crime I know he'd been involved with before. Neither of those options pays well, so that would also limit him to cheap housing – bad apartments or even worse motels.

The first place I try is the Mountain Bar, a solid box of red brick with a neon sign bearing the name and a rough approximation of Mount Mansfield sticking straight up from the edge of the roof above the door, 1950s style. It's only just opened. Even at this early hour the place is already home to half-a-dozen or so serious drinkers and two still-coherent regulars talking with the barman. As I reach the counter, the guy behind it breaks off his conversation. He's big, solid-looking, with short hair and a couple of ancient and unreadable tattoos on the back of his hands.

I slide the sheet with Webb's details and photos across to him. The barman picks it up, scans it for a few seconds, then says, '"Robin Garrett Associates – Licensed Private Investigators". Not a cop then?'

'That's right.'

'Why are you looking for this guy?'

'He hasn't been in touch with his family in Boston for a while and they're getting worried. Last time they heard from him, he was in Burlington.'

The barman purses his lips and shakes his head. 'Sorry, Mr Garrett,' he says, passing the sheet back across. 'I've never seen him before. Don't know the name either.'

'Keep it,' I tell him. 'If he comes in, give the office a call. We should be able to swing a reward for the information.'

'How big?' he says. It sounds like genuinely idle curiosity; I don't get the impression that he's holding out on me.

'Probably not much. We're not a rich company.'

'Not much?' He smiles and tucks the sheet on the shelf behind the bar. 'That doesn't matter. Every little helps.'

I get the addresses of the Hart and Cavanagh's from the phone book. The former is sandwiched between a convenience store and a small auto dealership in the north end of town, the latter occupies a basement underneath a terrace of brick houses converted into small apartments not far from the airport. Neither gives me any more information about Adam Webb, but in the Hart I get the names of another three bars it might be worth checking out, and the regulars in Cavanagh's give me the addresses of a couple of ultra-low-rent tenement blocks as well as the name of an employment agency that farms out menial jobs to the desperately short of cash. Both take a copy of Webb's details.

It's lunchtime and I'm growing tired of legwork. I post a couple of missing persons sheets up in the employment agency and a nearby hostel, and figure that's all I can, or want to, do for now.

I catch Flint in his office in the Waterbury Complex, the same place I spoke to him immediately after Gemma's death. Flint looks up from his computer as I walk in and close the door behind me. He clicks the mouse a couple of times, then leans back in his chair and regards me, half friendly, half irritated.

'What's on your mind, Mr Rourke? You said on the phone you might have some new information for me.'

I sit down without being invited. 'Have you had any luck finding who killed Gemma, or why they might have done it?'

'We're following up everything we can,' he replies in a tone that says he knows, just as well as I do, that this is a stock answer which means 'so far we've got jack'.

'Have you spoken to any of the staff at the hospital she worked at?'

'Some, not all.'

'How about Dr Frank Altmann?'

Flint shrugs. 'I don't think so. Who is he?'

'He had a thing for Gemma, though he apparently didn't try to do anything about it beyond being friends. He lives alone, he's been to Gemma's house before, and I don't think he has an alibi. I spoke to him yesterday but he wouldn't answer all my questions.'

I can see Flint groan inwardly before he says, 'What happened?'

'I asked him where he was when she died and he threw me out.'

'So if I speak to him now, he knows he's a potential suspect and that he needs to be careful what he says. Hell, he could lawyer up right from the start, for fuck's sake.'

'He said he'd be happy to answer any questions you might ask. I just don't think he liked speaking to me.'

'Well, that's just great then.' Flint scowls.

'And last night someone broke into Gemma's house. I don't know what they were looking for, but they certainly weren't a regular burglar. I didn't get a good look at them. Best I can say is I'm pretty sure it was a man. I chased them halfway around the lake, but they got away in a car.'

'Did you see the car?'

'No. Took a hit to the head, so I was out cold when they drove off.'

There's a knock on the door behind me. It opens and a woman muffled in a long winter coat leans through. 'No luck with Dyson, sir. Same with Peters. I suppose that's two we can take off your list.'

'Right. Keep at it, Fiona.'

'Yes, sir,' she says and disappears. I detect a hint of disrespect in her voice, but maybe she's just being extra polite.

'Gemma's case, or one of your others?' I say, wondering about this 'list'.

He sits still for a minute, still glaring at me, then seems to reach a decision and hands me a sheet of paper. Names, personal details and last known addresses, maybe fifteen in all.

'These people have the kind of mental problems that might, in theory, grow bad enough for them to kill. They could all also have had the opportunity to see Dr Larson and pick her as a victim. Paranoid schizophrenics mostly, though none of them bad enough to be institutionalized. It's not complete, and it's as wild a shot in the dark as you're ever likely to see investigated, but these people represent just about my only potential suspects unless your doctor guy starts to become interesting.'

'You're trying to find out if these people have been around Lamoille County recently?' I scan the list. Some of them look like they'll be hard to pin down. None of them lives there, either. 'Surely if they were going to kill, they'd do it nearer their homes.'

Flint shrugs. 'You're probably right, but there's always a chance they could have seen Dr Larson in Newport or out in Burlington. Like I said, until I have anything more concrete to go on, this is about as good as it gets. At worst, we'll eliminate this crowd. Fiona's handling most of them, but there's one in particular I want to speak to. If you're free, you could come along. You could see if he'd fit as your intruder.'

He hands me a photo of a man in his mid thirties with short brown hair. 'Reuben Wynne. Diagnosed as a mild paranoid schizophrenic ten years ago, still on medication but otherwise looks after himself. He was first picked up after he shot his neighbour's two cats with a .22 rifle; he told us he thought they had cameras for eyes and they were watching him. I was one of the cops who made the arrest.'

'That's a mild schizophrenic?'

'Apparently he realized what was wrong after he did it, so he can't have completely flipped. He volunteered for treatment, and that was that. Until four and a half years ago.'

'What happened then?'

'Some hooker called Carita Jenner got herself beaten to death in Burlington. Reuben was one of her clients and he didn't have an alibi. But there was very little evidence at the scene and we found nothing at his house, so we couldn't pin it on him.'

'You got a search warrant without evidence?'

Flint shakes his head. 'He said we were welcome to look around.'

'Doesn't sound like a guilty man.'

'Maybe he was just that confident nothing would be found. I don't know – I didn't work the case. The murder was never solved so whoever did it must've been clever.'

'Any other sign that he has a history of violent behaviour?'

Flint shrugs. 'No, but that doesn't mean Dr Larson wasn't his next big break with reality. Maybe the son of a bitch thought she was watching him like the cats.'

'Sure.'

'He's a borderline lunatic who's gone for his rifle at least once before. That's enough to make him interesting.'

'How long've you been a cop?' I ask, slouched in the most comfortable position I can manage in the front of Flint's Taurus. An hour later we're parked a little way from the entrance to a block of downscale condos in South Burlington. Flint has the engine turned off so the heater is dead and I have to wedge my hands beneath my armpits to keep the blood flowing. The wintry air wafting through his window, left open to stop the windshield misting over, isn't helping any either.

'Fifteen years. Six at my current rank. Why?'

'Just curious. You often deal this kind of thing?' I ask, trying to think about something other than my absent gloves, which are back in the 'Vette.

'I've worked serious crimes since I've been with the BCI, if that's what you mean. Murder's not common, but I've handled a few.'

'Anything major?'

'Nothing you'd have heard of in Boston. Some get solved, some don't. Shit happens. You can get away with anything if you're smart or lucky enough. Like Carita Jenner.'

'Perfect crime, huh?'

'It always is if you don't get caught. That's him,' Flint says as a Nissan compact that's definitely nearing the end of its serviceable life pulls up thirty yards in front of us.

Reuben Wynne is the kind of guy who fits half the descriptions ever given to the police – medium height, medium build, somewhere between twenty-five and thirty-five years old. He's wearing battered jeans and a winter coat that's starting to show a couple of threads, with a new woollen hat pulled down over his ears. He hefts a pair of grocery bags out of the trunk of his car and walks ponderously over to his apartment door. He's still fumbling with his keys when we catch up with him.

'Mr Wynne?' says Flint as we get within earshot. He brings up his ID badge in his left hand. 'I'm Detective Sergeant Karl Flint from the State Police. We need to ask you a couple of questions.'

Wynne stops playing with his keys and shifts so the weight of his bags isn't too uncomfortable. 'What's this about?' he asks.

His voice is clear and his eyes have widened a little on seeing the badge. He looks innocent enough. I remind myself, though, that this is a guy who was happy to wipe out his neighbour's pets just because he thought it was a good idea at the time.

'We just need to ask some questions, that's all. It won't take a minute.' Flint smiles, but without feeling.

'Sure, okay.'

'Where were you last Tuesday, between four and six p.m.?'

Wynne thinks before answering. 'I was sweeping the hall on Jackson Street before a meeting in the evening. I don't work Tuesday afternoons.'

'Meeting?'

'It's an art group. We do some work, mostly watercolours, but sometimes we talk about techniques and stuff like that, sometimes with other artists who come in to do short presentations. I always make sure the hall's tidy before the meetings.'

Flint nods. 'Is there anyone who could confirm that you were there?'

'Mrs Greiner – she manages the hall. Martha Greiner. She has to unlock it for me. Oh, and Amy, Amy Powell – she showed up at the same time as me because the heating sometimes cuts out and she wanted to make sure everything was warmed up before we began.'

'Whereabouts do you work, Mr Wynne?'

'Caffeine Shack on Church Street.'

'And you live here alone?'

'Uh-huh. What's this about?'

'Does the name Dr Gemma Larson mean anything to you?'

Wynne pauses a moment, thinking. 'No, I don't think so. Is that everything? I have to put these groceries away.'

'Sorry to inconvenience you, Mr Wynne,' Flint says, although it's perfectly clear that he isn't. Then, more seriously, 'You make damn sure you tell us if you're going to be leaving the state.' He turns towards me, expression one of frustration. I guess despite his bluster he doesn't see

Wynne being our murderer, although he'd like to. Flint's hopeful long shot has drawn a blank. I doubt he'll even bother checking the guy's alibi in a hurry.

So once we've gone our separate ways, I do it for him.

There's only one Greiner in the phone book. Powells are more plentiful, but nothing compared to the list I'd have got in Boston. I start with the one I know.

'Martha Greiner? This is Detective Jones from the State Police. I have a couple of quick questions if it's okay with you.'

'So long as they're quick.' She doesn't sound pleased to hear from me, but then some people just have a problem with cops.

'I understand you manage a hall on Jackson Street used by an art study group?'

'That's right. What have they done?'

'Nothing. Did you open up the hall for them last Tuesday?'

'For Reuben,' she says after a moment's thought. 'He cleans the place before they meet.'

'And what time was that?'

'I don't know. Four o'clock, something like that. He likes to get it done before he has dinner, not after. What's this about?'

'Routine questions, Mrs Greiner. Thanks for your time.' I hang up.

It takes several false starts before I reach Amy Powell. She sounds young, breezy. When I mention the art class she tells me she does it as a useful addition to the media course she's taking at UVM.

'Reuben had just started cleaning the place when I got there. He'd only been there a few minutes,' she says, confirming what he told us.

'And what time was that?' I ask.

'Around seven.'

Three hours *after* Wynne claimed. He lied to us about his alibi, about the three-hour gap in his afternoon.

A gap long enough and covering just the right time for him to have killed Gemma.

14

That evening, questions continue to loom over me. I haven't told Flint about the gap in Wynne's alibi, or the fact that what he gave us was bullshit. Neither by themselves is even close to proof – there's a lot of reasons someone might not tell the truth to the cops – and I don't want him to know I checked without him. I'll probably tell him once I've figured out what to do with Wynne. But more disturbing and awkward than that, there's still the voicemail.

I eat my lonely dinner in Gemma's living room, trying not to think about my cell phone and what I'll eventually have to do. The harmless lump of plastic-wrapped electronics waits, lurking at the centre of a dark cloud of conflicting emotions and desires. The drive to do everything I can to find the killer is at war with the aversion I have to reliving Gemma's last moments. It's a fixed fight and I already know the outcome, but it doesn't make it any easier to actually summon up the courage to play the recording again.

The clock on the mantel tells me it's now half past eight and I'm no closer to picking up the phone. I figure some extra cushioning of the inevitable impact wouldn't go amiss, so I grab my coat, making sure to lock up in case anyone tries breaking in again. I've already moved the kitchen table to block the back door as best I can.

The Owl's Head is pretty much empty. If Bleakwater Ridge has any serious drinkers, the cold must be keeping them at home tonight. Ed Markham is in, as always, but he's alone. Charlie either left early or he didn't make it out at all. I wave and wander over with my drink.

'Hi, Ed,' I say, taking the proffered seat.

'Evening, Alex. You look like you've been working a couple of late nights.'

'Kind of. I'm not getting much sleep just recently.'

'It's understandable, especially in winter. The old houses around here can get pretty draughty.' He takes a long draw on his bottle. 'You'll get used to it after a while, then you'll sleep like a baby.'

I don't share his optimism but I keep quiet. 'On the subject of old buildings,' I say, 'do you know much about North Bleakwater?'

Ed seems to think for a moment. 'You mean Echo Springs? That's what the people who lived there called it, most of them. My dad could remember when they were still trying to make it work as a town, even if it was already starting to empty. By my time, it was totally abandoned. In better repair back in those days, though.'

'What happened?'

'Science and weather,' he says matter-of-factly. 'From what my dad used to say, and my grandpa when he was still around, it started just as a hotel by the spring at the other end of the lake. Rich folk from New York, Boston, big towns all over used to come up here and half-a-dozen other places like it a hundred and fifty years ago to "take the waters". They'd stay at the hotel and knock back spring water like it was going out of fashion, then go home telling everyone how great they felt. Echo Springs was never a big player, I think, but it did well enough that people started putting up other buildings around the hotel until it was practically a new town.

'Then the water craze died out and people realized there was more to curing disease than just drinking. So science killed the hotel, and the rest of the town started to follow. But they still had the springs and Echo Stream, so they figured they could try becoming a mill and factory town. Nothing big, but enough to keep people in work. They'd just got their first couple of takers and things were going okay – my dad was even thinking of switching jobs to work there – when there was the Great Flood of Twenty-seven.'

'The town was flooded?'

Ed shrugs. 'Partly. But the main damage the rains did was cause a landslide that buried the springs and totally changed the course of Echo Stream, so the new businesses had nowhere to take their water from. With the Depression soon after, no one was in much mood to try rebuilding again, and people moved back here, or went south looking for better times. So, what's your interest?'

'Do people often go out there?' I ask, dodging his question so I don't have to explain what I was doing in the old town in the middle of the night. 'I guess any tourists passing through would want to check it out.'

'I guess. Not that we get many. Have you seen someone then?'

I shake my head. 'Tyre tracks. I just wondered if people regularly drove out there. Curiosity, that's all.'

Ed's eyes twinkle in a way that suggests he doesn't believe me, and that he knows or suspects more about the old town than he's letting on. 'Not that I know of. Maybe the occasional guy going fishing at that end of the lake, but not in winter. School trips in spring; I doubt there's anyone grown up here who hasn't been taken out to the ruins to learn the history of the area.'

Ed seems keen to return to the original subject of our conversation. 'You reckon the tracks you saw could've been anything to do with your girlfriend's murder?' His eyes haven't lost their glitter, and I find myself wondering how deep the old man's obsessive thirst to find his granddaughter's killer runs. To come in here, night after night for two years and hunch over a lonely beer, constantly searching for whoever murdered Stephanie, it must run deep and strong. No forgiveness. No desire to forget and move on. I'd have cracked under the strain long before; I'm already losing it and it's only been a week since Gemma's death.

'Did Stephanie ever go to visit North Bleakwater?' I say, half thinking out loud. Ed's eyes narrow slightly.

'What are you talking about?'

'Sylvia told me what happened, and I've read the news reports.'

'Did you now.' His voice drops several degrees in temperature. 'And what made you want to do a thing like that?'

'Whatever happened to her was in the same area as Gemma's murder. Both times there's no obvious motive. I was curious.'

Ed plants his hands firmly on the tabletop, like he's about to push himself to his feet and lunge at me. 'Don't go talking about her like that, Alex. You've got no right.'

'We've both been through the same thing,' I say, trying to calm him down. The few other patrons in the bar are starting to pay attention to our table and I don't want to be seen harassing an old guy. I still can't work out why he's getting mad. 'We've both lost people we cared about.'

'It's not the same! You never had to face the worrying, the wondering what had happened, where she was, why she couldn't be found. You didn't have to go through weeks of not knowing, of watching the cops lose interest. You didn't have your own kids calling you up to find out what the hell had happened to their little girl while she was in your care. Don't you dare go making comparisons you can't understand!' He stands, face red with anger, and snatches his coat from the back of the chair. 'You got to bury your girlfriend. You got to say goodbye. No one goes forcing their damn ideas on me until I've been able to do the same!'

Cold air spills into the bar as Ed storms out into the night.

'Hi, honey, it's me. Um, I thought I'd ring to ask you about the weekend. Susan's invited—' I ram a finger into the 'call' button to disconnect from my voicemail and take another gulp from the generous glass of vodka on the coffee table. I don't normally go near the stuff, but it was all I could find back in the house. A single, barely touched bottle; Gemma's sole stock for the rare occasions when she fancied something strong in the evenings. I don't drink much either and I don't want to be hopelessly drunk when I go through the recording again. I just need a decent cushion of alcohol inside me to take the edge off what I'm hearing.

Off what I'm being forced to relive.

Two and a half sentences in Gemma's soft voice isn't a good benchmark. I force down another couple of mouthfuls of vodka, then refill the glass. It may taste like antifreeze, but it seems to be doing the job. Warm fuzz is already spreading from my stomach outwards. I let it seep through my system for a few moments while I try to relax.

Then I pick up the phone again.

This time I make it through all of Gemma's last words, downing the occasional swallow from the glass and trying not to think about what I'm hearing and all the plans we could and should have made in an ideal world. Then there's the *crack* as the windshield goes and I lose my nerve again. Once more, I kill the connection.

I go to rinse my face with cold water from the bathroom, subconsciously hoping that some combination of this ritual washing and the alcohol will grant me a Zen-like calm, enabling me to listen in a state of complete detachment.

On my way upstairs, a sudden crash in the temperature makes my breath steam and my jaw clench. The draught or whatever the hell is causing this patch of cold now seems to have abandoned the landing in favour of freezing the middle half-dozen steps. The hazy vapour that billows from my mouth as I pass twists and swirls in half-glimpsed patterns and shapes towards the floor before dissipating altogether. For a second, some of those shapes look faintly recognizable, but I put that down to the vodka and continue on my way. The subsequent splash of ice-cold water against my face doesn't do much, certainly not enough for any Zen-ness, but I still feel better for it.

'. . . it's just started snowing again and I'd better keep my eyes on the road. I love you, honey, and I'll—' *Crack*.

I close my eyes and finish what's left in the glass, but I keep listening. Calm detachment isn't a possibility, but I'm doing my best to hold back my emotions.

A creak, maybe the seatbelt, and the pitch of the engine starts dropping. Gemma's foot must be off the gas. I try not to think of her slumping over the wheel.

Slushy crunching as the tyres leave the well-worn ruts left by other traffic along the highway.

The high-pitched rattle and scraping as the car rolls through the bushes by the roadside. A few seconds of muffled bumps and crackling – heading down the slope. Doesn't sound fast.

The *thud* as the car hits the tree and the last of its momentum is lost. Another faint seatbelt creak. I hope it's just tightening with the impact. I hope Gemma died outright. I pour another hefty shot of vodka.

The engine's idling hum continues for a while, a couple

of minutes at least. One faint swish of traffic passing by up on the road, but there's no other sounds, no further vehicles. I know, though, that the car's far enough downhill that I wouldn't necessarily be able to hear any more.

A couple of twigs snapping. Close by – they'd have to be, to be heard over the engine, which must be drowning out any footfalls.

Clunk. The door, opening. A few seconds later, the motor dies and I hear the jangling as someone takes their hand away from the keys in the ignition.

Breathing, slightly hard, huffy. Then, very faint, 'Uh-huh. Good.'

Man's voice. Not particularly deep, can't make out an accent, although something about it doesn't sound like native New England.

Fabric swish, barely audible. Not smooth, like nylon, but maybe wool or a fleece jacket. Faint metallic noise, maybe a pocketknife opening. Then more fabric noises and a dim scraping. The man grunts. The same metallic noise again.

A rustling sound followed a few seconds later by a couple of spongy thuds, then the squishy squeak of protesting – what? – seat stuffing. He's making or enlarging the bullet hole in the back of Gemma's seat. He's pried the bullet out with his knife and is now playing with the hole to make sure it looks as though the round passed through the car.

Some more silence, broken briefly by the rise–fall tone of a car passing on the road above, then the second *clunk* of a door opening, fainter than the first so I guess it's one at the back. *Chink*, *chink*, *crunch*, *crunch*. The rear windshield, being smashed by whatever implement the guy used on the seat.

Clunk. The back door closes. There are a couple of noises from the front, but he must have left that one open because I can hear him moving around outside the car.

Skittering? Sweeping?

The guy is doing a hurried job of hiding the tracks he's left in the snow. Doesn't sound like he's taking long over it – the noise quickly fades – but it must have been enough not to make his presence obvious to Sylvia and the other cop when they arrived on the scene.

Another car passes on the highway. Like the first, it apparently sees nothing because it doesn't stop. By the time it's gone, the sounds of the killer making his exit have faded completely and everything is silent again. Apart from the very occasional vehicle going by, it stays quiet until the recording reaches its automatic time limit and cuts out.

I breathe out hard as I put the phone down. Only then am I hit by what I've heard, what it means, and what could have been. Supposing one of the cars that passed while the killer was at work had spotted the crash. Supposing I'd listened to the message all the way through the first time I heard it. Supposing, supposing, supposing. Despite the whirl of questions and 'what ifs' stampeding through my head, I don't feel any fresh hurt from Gemma's death, only a sense of relief that she died instantly. I'm now closer to understanding the way her killer worked. The open wound deep inside has been cranked shut, just a notch or two, but it's a small amount of closure nonetheless. I understand what Ed meant, about how bad it is to wonder what happened but never actually to know. No surprise that justice or revenge – whichever it is he longs for, I'm not sure – eats away at him so much.

Gemma's murderer was waiting specifically for her, of that I'm positive. He'd picked a spot to shoot from and made sure he could get down to her car fairly quickly. There's certainly no audible shot, which suggests the gun was silenced, and he only needed to fire once, even though it was dark and she was a moving target. It's been years since I've handled a firearms case, but I know silencers cut the muzzle velocity of the bullet as it passes, dropping the round's penetration. That's why it lodged in the seat. He knew to search for the shell and take it away, and he then did a fair job of making it look like the round went clean through. He shut off the engine, probably to make the car harder to spot, and tidied up before he left. He came and went on foot, which means he either had a vehicle stashed somewhere nearby, or he was willing to hike miles in the snow at night, or he was a local. In any case, he must've been familiar with the area.

And he must have known she was coming.

15

Half an hour later I'm sitting in Gemma's kitchen with a cup of coffee, and I've started to understand the whole thing a little better. Time, place, and all the preparation the killer must have done to get them both right and make a clean escape. He knew where she was driving from and where she was heading. He couldn't just have followed her, not if he had time to set up an ambush. He knew what car she was driving and when she'd pass his position. So he had access to that sort of information.

Altmann would certainly fit the bill. He'd been to the house before and he could have checked her shift rota. Anyone else working at the hospital could also have known, along with any regular visitors she'd had to the morgue – undertakers and the like. Her neighbours and other locals would also know enough to make them possibilities. I don't see how Wynne, even though he lied about his alibi, could have done.

The voice I heard on the recording didn't sound like either Reuben Wynne or Dr Altmann, although I've only got one word to go on and that was at some distance from the phone. Wynne lied about his alibi and Altmann wouldn't even talk about it. What still bothers me, though, is why kill Gemma?

Maybe the murderer was a professional hired by someone else. His skill would then be just a part of the job, and the information he could've got from his employer. Maybe he was a nut who sees himself as an assassin, and stalks and kills every once in a while for fun.

I can't think why someone would get a pro to shoot Gemma. Sure, if this was New York or LA and Gemma was a money-broker for the Mob, it was a hit, no problem. But it's not.

A local backwoods psycho would have a familiarity with the area, but would he have that kind of skill with a gun? Could he have acquired a silencer and whatever night-time scope must surely have been used? And why kill only Gemma? The pathological types make a habit of it by definition.

Unless he didn't kill only Gemma. Stephanie Markham was last seen heading up the same stretch of road that Gemma died on. Maybe there's someone out in the woods around there who regards it as his territory, and death to anyone who trespasses. Perhaps Gemma wandered on to his patch but escaped without realizing he was after her, and so he decided to make sure she wouldn't be coming back.

The killer couldn't have hiked miles to the scene of the shooting, it doesn't make sense. So either he hid his vehicle nearby, or he lives here in town.

And where better to hide a car than the overgrown track that leads to North Bleakwater? It joins the highway maybe half a mile south of where Gemma died, and if Ed's right, no one much ever goes down there. Whoever broke into the house hid their car in the town itself. If the intruder was connected to the murder, then presumably they'd have been happy to use the same place.

I think of the tyre tracks I saw in the night, and the trail of trampled snow and dead winter weeds leading from what used to be the ghost town's main street up to the back door of the hotel. Could they be from the same guy? Not made at the time Gemma was killed; there's been plenty of fresh snow since then. But maybe the killer uses the old town for God-knows-what in his spare time.

And maybe Stephanie Markham took a detour on her hike, just to have a look at the old ruins, and saw something she wasn't supposed to.

That thought sends an excited chill running through me that no amount of vodka can dent. Stephanie might not have been lucky enough to escape when she wandered in. And the Haleys – they were hiking through this part of the country. They were tourists, just the sort to make the trip to a genuine ghost town.

If there's a problem, it's fitting Gemma into the scenario. She'd walked to North Bleakwater before, but as far as I know, not for a while. And she didn't disappear like the others.

To find out what, if anything, is going on in North Bleakwater I'll have to check it out tomorrow. Maybe then things will be clearer.

When I crawl off the couch next morning there's light coming in through the windows, but that doesn't mean anything much. The clock on the mantel is flickering as if the batteries are low. I try to work out how many days have passed since I got here, but I can't get the same answer twice.

Outside, the town looks dead, deserted. Glancing both ways down West Road I see maybe one or two cars still in people's driveways, but no more than that. Everyone else must have already left for work. I check my pockets twice, once for the keys, once more for the weight of the gun nestled inside my coat.

Since there's no way I can remember the route I took to North Bleakwater last time, I follow the road down to the lakeside, then trek around the shoreline until I reach the old abandoned town.

After half an hour or so, the shells of buildings start to

loom out of the trees and the snow-clouded spaces between. The L-shaped remains of a small factory or workshop of some sort. Two rows of high, narrow windows spaced irregularly in the brickwork, post holes to suggest where one storey ended and another began. Interior a mess of stonework and wood broken here and there by stunted black trees and a couple of remaining iron workbenches, all covered in a shroud of snow. A crumbling edifice of cracked grey stone that might once have been a kiln or large oven of some sort, now just a shapeless mass, leaning against the collapsed remains of the building that once housed it. The space beneath the bivouacked ruins is dark, a treacherous maze of crawlspaces half-filled with dirt. I can see the town's overgrown former main street running into the trees to the southeast, away from the lakeside headed for nowhere.

Past the newer additions to North Bleakwater, I come once more to the bridge over the dried-up bed of Echo Stream, the open space of the town's common and the hotel on the far side. The decaying structure has lost some, but not all, of the majesty it possessed after dark. In the grey light of day the small signs of neglect are far more obvious – dark patches of damp-riddled wood, runnels of brown-red from metal fittings, holes where bugs have made a meal of the timbers.

A lone figure in a puffy red winter coat and an insulated hunting hat is sitting on a pile of old timber outside the building. 'Morning, Alex,' he says.

'How's it going, Ed?'

'Okay,' he says, briefly glancing in my direction. 'It's going okay. I guess I should apologize for last night. I didn't have any call to go flying off the handle like I did.'

'That's all right, I understand.' I take a perch on the wood next to him. 'Why are you out here?'

'What you were talking about last night got me thinking,

I guess. So when I woke up this morning, I thought I might head out to the old town and see what I could see, you know, maybe jog a memory or something like that.' He coughs loudly and slaps his chest a couple of times to clear his throat. 'How about you?'

'I'm checking out the hotel. Someone's been here and I thought I'd find out what they were looking for. It might be nothing. You're welcome to come along.'

He nods and climbs stiffly to his feet. 'Sure.'

The trail of crushed foliage at the back of the hotel is just as clear as last time I was here. It seems strange for visiting hikers to hug the walls so closely. My knowledge of tracking is sketchy, but I take a look at the hard-packed ice anyway.

'What do you reckon?' Ed asks.

'Hiking boots, I think. The older marks aren't too clear with the fresh snowfall, but from the tread that's what I'd say they were.'

'That doesn't narrow things down any, not in this area at this time of year.'

There are at least two sets, one smaller and narrower, that could have been made at the same time – a couple of people, walking side by side. There are also other prints of a different sort, ordinary shoes, but there's not a lot I can tell about them. A man's, probably, about the same size or a little larger than mine. There might even be two sets of these, overlapping. All four print groups come and go the same way.

If there have been several recent visitors to the hotel, presumably none of them so far killed, my backwoods territorial psycho theory no longer seems to hold water. Unless they were friends of his, of course.

'Let's go see what everyone's come all this way to look at,' I say to Ed as I stand up.

I'm expecting a squeal of rusty hinges when I carefully

push the back door inwards, but I'm disappointed. There's a faint grating as the wood scuffles against the floor. The air is a little musty but not wholly stale; the gaps between boards and the occasional missing window have seen to that. I feel like I've dived down to the wreck of the *Titanic* and gone for a walk inside. There's the same sense of opulence gone rotten over the years, the same eerily empty feeling, a living monument to the past.

Ed whistles. 'Would you look at all that.'

'They must have closed this place without selling everything off first,' I say.

We're peering into what was obviously the hotel's dining room. Most of its original fittings are still here. A dozen tables or so, half of them overturned or leaning against the walls, another two or three little more than sodden firewood. Mildew-eaten carpet that must once have been a deep red, now black with damp. The wallpaper around the room has bubbled and burst with decay, drooping in strips like jungle fronds. A handful of paintings still in the crumbling remains of their frames. Years of rain and snowmelt have all but cleaned the canvases; paint runs in coloured smears down the walls beneath them. A pair of baroque brass chandeliers lie in verdigris heaps in the middle of the wreck. In the far corner of the room a grand piano sits forlornly, looking at first like it could still be in working order. As I move inside I see the broken strings dangling underneath and the faint sheen of frozen damp or slime running along its sides.

I switch on my pocket flashlight as we cross the room and away from the weak tendrils of watery light that leak through the cracked and smeared windows.

'Those footprints head that way,' Ed says. The old man's eyes are still sharp.

Shining the beam at the rotting carpet, I can see what

could be a line or several lines of depressions running towards a set of double doors at the far side.

A low wet creaking as we push through the doors to the hotel's main hall. The level of decay in the hallway is the same as it was in the dining room. When my beam flashes over the old reception desk, tucked away at the side, I can see where insects or rodents have gnawed at the wood; the paler fresh splinters glitter white.

The tracks trampled in the carpet run to the stairs. Ed looks at them, then back at me. 'Is it safe, do you think?'

'Without the tracks, I wouldn't want to risk them. But someone's been up and down them, so they've got to be reasonably sound.'

'After you then, Alex.' He grins in the gloom.

Gingerly at first, then with more confidence, I lead the way. To break the musty silence, I ask, 'Do you remember if Stephanie ever came here?'

'I don't recall. Can't remember anything at all about where she used to go, what she used to see.' Ed sighs and shakes his head. 'You can't hold on to the little things like that, no matter how hard you try. When you lose someone, you tell yourself you'll preserve every detail, the tiniest little elements of every waking moment you spent with them. It's like trying to hold a handful of water – it all slips away, it don't matter how tight you grip. All you're left with are a few drops, just the big events, the stuff with a bit more staying power. And even they fade over time.

'I keep watching, waiting, hoping I'll find the guy who took Steph away, but I can't recall exactly who I'm avenging, not any more, not the details. All I remember clearly are my own feelings since it happened. It leaves you kind of hollow.' Ed looks and sounds older, as though a decade or two of wear has just hit him, all at once.

'Take it from me,' he says, 'you want to find whoever killed your girlfriend before you get to where I am. Get your justice while you can still remember all she was. It'll make the forgetting a whole lot easier.'

I say nothing and keep climbing. There's a breeze blowing down from on high, cold and clammy. On the first-floor landing we come across the chandelier that once illuminated the stairwell lying twisted and corroded in the ruins of a reading table, along with some chunks of plaster. The electrical cord runs limply up into the gloom. The footprint trail cuts around the carnage and heads north, away from the stairs.

'Looks like the weight of the chandelier was too much for the ceiling's plaster to bear and the cord cut through it,' I say quietly. 'Whole thing must've come down like a wrecking ball.'

Through a door that opens on a short corridor with suites on both sides. The tracks don't deviate into any of these, but continue straight ahead until they come to another, much narrower stairwell. I shine my flashlight up, and from the height I guess we're now in the tower-like structure that juts from the western end of the hotel. As I swing the beam back to my feet to follow the trail upstairs, there's a sudden burst of noise from below.

Wood, splintering. Tiles, maybe, or a pile of other detritus, clattering and sliding against each other as they're disturbed. A dull thud, a brief glimmer of daylight and a high-pitched yelp.

'Jesus,' Ed says, hand over his heart. 'Goddamn animal scared by the light. Nearly gave me a heart attack.'

I breathe out and take my fingers away from the handgrip of my Colt. Then I bring the flashlight beam back to bear on the steps in front of us, flash a grin at Ed, and resume climbing.

'I know what you meant back there, about forgetting,' I say. 'My parents were killed five or so years back. Hit-and-run car crash while I was driving them to a restaurant.'

'That's rough. You find out who did it?'

'In a roundabout way, yeah, eventually. But I don't want to wait that long this time. You were wrong when you told me I could say goodbye to Gemma when we buried her. I can't say goodbye, and I *won't* start forgetting, not until I know whoever killed her gets what's coming.'

'And you think there's a chance what happened to her had something to do with what happened to Steph?'

'It's possible, maybe.' I shrug. 'This state doesn't see much major crime so it's more likely than if we were in a city like Boston.'

'How does this place fit in?' Ed asks.

'I'm not sure it does yet. A guy broke into Gemma's house the night before last and I chased him back here. He had a car waiting for him. The old town would make a good hiding place if you needed one. Just a theory.'

The tracks take us all the way up. The top floor of the tower is home to a single L-shaped suite that must once have been one of the largest and most luxurious in the hotel. Now it's a dank, almost empty chamber lined by grimy windows with several cracked or missing panes. There's a collection of mouldering furniture scattered around its walls and a hefty hole in the middle of the floor. The carpet is rolled up and leans, part collapsed, against one of the interior walls. Two closed doors – a second bedroom, maybe, and an en suite bathroom. No carpet means no tracks, so I'm left with nothing but instinct to go on.

'I'll check the floor's safe,' I tell Ed. 'Stay here while I have a look at the hole. If everything gives way beneath me, I'll need someone to dig me out of the wreckage.'

He nods as I step into the room. There's a six-inch void between the floor and the second set of boards that made up the ceiling below; both have been broken. The exposed wood around the edges is pale, and although it's a little frost-damp it still seems pretty sturdy.

'This damage looks fresh,' I call over my shoulder. 'Well, fresher than the rest.'

The remains of the boards that fell through are lying in the room below. I lie down and dangle my flashlight at arm's length to get as good a look at them as possible from up here. I get a prickly spiders-running-up-my-arm sensation as I peer down at the shards of hardwood below.

'You want to look at the room below, we can just go downstairs,' Ed says.

'If there's anything exciting down there, yeah. Otherwise I don't want to disturb anything I don't have to. It's no good if whoever's been here gets scared away.'

Scuff marks. Shallow dents in the wood, picked out as tiny changes in the shadows cast by the light. 'It looks like the floorboards were deliberately smashed,' I say. 'Like someone took a hammer to them.'

We search the rest of the suite. There's nothing remotely interesting in the disintegrating furniture and the roll of carpet is a solid mess of frozen cloth. I open Door Number One.

It leads into a second, much smaller bedroom. The furniture here is mostly intact, although the mattress and any linen are long gone, leaving just the rusted iron framework of the bed. A dresser whose varnish is pitted and bubbled with decay and a single wooden chair complete the set. The carpet is gone and the boards look pretty clean.

'It's almost like the floor's been swept,' Ed says. 'You know, sometimes, not very often, I've thought I've seen lights up here.'

I look across at him. 'Really?'

'Like flashlights, maybe. My house is on the north side of the ridge, so I've got a pretty good view across the lake. There's been nights when I thought I could see a light moving around town, maybe high in some of the buildings. Never very bright, and I can't remember there being more than one. I used to figure it was just kids messing around out here after dark. It makes you wonder.'

'It sure does.'

The last room in the suite is small and narrow, occupied mostly by an ancient enamel bathtub turned ammonia-yellow with age. The tub has a lattice of fine cracks and there's a solid-looking tuft of frozen moss growing from the plughole. The toilet and the chain-flush cistern are both empty.

I take a look under the bath and emerge with a brick-shaped package tightly wrapped in plastic and tape. Through the wrapping I can see white powder, here and there speckled with faint traces of brown. There's a second one tucked further back in the same hiding place.

'What's that?' Ed asks.

I hold it up to the light. 'About a pound of heroin.'

16

Half an hour later, I'm home and making some calls. Ed is back at his house, although he said he'd keep as good a watch on the old town as he could through binoculars.

'Okay, Alex, what can I do for you?' Flint says once we've exchanged pleasantries.

'What do you know about heroin?'

There's a pause. 'What?'

I describe my daylight visit to the mouldering structure that used to be the Echo Springs Hotel and everything I found there.

'Are you sure that's what it was?'

'Not a hundred per cent, but I can't think of much else you'd want to hide like that. The number of people who've been that way, it looks like a drop point. My guess is a buyer will show up before long to pick the stuff up.'

'That's interesting. But why go all the way up to the hotel and make all the effort they did? They could just take it straight to Burlington or wherever.'

'Maybe it's safer to do it in two stages and have a place where they can leave the dope for a while. Maybe it's a dead-letter drop system – the smuggler and the dealer never meet. Very secure. In the hotel you go up the main stairway first because anyone wandering in there is going to do that, so it doesn't look strange. But the main one might not be solid on the higher floors, not with the water damage and everything in there. So you go to the smaller stairwell. And you go all the way up because most people would chicken out of going so high in a building that could collapse at any time. If you don't want casual visitors to find what you're hiding in the top suite, you roll up the carpet and knock a damn great hole in the middle of the floor so they won't go into the room because it's obviously too dangerous. It's like a big "keep out or you'll fall and die" sign. And because there's no carpet, there's no easy way of seeing that you've been in there.'

Flint sighs. 'So what's this got to do with Dr Larson's murder? Unless it's connected to the case I'll have to pass the whole thing over to the drugs taskforce and they can handle it. This isn't Colombia and I'm not DEA.'

'Like you said, this isn't Colombia. North Bleakwater isn't big enough or famous enough that there's going to be a lot of criminal groups using it together. The other night I chased a guy who broke into Gemma's house all the way over to North Bleakwater, where he'd left his car. He knew how safe a hiding place it was, and he was looking for something at Gemma's. He's the connection. I think they might have been worried Gemma saw something or found something, which is what the guy who broke in was looking for, so they killed her.'

'It's a theory, but—'

I cut him short. 'Are you honestly going to say it's not as worthy of investigation as your list of whackos or the hunting accident idea? You've spent enough time on those.' I'm struggling to contain my frustration. 'Speaking of which, did you check that guy Wynne's alibi? He sounded kind of edgy to me.'

'No, not yet. Maybe later.' He stays quiet for a while, then says, 'Okay. Hold the line for a minute, I'll bring Fiona in on this.'

Scattered sounds in the background, fuzz of white noise.

Then voices, close by and a sudden change in tone and volume. Echoing. We're on speaker, I guess.

'Alex,' Flint says, 'this is Detective Fiona Saric. I don't know if you've met.'

'I think I saw her at the office yesterday.'

'Good morning, Mr Rourke,' she says.

'Fiona was on the Northern Drugs Taskforce for a while before moving back to the BCI. Describe these packages again.'

'White powder, maybe a few brown-white impurities, sealed in plastic. About a pound, I'd guess.'

'They haven't been opened at all?' Fiona asks. 'This isn't some big-time junkie's stash?'

'They're so tightly covered they could've been shrink-wrapped,' I say.

'And you left them where they were?'

'Put them back right where I found them, under the tub.'

'Good,' she says. 'That was the right thing to do. I think we should stake the place out for a couple of days and see who collects the dope.' This last, I guess, to Flint.

He goes quiet for a moment, then says, 'Okay, I'll go with that. I won't ask forensics to check out the room you found, Alex, not yet; I don't want to risk being spotted and scaring away whoever's using the building.'

'Sure, I understand. How about just looking for prints?'

'If they're smart enough to go to hide everything the way they have, they're smart enough to wear gloves. Hell, Alex, it's winter – *everyone* wears gloves.' He switches to addressing Detective Saric. 'Can you think of anyone to rotate with us on stakeout?'

'I don't think there is anyone,' she says. 'Everyone in the BCI has their own cases to work and Patrol Division's tied up with the usual winter rush of accidents. I think it might have to be just you and me.'

‘Any objection if I join you out there?’ I ask. ‘I can show you the lie of the land, how they get into the hotel and so on.’

‘Knock yourself out,’ Flint says. ‘I’ll give you a call on our way through Bleakwater Ridge. We’ll pick you up.’

The line goes dead. I sit back in my chair, head buzzing with the flush of adrenalin that comes with any major break in a case, tinged with a small kick of pride. I light up a cigarette and, for the first time in a while, actually enjoy the flavour and the rush of nicotine.

‘Do you have to smoke those in here?’ Gemma doesn’t sound too exasperated. This is probably just part of her continuing efforts to get me to quit.

‘It’s a long drive and I haven’t had a cigarette since this morning.’

‘Don’t you have the willpower to wait until we get there?’ She opens the window a crack and air blasts into the car in ruffled billows.

I smile and refuse to rise to her challenge. ‘No, afraid not. One stage at a time. Get me down to a pack a day and then we can cut them further from there.’

‘You’re impossible,’ Gemma says, shaking her head with a wry grin on her face.

While I’m waiting for Flint and Saric to arrive from Waterbury, I fill some time by calling Sylvia.

‘Ehrlich,’ she answers on the fourth ring of the phone.

‘Sylvia, it’s Alex Rourke.’

‘Hi, Alex. What’s up?’

‘Can you remember if there’s ever been any trouble, or if your department has ever had any calls about North Bleakwater?’ I say.

'The old ghost town? I can't remember anything myself. Hold on.' There's a muffled *whoosh* noise; I guess she's just put her hand over the receiver. It's not a hundred per cent effective because I can still hear her ask, 'Ben, can you remember anytime we've been called out to anything in North Bleakwater, the deserted place up by Silverdale Lake?' After much mumbling from Ben, Sylvia comes back on the line.

'It doesn't look like it. Ben says he's occasionally heard about tourists trying to drive down the old road off Route 100, but that's not against the law. He says there was talk four, five years ago, just before I joined the force, of doing regular vehicle patrols through the old town. Apparently, some of Bleakwater's good citizens thought the place might be attracting kids or vagrants. Anyway, there was some discussion with the State Police, nothing was found and the idea got dropped. That's about it.'

'Uh-huh.'

'So what's going on, Alex? I figure these questions must have a reason behind them.'

'Some guy broke into the house the other night and I chased him out there. I just wondered if anyone else ever reported anything to do with the old town.'

'Broke in? Did he take anything?'

I pause for a moment. 'I don't think so. I had a quick look at the place when I got home. Didn't spot anything then and I haven't since, so I don't know what he was after.'

'Did you get a look at him?'

'No. He cracked me on the head once we reached open ground near the buildings. Before that it was too dark. By the time I woke up, he was gone.'

'Ouch.' I can hear her wincing. 'Are you okay?'

'My head's still a little sore and I was pretty out of it for a while, but I'm surviving. If I catch the guy sneaking around here again I'll be sure to pay him back in full.'

'Give him one for me, too.'

'I will. On the subject of North Bleakwater, did you check there when Stephanie Markham disappeared?'

'I think so,' she says. 'One of our cars drove out there, but I can't remember whose. They couldn't have found anything. So what's this about? Do you think there's a connection between Markham and Dr Larson?'

'Well, both incidents happened in the same area. I think both might have been something to do with the old town. But I don't know how or why just yet. I'll let you know when I'm certain I'm on the right track.'

'You be sure to do that,' she says. 'Take care.'

'You too.'

Flint's car pulls up outside an hour later and I climb in. Fiona Saric's Neon is waiting, line astern. When we make the turn off Route 100 and on to the stony dirt track that runs out to the old town, I'm thankful I never tried bringing the 'Vette down here. The ground is rough and broken, with potholes and hidden humps that threaten to take out the bottom of the car more than once.

'You know, I've been here before,' he says as we bounce over the track surface. He seems eager, happier than when I saw him question Wynne. It could just be edginess over the case – his eyes are sunken, cheeks hollow, like he's been working a couple of late nights. 'When I was at high school I went out with a girl from Bleakwater. We came here a couple of times in summertime. There was a little more of it still standing back then, but it's not that different.'

'I didn't realize it was a make-out spot.'

'It wasn't, not in my day anyway. Jessica's dad used to

paint down by the lakeshore in his spare time. Since that was where everyone hung out, we couldn't; he didn't like me much. It was sometimes hard to take her back to my place – my older brother Jack was an asshole. Drunk, usually, or worse. So we ended up here.'

'Did it last?'

'No,' Flint says, then shrugs dismissively. 'But that's what high school is all about. Not much different to how it is when you get older. Best that way, y'know? Having women in a relationship is more trouble than it's worth. How about you, how did you meet Dr Larson?'

'I was helping with a murder case in northern Maine, what, a year and a half ago. She was the medical examiner who autopsied the victim. We hit it off pretty much straight away.' I smile, half-happy at the memory, half-sad that that's all it is now. 'Funny, really.'

'What is?'

'She changed jobs, moved to Vermont so she'd be closer to me. If we'd never met, she'd probably still be alive.'

'Tough break,' Flint says. I can't tell if he means it. 'Makes you think.'

The Taurus emerges from the morass of leafless forest that surrounds and entwines North Bleakwater. I can hear the snow crunching beneath the tyres as Flint lets the car roll slowly into the decaying remains of the town. He pulls up on the far side of the bridge, some way from the hotel, then climbs out. Saric stops next to us and does the same. She's wearing a long winter coat and gloves. Probably a year or two younger than me, fairly short with quick dark eyes. Looking at her, I get the impression she can really focus if she needs to, able to pour all her concentration into tackling a problem.

'Fiona Saric,' she says to me, extending a hand. She has

quite a deep, husky voice. 'Pleased to meet you, Mr Rourke.'

'That's the building, huh?' Flint asks, pointing at the hotel. 'What made you want to go looking around in that dump?'

I tell the two cops about finding the tracks outside the building and what I found when I came here with Ed.

'We should speak to Mr Markham,' Saric says.

Flint nods, frowns. 'Yeah, you do that if you want, Fiona.'

'Yes, sir.' She glances in my direction.

'Do you know if the dope is still here?' Flint asks me. 'It's been, what, over two hours since you were here.'

'No idea.'

'In that case I'll go check it out. Just to be sure.'

Saric speaks up before Flint leaves us. 'Do you mind if I come too, sir? I'd like to see the building and have a proper look at what we're dealing with.'

'Sure.' Flint shrugs. His shoulders drop in irritation. 'In fact, if you do that, you can see if the dope's still in place. No sense in us both going.'

We watch Saric tramp off through the snow. Flint stays leaning against the side of the car, watching her.

'Is there much of a drugs trade in Vermont?' I ask him. 'You guys must work with the Border Patrol, like they do in Maine. Is there much that comes down from Canada, or goes the other way? I know the whole area's always been big on smuggling in the past.'

Flint thinks for a moment before answering. 'Some, I guess, but not very much comes cross-border. Most heroin supplies come from New York and other places to the south.'

'But it does happen?'

'Sure.'

I fall silent again and take the opportunity to light a cigarette. 'Have you spoken to Dr Altmann yet?'

'Yes, I have. The doctor says he was home all day cleaning

out his kitchen when Dr Larson was killed, so no alibi. He was offended by the fact that anyone could think he'd do anything like that, especially to her, is what he said. He complained a lot about you, Alex. It's a damn miracle he told me anything at all.'

We stand in silence for a few minutes until Saric emerges from the hotel and walks back to our position. 'It's just like Mr Rourke said,' she tells Flint. 'The heroin is still there.'

'Probably won't be long before the buyers come to collect,' he says, nodding. 'Fiona, you take first shift watching this place. I'll come take over about one in the morning.'

'Yes, sir.' She doesn't look pleased by the prospect.

Flint gazes at the buildings around us. 'There's a gap over there that should make a good place to park,' he says. 'You should be able to see the hotel without anyone spotting you. Alex, you want a lift home or are you going to stay out here for a while?'

'I'll stay with Detective Saric, if that's all right.'

She nods. 'Sure. At least I won't have to start on the paperback I brought, at least for a while.'

'In that case, I'll see you both later. Just remember you're supposed to be working out here. Save play for after.' Flint leers, half-smiling in our direction, then drops into his car and cruises away.

Saric shakes her head and mutters, 'Prick.'

I help her reverse her Neon into the jumbled ruins. She lines the car up so it's possible to watch the hotel through a narrow window in the shattered building next to us.

'All that "yes sir, no sir" stuff is kind of formal,' I say to her. 'I thought you two worked together fairly regularly.'

'We do. Karl has a short temper and he tends to get grouchier as the day wears on. Starts off okay, but it's all downhill from there.'

'Now you mention it, he was in a lousy mood when I saw him yesterday. He seemed happier today until we got out here.'

'I know people who aren't good at mornings; he's fine with them, it's the rest of the day that's his problem. He likes to be reminded of the fact that he outranks me when he's in one of his moods.'

'It sounds like he should lay off the caffeine.'

She laughs, sounds bitter. 'The least of his problems.'

'Really?'

'Five years ago he was nearly kicked off the force. Went off the rails for a while. Drink, more if you believed some of the wilder rumours.' She looks at me. Her gaze is curiously flat. 'I don't. I like to think I'm a good judge of people, and while I'd say Karl Flint is an idiot and at times only a mediocre cop, I don't think he'd be stupid enough to mess with anything illegal. He brings the stories on himself. Hangs out with some rough types in some rough places, but I'm sure that's just so he can keep his ear to the ground.'

A couple of snowflakes drift past the car. 'Why'd he go off the rails?'

'Did you hear about the Damien Ackroyd case?'

I shake my head. 'If this was five years ago, I'd have been working out of Quantico. Unless he was a major violent criminal, I'd have missed him.'

'I don't know about violent,' Saric says, shrugging. 'But he was certainly a big-time scumbag. He was like a criminal version of one of those big Japanese conglomerates – he did a little bit of everything. His main thing was selling runaways and impressionable girls who thought they were going to be models into the sex trade in New York, then bringing heroin back in return.'

'Doesn't ring any bells with me.'

'Oh well. He wasn't even smart enough to hide the fact that he was a crook. He had a big house in Burlington's Hill District, three sports cars, the works. People were getting suspicious of his business dealings when one of his girls escaped from a brothel in New York and told her parents everything. Big media coverage, and we got involved. We went after Damien Ackroyd. The girl identified her handler and NYPD picked him up. He led us to the next rung on the ladder, and she gave us the name of Isaac Fairley, Ackroyd's number two. Without him, we could've busted some minor crooks, but we only had circumstantial evidence on Ackroyd. Certainly nothing that would've made for a conviction.'

'And Flint failed to bring in Fairley?' I ask.

Saric shakes her head. 'No, he found him wherever he was hiding out, subdued him and brought him in for interrogation. Fairley gave us a full statement implicating Ackroyd, all the details, held nothing back. We made the arrest. When the case came to trial, Ackroyd's lawyers – who coincidentally also represented Fairley after his initial interview – produced photos of Fairley's chest, covered in welts and bruises. On the stand he said Karl beat the confession out of him. The statement he gave us became inadmissible and the case collapsed. Ackroyd was busted on some minor possession-with-intent charges and escaped without punishment for the whole prostitution ring. He kept his big house and all his cars, although he moved away not long after his release.'

I nod. 'I bet your superiors weren't happy about that.'

'*No one* was happy about that. Karl denied everything, but he was suspended, investigated, and might have been fired. As it was, the only proof was the photos of Fairley's injuries, and Ackroyd could've had him beaten after the interview, both to get the pictures and to threaten him into retracting his statement. Karl was reinstated, but for a few months he was out on the ragged edge. I remember one night I went for a drink with him in Burlington, just to see how things were – I didn't know him then as well as I do now, otherwise I wouldn't have bothered. I don't think he drank much, but he was in a *mean* mood all the same.' She shakes her head. 'Maybe it was the summer sun, y'know? Affects people all sorts of ways. This was a couple of weeks after Fourth of July, so the party spirit was long gone. Karl got kicked out of the Bar None for getting in a fight with a couple of guys. I had to drag him away.'

'But he's not like that any more?'

'No, not really. He's regained his inflated ego since then. I think it's calmed him down.' Saric smiles, belying the acid within. I get the feeling it wouldn't be much fun to be on her bad side.

The car falls quiet for a while. Fiona and I chat sporadically, but not about the job. She seems quite withdrawn, happy to talk about other people, but saying comparatively little about herself.

Night comes down but I see little point in heading for home just yet. My watch tells me it's just gone six-thirty.

Then Saric leans towards the window and says, 'Alex, have you got a gun on you?'

'Yeah.' I frown. 'I've got the proper permit, if that's what you're wondering.'

She shakes her head. 'I might have to use you as backup. There's someone out there.'

17

I strain my eyes over Saric's shoulder. She's right. A figure picked out dimly against the snow, outside the hotel. Beyond the fact that someone's there, it's too dark to make out any details.

'How long's he been there?' I ask quietly.

'I think I saw him coming out from the back of the hotel. He could already have been inside. I haven't seen a car's headlights. He must have killed them before he arrived.'

'Maybe he walked here or he parked on the track before it left the woods.' I glance at her. She's straining her eyes, trying to make as much out as possible. 'Do we grab him?'

'I don't see anyone else out there.' She thinks briefly, then nods. 'Okay, let's get him. You back me up, but remember you're not a cop so don't go waving guns around just yet, not unless this goes really bad. Officially, you're here to help ID those involved.'

'Sure.' I check my Colt, just in case.

We swing out of the car and scuttle quickly towards the bridge. I'm uncomfortably aware of how loud everything is in the stillness. We've crossed the dried-up stream bed and are only thirty yards or so from the suspect when he spots us. He stiffens and moves his head, like he's craning for a better view. Then he turns and runs.

Saric instantly breaks into a sprint and brings up her gun in both hands. I follow her. 'Hey!' she yells. 'Police! Stop where you are.'

The suspect keeps going so she repeats her warning, louder

and more urgently. This time, the figure stops and turns around. 'What's going on?' he asks in a voice I recognize. 'What did I do?'

'Just keep your hands where I can see them,' Saric says as we approach Reuben Wynne. He's wearing the same winter coat as last time I saw him. A notebook protrudes from one of the pockets. He looks scared.

Saric asks him if he's carrying any weapons, then frisks him to be sure. She looks at me and says, 'He doesn't have anything on him.'

No drug packages. To Reuben, she says, 'Who are you, sir? What are you doing here?'

'My name's Reuben Wynne. I was supposed to meet some people about some work. They want me to paint pictures of this place.' He gestures at the old town. 'It's going to be in a magazine. They're going to pay me fifteen hundred dollars for it. They're going to show me what they want painted, and then we're going to have something to eat and a drink in the town on the other side of the lake and discuss things.' He smiles proudly. 'It's my first commission as an artist. They said they were impressed with what I'd done at the class.'

Saric looks at me, raises an eyebrow. 'It's dark. Why would they want to meet at night?'

'They work during the day and so do I, so they said it would be easiest if we met in the evening. They said it didn't matter that it was night because I could still see what they were talking about. Six thirty, they said, but I'm a few minutes late because I couldn't find the road.'

'Where's your car?'

'By the side of the track, just before the first buildings. They said the ground was really bad here and I'd be best parking before I got to the town. The track was bad enough.'

'Who's they?' I chip in. 'Who are you meeting here?'

He flicks through his notebook. 'Mr Delaney was the guy I spoke to on the phone. He's coming here with two other people from the magazine. It's called *Green Mountain Life*. They want pictures of scenes all over the state by different artists. They want me for this and maybe Lake Willoughby as well, although they said they might have someone else in line for that job.'

'I've never heard of the magazine,' Saric says. She holsters her gun.

'Mr Delaney's number should be in my cell phone calls list.'

'And he told you to meet here at six-thirty?'

'He said they might be inside the old hotel because the interior is one of the places they wanted done. Otherwise they'd meet me out here. I had a look through the back doors, but there wasn't anyone there. I guess they must be late as well.'

Saric takes Wynne's personal details and copies down Delaney's number from his phone. When she calls it, there's no answer. We check his car is where he said – the battered Nissan sits on the track twenty yards or so inside the treeline – and Saric asks him for permission to search it, which he gives. Nothing to show he has ever had anything to do with the drugs trade. No weapons. No cash.

Mr Delaney and the magazine people still haven't shown up. Saric and I are both thinking the same thing – someone tricked him into coming here.

'No sign of your people,' she says to Reuben. 'Rather than freezing to death out here, it might be a good idea to go home. If they show up, we'll explain to them what happened.'

He looks disappointed, but he does as he's told. 'I'll check his alibi for Dr Larson's murder and his record for anything drug-related,' Saric says to me as he leaves. 'Just to make sure he's not involved in any of this. Unless coming here was an elaborate ploy of some kind, I don't see it.'

'Flint told me he was a suspect in a previous murder,' I say as we walk back to the car.

She nods. 'Carita Jenner. He was one of her clients and he didn't have an alibi. No evidence to suggest he'd done it, though. He was questioned, like a bunch of other people, but he was never charged with anything. The murder was never solved.'

'Who handled the case?'

'I don't remember.' Saric puffs out her cheeks. 'Makes you wonder. She'd still be alive if she hadn't turned hooker to keep up with her heroin addiction. I hate it when people let the dope take over.'

'You do?' I keep my tone neutral, detecting something deeper in what she's saying.

'My older brother Dan OD'd on the stuff when I was twelve.' She smiles. 'Don't worry about it. It's my hang-up, not yours.'

I stay quiet. When we reach the car she says, 'Do I have the pleasure of your company for any longer or are you going to call it a night?'

'I might head for home. In fact, I might head for the bar. If whoever sent Reuben here is in the area, maybe they'll stop for a drink. It'll give me a chance to grab some dinner, too.'

Saric laughs. 'Don't rub it in. I've got a couple of sandwiches and a flask of coffee and that's it.'

'I don't think the Owl's Head does take-out, otherwise I could bring you some.'

'You just enjoy yours. I'll try not to think about it, out here in the cold.'

We say our goodbyes and I hike back alone around the lake through the darkened woods.

The bar is almost busy, by local standards anyway, when I shuffle in out of the cold. People have returned from work and come looking for food. Anonymous faces, some in couples but most alone. A patter of faint conversation. No suggestion that any of them are Reuben's mystery caller, Mr Delaney.

I've finished my dinner by the time I realize that Ed hasn't come in tonight. The tiny complement of regulars are all here, along with the usual handful of other people from around town, all of them strangers to me, but the one face I'd expect to see is absent.

Almost without noticing, I fall into the same pattern as Ed over the past two years and let my eyes drift over the faces of the other people in the bar. Unlike him, there's no one in town I know and trust, and can thus ignore. But since I think Gemma's killer is fairly local, I don't see that as a big problem. No one's earned the right to be trusted.

A woman in her late forties. Strawberry-blonde hair pinned back. Still wearing a dark coat and a uniform of some sort, though she's taken her gloves and scarf off. There's a gold ring on her left hand, a thin silver watch on her wrist. No other jewellery and no make-up of any sort. Her mouth puckers as she sips soup from her spoon.

A guy past fifty, with a well-receded hairline and sagging features. Tired eyes look out over a downturned mouth. He's wearing a thick sweater and has a winter coat and a fur-lined hat lying on the seat next to him.

A middle-aged couple both wearing suits – his grey, hers very dark blue. She has a narrow face and eyes that are deep-set below her short brown hair. He has similar hair, glasses, the beginnings of crow's feet and a dimpled chin. As they talk, she calls him 'Ross'.

A guy who looks maybe ten or eleven years younger than me, wearing a Celtics baseball cap beneath which I can just make out strands of short blond hair. A heavy brown coat, gloves to match and jeans. Almost hunched over his Bud, dark eyes staring blankly at the space in front of him. Occasionally, his gaze flicks towards me as if he's doing the same calculations about me as I am about him, then just as quickly flicks away. I try to remember when he came in, but I can't.

When I leave, the young guy watches me go, following me with his eyes without moving his head. It's another bitterly cold night and slow, heavy flakes of snow are drifting lazily out of the sky, but I take a moment to check the parking lot at the back of the Owl's Head. Two cars, and a third with enough packed ice on it to suggest it belongs to Bella or the bar's owner and doesn't get moved much. One of the more recent arrivals is a heavily used pickup with a bundle of tools covered in a tarp in the back. The other is a fairly old tan Toyota Paseo devoid of accumulated junk. There's a couple of pieces of paper wedged in the closed door of the glove box; I can just make out the corner of what looks like a photo on the uppermost of these. A couple of cans of Coke in the passenger footwell, empty. Both vehicles have Vermont plates.

On my way back past the front of the Owl's Head, I take a glance through one of the windows. The young man has left his seat and is talking with Bella behind the bar. She's shaking her head and shrugging.

18

That night I lie on the couch in the dark, trying to relax, Gemma's house moaning around me. My body is so numb I can't feel the couch beneath me and I float in lukewarm air, hovering in the centre of a room that I once regarded as a happy place, somewhere I could meet and be with the woman I loved. Now it holds nothing but an ever-increasing desert between the lands of sleep and wakefulness that every night I must try to cross on ever-wearier legs. With each breath in and out, I rise and fall on my cushion of air like a boat on the ocean. With each breath in and out, I force myself to take another step across the sands.

Sometime in the dead hours of morning, I drift into an uneasy and all too short-lived doze. I dream I'm back in my office in Boston, only somehow it's much bigger and I'm alone. Huge stacks of paper and bundles of manila files surround me on all sides, towering cartoon-like above me. More piles lean against each other on the floor all around my desk, along with photographs, tapes, plastic evidence bags tagged with names and dates. An entire career's worth of paperwork and investigation. And I'm working my way down each stack, looking for mention of Gemma. I know I've got her case notes here, but I can't find them, and I don't know if she's included in any of the others.

On the far wall, hanging above where Rob's desk would normally be, there's one of those big clocks I used to see sometimes at public swimming baths or in the high-school swimming pool when I was a kid. The kind that only has a second hand and no numbers and just ticks round and round and round so swimmers can see how long it takes them to do each length. Only I'm not working fast enough; each page of each file takes an age to read through, and every time I look up the clock is still whirring around and the piles of paper seem just as big as before. So I try to speed up, but it makes no difference and I'm still too slow.

Open my eyes and it's still dark. It also seems as though a window has blown open somewhere; the room is bitingly cold and where I was once floating on air, the couch now feels like a cold, clammy mouth trying to swallow me whole.

I sit up and rub my forehead, wondering where on earth my subconscious dredged all that up from. The LCD clock with the fading batteries has at last gone stubbornly blank and I can't immediately remember where I left my watch. Looking around for it, shivering with the cold, I catch sight of my collection of newspaper photocopies and Gemma's files, along with my notes on the crime scene report from the crash site, the stuff I got from the journalist Elijah Charman, little notes and scribblings, fragments of facts and ideas. I can imagine the look on Rob's face if I told him I did it because I'd just dreamt something similar, but I step over to the papers anyway and hunker down next to them.

I read, re-read, sifting information, looking for connections. As I read, I begin to spread the papers out into different patches of floor around me according to who or what they refer to.

Stephanie Markham.
The Haleys.
Gemma.

I picture Elijah shouting for the attention of a couple of cops as they walk up a trail blocked by a patrol car, following a string of state troopers. 'Detective, Detective! Are you expecting to find her today?'

For some reason, I see him wearing his huge swathe of cold-weather clothing and his woollen hat, even though it's summer.

The two cops stop and turn around. 'We're hoping she'll turn up alive and well. We *always* hope we'll find her,' Flint yells back.

'Ask us about it again this evening,' Detective Saric adds. 'We think she might be up on the Long Trail.'

Lamoille County.
Orleans County.
Photos.

I picture the young, nervous-looking manager of a car rental dealership in Waterbury looking at the blue Volvo parked in the garage, checking the booking forms and going to make a phone call. 'Is that Helen Haley? This is Bowman Auto Rentals in Waterbury, Vermont. We have a car reservation for a Mr William Haley, but he hasn't come in to pick it up . . .'

Outside, daylight leeches over the horizon. I light up another cigarette and keep going.

Crime scene reports.
Forensics.
Plans.
Diagrams.
Position of body at scene of death.

Gemma slumped over the steering wheel, a trickle of drying blood running down her back, underneath her coat. Eyes open. One hand limp at her side, the other still caught up in the wheel.

Have another cigarette, then take the laden ashtray out to the kitchen like a crematorium jar and empty it in the trash. Return with a cup of coffee.

The living room is awash with papers, covering the floor in an overlapping mess of black and white with a single hole at its centre – my perch. Only when I step rather awkwardly into it, trying not to disturb the array of information around it, do I realize how cold it is there. I clasp my hands around the coffee for warmth and keep reading as the morning wears on and the pale sun climbs higher in the sky.

Adele Laine, unattended death.
Arthur Styles, unattended death.
Lester Hoffman and Kate Wylie.
Rosemary Saunders.
Eric Burns.

'I might have to do an autopsy on a kid killed in a hit-and-run when I go back on Monday. The State Police think it may have been something to do with the heroin trade . . .'

Eric Burns, 20, suspected homicide. Hit-and-run victim, the last post-mortem Gemma carried out. Killed by blunt trauma consistent with vehicle impact. Preliminary results of blood screening indicate small amounts of heroin or a similar opiate in his bloodstream.

A notation at the bottom of the page mentions the personal effects found on the deceased, which were taken away as evidence on Tuesday, the day after the autopsy, the day Gemma died. Three hundred and seventeen dollars in cash. Watch, a couple of bits of personal jewellery. Cell phone, more or less destroyed by the impact that killed him. Wallet with all the usual crap. Including two scraps of paper, folded away inside one of the credit card pockets.

The first read: *You'd better be ready to deal with the big boys, or you'll have to deal with the consequences. Don't think you can hide from us.*

Gemma's notation adds that the note had two puncture marks in it, similar to staple holes. Nothing was found to match, but my first guess is that if you want to threaten someone with 'consequences', how better to do it than with a photo of someone who wouldn't play ball?

The second note reads: *Corner of Fourth and Dougan, 10.00 p.m. Delaney.*

That name again.

Could be coincidence, but I doubt it. This time, the set-up resulted in Eric Burns's death. Reuben Wynne may have got off lucky.

There's no photos of either note in the copied file, so it's hard to know what to make of them. Could the fact that Gemma found the reference to Delaney have made him want to silence her? Why do that if it's mentioned in a report sent to the VSP, though? And wouldn't he have searched the body if he could, or been more careful when using his name in the first place?

I'd need to see the notes, or speak to someone who had, to narrow down the options. I dial the number of Kingdom Hospital and ask for the mortuary. After a minute or so waiting for an answer, I give up. It seems Ashley and Clyde are both out or busy. They're the only ones I know who might have seen the notes and who might be able to tell me more. For a moment I wonder whether or not to try again later, or to go there myself and catch them once they've finished whatever it is they're doing. I try the phone one more time, with the same result, and reach for the keys to the 'Vette.

Snow whirls uncertainly from the sky. Fat wet lumps of the stuff first pepper, then blanket, then pepper the windshield of the car again. The sawtooth landscape is hidden behind a fog of white and even though I'm keeping the 'Vette's speed down, I'm having to fix my eyes firmly on the road. I've got Billy Flynn playing quietly on the stereo and I'm thinking about Mr Delaney. Him and the tan sedan I occasionally glimpse in the mirror between snow flurries, holding station a couple of hundred yards back.

It might be I'm just being paranoid. After all, it's not as though there's much choice of destinations on this lonely stretch of state highway. There's a fair number of minor roads branching off every once in a while, heading for towns probably even smaller than Bleakwater Ridge, but otherwise the only options are Newport, Orleans, a few miles south, or the Canadian border.

Even so, it looks like the Toyota I saw at the bar last night, and I keep an eye on it. If it is tailing me, it's not a pro driving; no way they'd let themselves get spotted so easily. No need to follow me at all, as far as I can tell.

It keeps up with me all the way, as the road curves from north to east towards the sluggish, partially frozen sheet of Lake Memphremagog. I finally lose track of it as I reach the outskirts of Newport. I can't tell whether it's a deliberate move on the driver's part, or if he just got stuck at an intersection. It still hasn't returned by the time I reach the hospital and park the 'Vette.

I've just done so when my cell phone rings. 'Morning, Alex,' a woman's voice says when I pick up.

'You sound beat, Detective Saric,' I say. 'Did you get much sleep last night?'

'Not enough. And call me Fiona. I'm too tired for formalities.'

'Sure.'

'I thought I'd let you know I checked Reuben Wynne's

alibi for the time Dr Larson was killed. He told you and Karl that he was cleaning the hall used by his art class, right?'

'Yeah.' Having already checked myself, I know what's coming. 'He lied, right?'

Saric pauses. 'How did you know?'

'Just a guess,' I say, smiling. 'Good instinct for these things.'

'Mrs Greiner, the woman who manages the hall, unlocked it for him at four, like he said. The next person to arrive was Amy Powell, but she didn't get there until seven, about half an hour before the class starts. She told me he'd only just arrived, or at least that's what he'd said, and he hadn't got far with the cleaning.'

'So there's a gap.'

'A big enough gap for him to have killed Dr Larson,' Saric says. 'But I went to speak to him in person to find out why he lied to you. I don't know if his little run-in with us in North Bleakwater has made him worried about police persecution or made him think we're out to get him, but he was surprisingly co-operative. It turns out he spent a couple of hours that Tuesday in the hall with a prostitute called Judy Cross. He's done it a few times in the past with various hookers. He doesn't like to be seen bringing them home. He lied about it because he was worried the story would get back to Greiner, and because he thought telling us might dredge up a past encounter with the cops concerning a hooker.'

'Carita Jenner.'

'Right again. And he figured that would mean a lot of trouble for him. He was just one of several suspects in the Jenner case, but then I suppose he is a *paranoid* schizophrenic.' She sighs. 'Anyway, I spoke to Ms Cross, and she confirms what he told me. Unless he hired someone – and he freely showed me his most recent bank records to demonstrate otherwise – he had nothing to do with Dr Larson's murder. Someone who knew him from the Jenner murder must've been trying to use him as a stooge.'

I nod to myself. 'Delaney?'

'So far I haven't had any luck tracing him. I'm assuming "Delaney" isn't his real name, not unless he's a total idiot. The number he called Wynne from turns out to be a payphone in Waterbury. It's out of sight of any CCTV. Barring spending a long time trying to find someone who saw him make the call, that's a dead end.'

I nod. 'What about Dr Altmann? He's about the only other suspect by name, and even he's a long shot.'

'He's Karl's business. He might do more work on him when he comes off stakeout, but don't hold your breath.'

'That's okay. I don't think it's likely to have been him. He knew Gemma. If she'd been killed at home by someone she'd let into the house, he'd be a strong suspect. Sniping doesn't feel right, and if it wasn't him that actually pulled the trigger, how would he know how to hire a pro? Plus I don't know if he's the type to do anything like that.'

'Well, we'll get back to the hunt. I'll keep you posted.'

'Thanks, Fiona.'

'Don't mention it.'

I hang up, then head inside.

A whistled rendition of the 1812 Overture, echoing and hollow, greets me as the steel elevator doors slide open. The hospital building, especially the basement, is quiet, almost empty. I turn the corner to see the janitor at an intersection twenty or thirty yards further down, cheerily attacking the floor with a mop and soapy water that's giving off bleach fumes I can smell from here. He stops whistling as soon as he notices me and gives me a strange half-askance stare for a couple of moments, like he's listening to a conversation I can't hear. Then he seems to relax.

'You don't look so good,' he calls out. His mouth breaks into a grin, the kind doctors use when they tell patients, sure, you've got cancer, but look on the bright side.

'Thanks,' I say. 'Maybe I should've worn a tie.'

He laughs, with me or at me I don't know. 'They know you now. Inside. They want to ride, get what's theirs. Bad now, the look.'

He shakes his head and goes back to whistling and attacking the floor with the mop. I wait for a moment, wondering if that's all. Since he continues to ignore me, I figure that's all I'm going to get out of him today and resume my journey to the morgue.

I stop outside the mortuary office as the door opens and Ashley Lynch hurries out carrying a cardboard box. There's a *glink* of glass knocking against glass as she pulls up short in front of me, a baffled look on her face.

'Hi, Alex,' she says after a moment's pause. 'Look, we're really busy right now. I don't suppose this can wait until tomorrow?'

'Not really.' She starts to protest but I hold up a hand to cut her off. 'I know you're busy – I tried to get you on the phone earlier – but this won't take two seconds. Then I'm out of your hair.'

'Okay. What is it?'

'Before Gemma died she did a post-mortem on a hit-and-run called Eric Burns, right?'

'On the Monday, plus some lab results and cataloguing, paperwork and so on, on Tuesday.'

'His case notes said there were two notes found in his wallet. Do you remember them?'

She thinks for a moment. 'Yes. They were only small,

folded up and tucked away. We only spotted them on the Tuesday when we were properly outlining what he had on him at time of death.'

'What did they look like?'

'Uh, both handwritten, I think. If I remember right, it was two different sets of writing. The cops dealing with his case thought there was a photo attached to one and that we'd mislaid it.'

'The report said it looked like something had been stapled to one of them.'

'That's right. They must have thought we'd pulled the staple out and separated whatever was there, although we didn't. Right at the end of our shifts, too; Gemma and I were supposed to be heading home. In the end we left the problem with Clyde since he was working late. I think they realized their mistake eventually.'

'Thanks, Ashley,' I tell her. 'I don't suppose you've heard how the investigation into his death is going?'

'No reason why we would. You'd have to speak to the VSP if you wanted to know more. The name of the cops handling the case should be in the file somewhere.'

'Thanks, but I can't ask the police. They'd know someone had shown me the autopsy report. It probably doesn't matter. I don't suppose the name "Delaney" means anything to you?'

She shakes her head and smiles wryly. 'Sorry. What's all this about?'

'Some other time,' I tell her.

I'm walking away when she calls after me, 'Have you seen Frank Altmann yet?'

'Yeah,' I reply, looking back at her. 'The other day. A cop from the VSP spoke to him too.'

'How did he look?' Ashley says.

I frown. 'What do you mean?'

'I was just wondering how he's holding up. He's called in sick the last couple of days. Stress, I think. I haven't been able to get in touch with him.' She smiles. 'I just hope it's nothing serious.'

19

All the way to Barton I try to make sense of everything. Somewhere I'm sure there's a connection. The tan Toyota doesn't put in a second appearance, so I'm left with a mind free to wander. I have no firm proof that this 'Delaney' guy is connected to Gemma's death and any of the disappearances, but his name has now come up twice. And if there was a photo attached to one of the notes, where did it go? Presumably, the cops spotted it at the scene but didn't investigate fully. I'd like to ask Flint to check for me, but I know I'd face a string of difficult questions if I did.

Standing at the foot of Altmann's driveway, gazing through the snow flurries at his house. The gnarled beech that dominates the front yard creaks alarmingly in the blustery air. I scan the front windows through the cover of its branches, looking for any signs of movement, but I'm not optimistic. Altmann's car isn't in the driveway – though it could simply be in the garage – and there's no fresh tyre ruts or footprints anywhere on his property. The whole place feels empty, lifeless.

Seeing no sign of occupation, I make my way up to the front door. Ring the bell a couple of times, pausing in between button presses to listen for sounds of movement in the house. Nothing.

I run my hand through my hair to brush the worst of the snow out of it, then go talk to Altmann's neighbours. There's no response at the house to the west, but a middle-aged woman answers when I try the other adjacent property.

'The last time I saw him must've been a couple of days ago,' she says when I introduce myself as a friend of the doctor's from Boston. 'He drove off to work, same as usual. I don't remember seeing him come back. Are you sure he said he'd be in?'

'Positive,' I say, looking suitably confused. 'He said he had the whole day off work when I spoke to him at the weekend.'

The woman shifts her weight, eager to wind up the conversation and get out of the cold. 'Maybe something came up. You know how it is with doctors.'

'I'm sure he would have called me. You're sure he hasn't been around at all? How about anyone else? He might have asked one of his friends to check in on his place if he had to leave suddenly.'

'Only person I've seen has been the postman. I'm sorry.'

'Well, thanks anyway,' I tell her. 'Sorry to have bothered you.'

One last look at Altmann's house confirms that there doesn't seem to have been any kind of break-in. I can't tell if he packed a lot of stuff when he left, but if he hasn't been back in two days, he's presumably skipped town. I climb back into the 'Vette and go looking for an internet café.

It's frighteningly easy to find out all sorts of background information on people over the net, thanks to the age of computerized records. Some of it is available through public access systems – usually the more basic data like address and phone number, sometimes more. For everything else you have to subscribe to various background check service providers. As an investigative agency, particularly one that deals with missing persons, we have accounts with a couple of the more reputable ones. A full report giving a complete life history – employment, property, credit, criminal records, all surviving family members and known associates – usually takes up to twenty-four hours. It's mostly only the Adam Webbs of this world who don't leave a trail to follow. For the Average Joe with a steady respectable job, a mortgage and a couple of credit cards, it's a piece of cake. For what I want to know about Altmann, mostly property owned in his name and relatives living reasonably close to the area, the search is more or less instantaneous.

Vermont is one of the more restricted states when it comes to information access, but I still get enough. Altmann's home in Barton is the only one in his name, but his father Sam owns a house near South Hero on the largest of the three main islands in Lake Champlain. Nice area; the family must have a fair amount of cash. No other nearby relatives are mentioned, so if he's hiding out with his folks he's either at his dad's or he's left the state entirely. I order a full background check, just in case there's anything more interesting in it, then hit the road.

The snow has slowed almost to a stop by the time I reach the end of the flat highway that makes up the Sand Bar causeway, linking the state's three main islands to the mainland. Stands of leafless trees interspersed with elegant, expensive houses by the lakeshore; summer homes for the most part, I guess. Many have jetties and private docks. On one of the minor roads leading away from the main highway towards the water's edge I spot the sign I'm looking for: *Altmann.* Underneath is a second, warning that from this point on the road is a private drive and not a public thoroughfare. I park up and finish the journey on foot.

Sidle cautiously down the side of the gravel track. The house is visible in patches through the screen of trees. White walls, black roof. High windows and plenty of them, probably more on the lake side of the building to make the most of the view. It's not the nicest or largest property on the island, but it must still be worth a lot of money. Light shines pale and yellow through some of the windows; the overcast day must make it gloomy inside. The only sound in the frost-cleaned air is the crunch of my footsteps.

I ghost up to the detached garage next to the house and peer through the ice-dusted glass panes at the top of the door. Altmann's Audi is inside. Movement at one of the house's windows and I press myself back against the garage wall, trying to will myself into invisibility. A glimpse of Altmann's face as he passes the glass, seemingly paying no attention to me or the world outside the house, then he's gone. I give it a minute or two, then make my way back up the drive, trying to keep to cover as much as possible.

Back at the 'Vette, I call Flint. 'Altmann's gone to ground,' I say as soon as he picks up. 'He's hiding out at his father's house near South Hero. I don't suppose he told you where he was going, did he?'

'It's not Dr Altmann, Alex,' he replies. He's talking fast. 'We've had a breakthrough. We had a guy come forward saying he was on Route 100 at about the time Dr Larson was killed. He said he drove past the spot a few minutes before it started snowing again – so a few minutes before she did – and there were two vehicles pulled over at the side of the road. One was a blue pickup or SUV – he wasn't sure – and the other was a tan sedan.'

'Tan?'

'That's what he said. There were two guys standing between them, looking like they were checking under the hood of the pickup. One of them was carrying a gym bag. The witness slowed down, thinking they might have had a breakdown or something, but then one of the guys stared at him and twitched his jacket open to show he was carrying a gun. The guy drove off, but he tried to get their licence plates, since they'd threatened him. He couldn't see the pickup's, but he got the sedan. It's registered to one Randy Faber. That name ring a bell with you?'

'Should it?'

'I doubt it, unless there's a TV show called "Scum of the Week" that I haven't heard of. He's originally from San Francisco and he's got a record – nothing big, a couple of weapons violations, a charge for threatening behaviour that was later dropped. But his name's come up in SFPD and FBI investigations into a bigshot businessman and criminal boss called Curtis Marshall. Apparently, they think Randy used to be a hitman for Marshall but had to leave a few years ago when the local PD busted one of Marshall's crystal meth plants. Although they couldn't prove anything, the story goes that Randy was so eager to get away that the son of a bitch fired on a couple of his own guys who wanted to escape in the same car as him. One of those killed was Marshall's nephew Joel and his uncle has been after Randy's blood ever since. We figure he came out here, as far away from trouble as he could get, and set up his own operation. Dr Larson must have driven past while he was making a deal and he thought she saw too much.'

'Doesn't—' I begin but Flint cuts me off.

'We got a tip from an informant that Randy is supposed to meet one of his distributors at an old farm south of Bakersfield near Route 108 in just over an hour's time. I'm taking some men up there now but I thought you might like to tag along. You won't be able to take part in the arrest, of course, but I thought you might like to see us get the little fucker. Whereabouts are you now?'

'South Hero.'

'Drive to Jeffersonville and we'll pick you up. We're

meeting up with some troopers from Patrol Division there. Give me a call when you get there; it should be about the same time as us.'

I dive in before Flint can start up again; he's talking at such a rate I don't know when I'll next get a chance. 'You want to take a civilian to the arrest of an armed suspect,' I say. 'I hope that's been cleared by everyone in charge.'

'Sure. I told them you were happy to act as bait if we needed something to draw him out. Don't worry,' he adds before I have a chance to reply, 'there's no danger of that happening. You'll stay in the truck. I just wanted you to be there as a favour. Look, I've got to go if we're to make it there before Randy. Call me when you get to Jeffersonville. We've got the son of a bitch, Alex. We've got him.'

20

Jeffersonville, named somewhat ironically for President Jefferson, who turned half of Vermont into smugglers by imposing a ban on trade with Canada during the war of 1812, is ideal postcard material. Old houses converted into bed-and-breakfasts, art galleries and antiques shops. I manage to find a parking space outside a craft store selling overpriced furniture and call Flint.

'We've just picked up our troopers,' he says. The rumble of an engine fills out the background and forces him to shout. 'Whereabouts are you?'

'Outside a store called Powell's Crafts. Look for the 'Vette.'

One cigarette later, a pale grey Ford E-150 van pulls up next to my car and Flint emerges from the back. I can see Detective Saric driving with a uniformed cop next to her. Flint waves me over and I climb into the back of the van. There are another four state troopers already in there, all armed and ready. The back is hot and the air gushing from the heater reeks of burnt dust. All of the cops look young and inexperienced. Jumpy, most of them. Strange choice for a homicide arrest that could turn bad.

'Welcome aboard, Alex,' Flint says, settling back on one of the bench-like seats running down either side of the van. He's not smiling, and his eyes have an edge to them, narrow and dark. He looks tense, sweaty. Wired. 'Glad you could join us.'

'Where exactly are we going?' I ask him, without bothering with pleasantries.

'An abandoned dairy farm a few miles south of Bakersfield.

Technically it's been on the market for a few years, but no one's bought it. Agriculture doesn't earn what it used to around here.'

'How reliable is the witness who saw your suspect's licence plate?'

'He sounded solid enough to me. I've got no reason to doubt him. Why?'

'Doesn't it strike you as pretty fucking strange that a guy who knows of a convenient derelict farm would choose to do his drug deals by the side of a public highway? And what about North Bleakwater? Your witness's description of events seems kind of weird.'

I see some of the troopers exchange glances. 'It's my goddamn theory and it makes sense to me,' Flint says. 'The witness puts an armed guy at the scene of the shooting and we've identified him. That's all I need. When the fucker's in interrogation we can find out what happened for certain. We'll have plenty of time for that.'

'I guess,' I reply, my misgivings still intact. 'What about the stakeout?'

'If we need to, we can go back to it after I make the bust. Fiona can go back on duty.'

'What if someone shows up to pick up the dope in the meantime?'

Flint looks away, peering through the front of the vehicle when he answers. His voice rises a little when he answers. 'That would be unfortunate. We won't be gone long, though. I had to be here for this – it's my case.'

The interior of the van falls silent again until the engine's pitch drops and packed snow begins to crunch beneath its tyres. I wonder whether whatever dirt track we're on had wheel ruts in it before, and if not, whether our suspect will notice them and turn around before he gets there.

'Okay,' Flint says, addressing the state troopers at a near-shout to be heard clearly over the engine. 'When we get to the farm, Detective Saric will conceal the van at the back of the buildings. You will deploy close to it and wait for my signal to move in and make the arrest. You've all seen photos of the suspect we're after. Remember that we think he's armed and he's a pro who's shot his way out of a police raid before, so be alert and don't risk taking a bullet. Take him down if you think you're in danger. The same goes for the person he's here to meet, if he arrives.'

He checks his pistol, then leans back in his seat, looking even more nervous than he did earlier. Pale, drawn. The cops with him look just as edgy. If Randy shows up, I doubt it'd take more than a single wrong move or misunderstanding to turn the arrest into a shooting match.

Unkempt buildings emerge from a stand of snow-wreathed trees in front of the van as we round the final turn in the track and reach the farm complex. It's small – no bigger than Sylvia Ehrlich's property – and from the weeds and the general sense of rot and decay, I'd guess it hasn't been occupied in at least ten years. Saric swings the Ford behind a wooden barn that was once painted red, now merely flecked with scraps of crimson.

Flint and the others jump out. With Saric, he barks orders, directing the troopers to take up positions surrounding the farm's central yard. One stays with me, to act as driver and call for backup if need be. Having nothing better to do, I light up a Marlboro. The cop flaps a hand in my direction and says, 'You're going to reek out the van with that.'

'Sorry. Is it okay if I stand by the door and smoke it outside?'

He frowns, then shrugs. 'Sure.'

I clamber out and lean against the vehicle's hood, just in

front of the passenger door, listening to the last sounds of movement coming from the other side of the barn. Shuffling feet, crackling snow, then silence. The air is cold and still, quiet enough for me to hear the tobacco charring at the tip of the cigarette. My sense of taste is still shot and all I get is hot cloying ash wrapped in nicotine. Maybe it's the other way around and my taste is improving. In any case, I grind the butt out in the snow while there's still a good half-inch left and wait for something, anything, to break the tranquillity and indicate that Randy Faber is on his way.

The back of the farm complex is hemmed in by a belt of sloping snow-covered pasture maybe half a mile long and three hundred yards to the trees that line the far side. During the interminable wait by the van, I think I see movement in the bare branches and the gloom, once or twice. I don't know what, if anything, it is so I keep my mouth shut and one eye on the treeline, just in case there's any more.

Thirty minutes tick by. My toes are now wholly numb and my face is feeling like stretched rubber. Still nothing. Another ten minutes and Fiona Saric comes scooting around the side of the barn, keeping low in case anyone is watching.

'He's late,' she says when she reaches me. 'I hope Karl hasn't jumped the gun on this one. He's going to look real stupid if his information turns out to be nothing.'

I nod and, through frozen lips, say, 'Yeah.'

Saric climbs into the Ford and spends a minute or so talking on the radio. Then she gets out, shrugs and says, 'I guess we keep waiting.'

'What about the guy Faber was supposed to be meeting?'

'Don't know. The way Karl's set this up, they'll both be lucky not to get shot dead the moment they get here. It'd be nice to take them alive so we can make sure they're really who we want.' She shuffles quickly back around the other side of the barn before I can ask her anything further.

More time passes. Ten, twenty minutes. Every now and then I rock to and fro on my toes, just trying to keep their circulation going. I could get back in the van, but I prefer the cold fresh air to warm blasts from the heater. Sometimes I hear traffic passing the road at the end of the long track leading to the farm. Some goes straight past, some of it slows, but none makes the turning, so I suppose those drivers are just being cautious on a dip or bend.

We've been at the farm for an hour by the time Flint and Saric return to the Ford together. Flint is scowling, his hands wedged sulkily in his coat pockets. Saric's face is carefully blank.

'I'll call in,' Flint says when they reach me. He opens the door and climbs into the van.

'All this for a lousy tip,' Saric says to me, keeping her voice low. 'I only hope Randy doesn't skip the state now he presumably knows we're on to him.' She rubs her gloved hands together. 'I'm frozen stiff.'

Flint says nothing for a moment when he emerges, glaring at the barn, at the fields, at anything as if hoping his suspect will miraculously appear.

'I don't know why the fuck he isn't here, Fiona,' he says to Saric. His face twists in frustration and he half-kicks half-stamps at one of the van's tyres, pounding his foot into it, full force, once, again, three times. If it hurts at all, he doesn't show it, he's too pissed. 'Where the fuck is he?'

Nothing we can say in reply.

He breathes out carefully a few times. 'I've put out an alert on his car,' he says eventually. 'If anyone from Patrol Division spots it they'll call it in, but I've told them not to pursue or stop him without orders, just in case I can get there first.'

I turn, glance in the direction of Saric, raise an eyebrow. At the same time, there's a snap of splintering wood as a bullet punches into the wall of the barn next to me.

21

It takes a moment to realize what's happened. No gunshot *crack*, just a distant pop like a limp firework. I look at the hole in the barn's wooden boards. Shredded, uneven. Tiny motes of dirt, sawdust and frost still hanging in the air. Hard to say who it was aimed at, no way to judge angles. I start to turn, diving around the van, the only obvious cover. Off to the left, Saric shouts, 'Gunshot!'

A second slug buries itself in the hood of the van and I realize I'm the target. Get down behind the wheel, engine block hopefully between me and the shooter, and I draw my gun.

'You see anything?' Flint yells. I don't know if he's asking me or Saric. Inside the van I can hear the state trooper's panicky voice as he radios in. Splinters of black plastic burst over my head as a third round punches into the base of one of the wiper blades.

Looking around, I see that Flint and Saric have taken shelter behind the vehicle, same as me. Fiona is bobbing and weaving her head as she runs her eyes over the treeline opposite, peering around the side of the van. I can see one of the four cops who'd been in position out front scooched down at the corner of the barn beyond her.

Glancing to the right, my field of vision is restricted by the building on one side and the wheel arch of the van on the other. An empty tract of farmland, with trees in the far distance. No sign of movement.

'Nothing,' Saric says. The trooper beyond her shakes his head, eyes wide.

I risk the briefest of peeks around the front end of the vehicle. A blur of snow-covered fields, dark forest encrusted with white. That first glance is held like a snapshot as I duck back. Nothing is out of place.

There's no answering shot and I take another, longer look, this time over the top of the van's hood. Two-fifty, three hundred yards away, the dark gaps between the bare branches of the treeline are still and empty.

I flick my gaze back to the cops. The couple of troopers I can see look scared – only natural when someone's firing guns at you, but not helpful. I'd guess none of them has ever been in this kind of situation before. Flint is keeping his head down, and seems to be just as pale as he was on the way here, flush of anger gone now. Not nervous any more, which seems odd. Saric is alert but steady.

'We've got to get over there,' I call across to her. 'Can't hang around here, hoping for backup, while the guy repositions and gets a bead on us.'

'What've you got in mind?'

'We get back into the farm buildings, then break right into the treeline. Work our way around to him in cover.'

She frowns. 'You and me?'

'It's that or you and Flint.' I look at him and he shakes his head, stays down. 'So it's settled then,' I tell Saric.

I walk in a crouch down to her end of the van. Check we're both ready, then run, keeping low, towards the barn. As we round the corner, there's another muffled shot and the trooper waiting there, right next to us, goes down clutching at his arm.

He backs out of the line of fire, and one of the cops behind him hurries over to check his injury and stop the bleeding. 'It doesn't look too bad,' he says. 'I think he'll be okay.'

'Hurts like a fucking bitch,' his companion says through gritted teeth.

'Faber's not aiming too well today,' Fiona says as we cut through the derelict buildings towards the trees, away from the old pasture.

'Probably got jumpy when he saw all those cops,' I reply in between breaths. 'It'd throw anyone off their game.'

Once in the cover of the forest we double back, around the edge of the field, trying to keep as quiet as possible. The ground is rough and broken, peppered with fallen branches and old stumps. The carpet of snow is enough to deaden the noise of snapping twigs but there's still plenty of crunching and scraping as we stalk through the trees. Everything around us is quiet.

At a spot behind a frosted holly bush opposite the van, cops still visible clustered in cover nearby, we find the shooter's trail. Footprints, a rectangular patch of packed snow where Randy Faber – presumably – lay down at the base of the holly to fire. Good position, plenty of cover. Dimpled scuff-marks off to the right, look like fingertips.

'He picked up his brass before he left,' I say to Fiona. 'Smart guy.'

'His tracks leaving follow the same path as the one he took to get here,' she says, pointing at the footprints heading west through the forest.

Almost certain that he's not hanging around, we hurry through the trees at a jog. The trail is easy to follow and takes us for a quarter of a mile or so through the woods. As we start to see a lighter patch up ahead, the suggestion of a gap in the trees, I think I hear an engine, fading away into the distance.

'Car,' I say without breaking stride. 'Could be him.'

We break out on a gravel road that runs north–south,

following the line of the mountains. One lane wide, a lane and a half at most. Fresh tyre marks in the snow, curving in to the shoulder where Faber parked his car.

'He's gone,' Saric says, dropping her hands to her knees and breathing out hard. 'We missed him.'

Backup has arrived by the time we return to the farm buildings. A crime scene unit follows a while later to detail the scene and go looking for bullets, and someone brings a second van so we can all go home. Flint asks us what we found and doesn't look overly pleased with what we tell him.

'No shell casings? Nothing at all?'

I shake my head. 'Not that I saw. How's the trooper who got shot?'

'He'll be fine.'

Saric leans close and murmurs, 'Faber must have seen our tyre tracks on the way to the farm and figured something was up. He's careful.'

'Maybe we'll get lucky with the examination of the area, get something we can trace him with,' Flint says, apparently not hearing her. He turns towards me with faux cheeriness written all over his face. His eyes are flat, almost desperate. 'Well, I'm sorry about all this, Alex. I was hoping we'd have a show for you today, but I wasn't figuring on this for the main attraction. It was supposed to be much easier than this. Full refund on all tickets.'

'No sweat. There'll be another time.'

'I'm sure.' The smile fades. 'Let's get the fuck out of here. Nothing more we can do.'

We pile into the interior of the van, oven-like after the cold outside, and sit in near-silence all the way from the farm, back on the highway and south into Jeffersonville.

When I climb out next to my 'Vette in the deepening

twilight, Flint follows. He takes a photo from his pocket and hands it to me. 'That's Randy Faber,' he says. 'Remember what he looks like. If you see him at all, you call me straight away. Don't approach him, especially after today's events. We already knew him for a dangerous man and now I think we can be certain of that. You see him, you're liable to end up having to defend yourself. I'll call soon, Alex. We'll have to get a proper report on what you did and saw today.'

'Sure,' I say as he gets back in the van. Did he just suggest he'd happily accept a claim of self-defence if I killed Randy? Is he advocating revenge? Flint really does seem to like the idea of Randy dead.

The guy in the five-year-old photo looks young. He'd be twenty-seven by now. Blond hair, dark brown eyes. Lean and fit-looking without being heavily muscled. He doesn't have a particularly intimidating look to him, but then I knew that already. I saw him last night in the Owl's Head, hunched over his beer and trying not to make it obvious he was watching me.

By the time I get home again, I'm thinking back to the events of last night. Reuben Wynne brought to North Bleakwater by 'Mr Delaney', presumably an attempt to use him as a scapegoat because of his past. And now Randy Faber. I know he's been shadowing me. I also know the voice on the recording of Gemma's death had an accent that wasn't north-eastern, and he's from California. Did he really kill Gemma?

He might have shot at us – at me – because he knew who I was and that we were on to him, but just as easily he could have done it because he's a career criminal who saw a bunch of uniformed cops and three people who looked like detectives at the place he was supposed to be doing a drugs deal. Flint pulled his name out of somewhere, but I wonder if, like Wynne, he was just another convenient stooge for a crime that was nothing to do with him.

I call Elijah and ask him what he knows about the murder of Carita Jenner four and a half years ago.

'Well,' he says, 'we're going back a ways here.'

'Did you cover the case?'

I can hear the smile in his voice. 'My first murder as crime editor. I handled it with Heather Rycroft, one of our staffers at the time. Big coverage; it's not every day there's a brutal killing in Burlington.'

'What happened?'

'Carita was a hooker and a junkie, twenty-two or twenty-three – I can't remember exactly. She'd been picked up several times by the cops during the three or four years previous. Anyhow, she was working her usual area one night in July – the seventeenth, I think – when she was beaten to death with something blunt. A baseball bat, iron pipe, along those lines. She was found the next morning in an alley near Stageway and South, a few blocks from where I used to live. Been dead a few hours. A real mess.'

'Did they figure out why she was killed?' I ask.

'I don't think so. As I recall, she still had her night's earnings on her. She didn't have a pimp as such, and I don't remember there being anyone with an obvious grudge against her.' He pauses. 'I did hear a rumour that she was seeing a cop, I guess feeding him information. Maybe someone wanted to silence her. Maybe he was wanting more than talk from her and she said no. Anyway, they tried to check her clients and look for witnesses, but nothing ever came of any of them. The weapon that was used was never found.'

'Have there been any similar killings since?'

'No. Burlington's a quiet city. Carita was one of a kind.'

'Thanks again, Elijah.'

'No problem,' he says. 'Why'd you ask?'

'One of the suspects in her murder has popped up a couple of times in some things I'm looking at. I've heard of the case, but I didn't know the details.'

'I'll see if there's any more that I might have forgotten by now if you like.'

'Don't kill yourself doing it; it's probably nothing. But if you have a spare half-hour or so, that'd be great.'

'I'll let you know what I find,' he says.

The phone rings again a couple of minutes after I hang up. At first I think it must be Elijah again, but the number on the screen belongs to the office back in Boston. I pick up.

'Alex,' I say.

'It's me.' Rob Garrett, my partner. If ever a voice could wear a frown, his would. Whether from worry, concern or annoyance, though, I can't be sure.

'Hey, Rob, how's things?'

'I was going to ask you the same thing. Haven't heard from you in quite a while, Alex. Not since the funeral. Are you okay?'

'Yeah, more or less.'

'Would I be right in thinking you're in Vermont right now?' Whatever emotion I'm picking up in his tone must be genuine. Normally Rob, an avowed urbanite, would have cracked a joke or two about the backwoods as part of that question. Not this time.

'I'm at Gemma's place.'

'Are you planning on staying much longer?'

I try a smile. 'Don't tell me you're missing me. If I'd have known, I'd have sent a postcard.'

'Not a bad idea, if they're not still using the Pony Express.

Seriously, I know how tough all this has been, and still is, and I'll cut you all the slack you need to get back on your feet, but with just me and the kids handling the load at the moment, we're busy as hell. If you're in Vermont, there's something I want you to do; I've got no one spare for long-distance work.'

'I've already checked for Adam Webb in Burlington, if that's what you mean. I spent a few hours asking around the bars and crummy apartments. I left flyers with his details on. No dice. Pretty good under the circumstances.'

'Colleen Webb wants to know where her son is. I've explained your situation to her, and she's sympathetic, but she's also a mother who's worried about her boy, and getting more worried all the time. I need you to make a serious effort to track him down. You've done some checking, so do some more. A few hours is never enough to find someone. And who knows, having something else to occupy you might even help get things back together again.'

'I've already got plenty,' I tell him. I run through everything that's happened since I came to Vermont. Intruders, drugs, disappearances, old murders. Suspicions and conjecture. I want Rob to understand that there's something here I have to get to the bottom of.

He listens to it all without interrupting, then says, 'You have been busy.'

'So?'

'Are you anywhere near a solution? Do you have any evidence, suspects?'

I sigh. 'No, not yet. I've got a recording of Gemma's murder, plenty of information and a few names, but I can't even tell what's connected and what's not.'

'Do you think you're likely to get any breakthroughs soon, like within the next twenty-four hours?'

I shrug. 'I don't know.'

'In that case, I want you to try and find Webb,' Rob says. 'I doubt the extra delay will make any difference, not now. I know you didn't think it would take long – either to find out what happened to Adam and where he is now, or to realize he'd vanished for good.'

I imagine abandoning my pursuit of Gemma's killer to spend a couple of days doing aimless legwork around Burlington. 'Can't you tell Mrs Webb to leave it a few more days? Just till I've finished.'

'She's a paying customer who wants our help,' Rob says, more firmly than before. I can't remember the last time I stretched his patience. 'You know how much we rely on our reputation to attract business. We can't afford to throw her case away now we've said we'll take it. So I'm sorry, but I *need* you to do this for me. That's all there is to it.'

'I've got to find out who killed Gemma and why.'

'And she's got to find out what's happened to her son! She's going through the same thing that old guy you mentioned did with his granddaughter. If something's happened to Adam and you let her down, you'll be leaving her to months of worrying and thinking, and maybe she'll never find out where he is.'

I consider refusing, walking out on Rob, quitting the agency just so I don't have to give up on Gemma. I imagine how it would sound, saying the words 'I quit'. I imagine his reaction. I imagine how it would feel, turning my back on my own life in order to avenge Gemma's. I'd have nothing left at the end, but it wouldn't matter. The great romantic quest fulfilled. Ashes to ashes.

It doesn't last. It might not be a great life, but I see little point in throwing it away. Besides, Rob knows exactly what buttons to push. Mrs Webb has as much right to know what's happened to Adam as I do with Gemma, and try as I might, I can't ignore that.

I break the silence. 'Okay, sure, I'll do it.'

'Thanks, Alex.' Rob sounds relieved, relaxing again. 'I wouldn't ask if I had any other option. Call me if you find anything. Just not too early; I need my beauty sleep.'

'More than ever these days.'

He chuckles. 'Look who's talking. I'll speak to you soon. And Alex, be careful. The heroin business isn't known for its soft touch.'

'Yeah, I've noticed.'

I hang up and let the phone drop on the couch next to me. I rub my eyes and try not to think how close I came to walking out on just about everything I've got left, a life that came as a second chance after my failed Bureau career. Instead, I make a list of the remaining places I should check for Adam, then boot up Gemma's computer to see if the check on Altmann's background has yielded anything.

It seems that the doctor's father Sam is in a nursing home; his current contact address is given as 'Cedar Grove Assisted Living Apartments'. Presumably Altmann Senior left his son with full use of his house by the lakeshore. The few other surviving relatives listed are all living out of state. Dr Altmann himself looks to have led a quiet, ordinary life. No criminal record, not even a speeding ticket, no court liens, nothing. The Audi is the only car in his name. He's worked at Kingdom Hospital for a little over ten years. Before that, he lived in Burlington and worked at Fletcher Allen. Only one thing stands out in his employment history. Back in the days when I guess he must have been either a medical student or perhaps starting out on his career, he's listed as having worked as a civilian for a few months with the Burlington PD in administrative services. A long time ago and it didn't last long. It wouldn't have been strictly true and most people wouldn't have believed him, but at one time Altmann could have claimed to be a cop of sorts. He would have known how to talk like a cop. And maybe, several years later, he would have used that knowledge again, if he'd been trying to intimidate one of the local hookers into playing ball.

22

Night, and I dream of the lake house. Clouds roil overhead as two figures in police uniform escort my casket and the gun carriage it sits on down the gravel drive. I sit up and watch as Randy Faber gives a military-style funereal salute with his rifle, firing three rounds over my head. Both cops keep their eyes on the floor, respectful. At the garage they stop and unload my coffin, hauling it between them like a bag of cement, occasionally bumping and scraping against the ground. Altmann watches us from one of the windows, Adam Webb standing by his side. The cops carry me down to the water's edge and carefully lower the casket so it bobs on the surface, rising and falling with the waves as they lap against the stones and mud. Without looking at me, they give the coffin a stern push and I go floating out over the lake. The shore rapidly recedes behind me and I can hardly make out the line of the land opposite, such is the gloom.

I glance down over the side and see movement in the water beneath. A woman, dark hair drifting around her head like a black halo, reaches both hands up towards me, like a reflection trying to claw its way through a mirror. I can't tell whether she wants to reach the surface or if she wants me to join her. I lean closer, feel the coffin tilt, tip and spin. Gravity takes over and the water rushes up to meet me.

Wake with a crack as I hit the floor next to the couch.

Thick grey clouds threaten snow over Burlington. I'm trying some tenements I didn't visit last time I searched for Adam

Webb. The first is a three-storey block clustered around a central courtyard. There's no sign of the building's manager and I have no luck trying to reach him by phone, so I content myself with sticking up a couple of missing person posters, then leave.

The second place, over the river in Winooski, looks like converted industrial space, a long hulk of crumbling brickwork with dozens of high narrow windows. A similar structure on the other side of the street has yet to undergo redevelopment. There's a couple of dozen buzzers on the intercom system by the front door, all numbers, no names. A separate bell underneath is marked 'manager'.

Ring once. Twice. A solid blast for thirty seconds or so. Eventually, a sagging man in his forties opens the door, wearing a dark blue jogging suit emblazoned with the UVM logo. His face is covered in sweat, so I guess I've interrupted a workout. He looks me up and down.

'Sixty dollars a week, first week in advance,' he says gruffly. 'No pets, kids by arrangement only. Electricity and water are included. Trash gets picked up Tuesdays.'

'Thanks, I'll bear that in mind. I'm not looking for a place to stay, though. I'm looking for someone, wondering if you can help at all.'

'I don't mess with residents' privacy.'

'I'm a private eye from Boston. The guy I'm looking for isn't in any trouble and I'm not here to hassle him. If there were names next to the buzzers down here maybe I wouldn't be asking you at all. I guess people come and go too quickly for that, huh?'

The guy frowns. 'Look pal, there's plenty of people in this city who need cheap housing. This place ain't great but it's affordable, I keep an eye on everyone in here and I don't fuck around with the tenants. If this guy isn't in any trouble, why're you looking for him?'

I try a smile. 'Would you believe me if I told you his mom was worried about him?'

'Serious?'

'Yeah.'

He thinks for a moment, then nods and his face relaxes. 'Okay, fair enough. Who are you after?'

'A guy called Adam Webb,' I say, showing him the report. 'The last time anyone heard from him was a couple of months ago. He said he was working as a tour guide, but that doesn't seem likely to me.'

'Are these pictures the best you've got?'

'Afraid so.'

We shuffle aside to allow one of the residents, a pale woman in her early twenties, to sidle past and out of the building. The manager looks up as she passes and says, 'Is your stove working okay now? I don't know how good a wiring job I did on it.'

'Yeah, it's fine now, thanks,' she says, looking back over her shoulder at us. Pretty enough, if rather gaunt and drawn. Dark hair, deep-set eyes. Healthy, though thin, physique. Must get plenty of exercise. She's wearing a fleece and hiking boots. Her gaze wanders briefly over the paper in the manager's hand, which he's dropped down to his side while he's talking, then flickers over me. I don't know what she reads there, but she pulls on a woollen hat and a blue scarf, then turns and hurries down the street.

'I don't remember having anyone stay here under that name,' the manager says, talking to me again. 'I'll check the records just to be sure, but it doesn't ring any bells. Same with the face, but the photo's so blurry I doubt I'd know him if he showed up in person right now.'

'Would you mind posting a couple of these in the hall? Just in case anyone living here recognizes him.'

'Sure, sure. If you give me a couple of copies I'll take them inside and check my records. It won't take a minute.'

The guy vanishes into the gloomy building. I pass the time until his return with the aid of a cigarette and let my mind wander. When the manager returns, he's shaking his head. 'I don't have any Webbs staying here, not in the last two or three months, anyway. Only one Adam, and he's too old to be your guy. But I'll stick up the description; maybe someone knows him.'

'Thanks for your help,' I tell him.

'No problem.'

I'm on the way back to the car when I see the woman from the tenement building again. She's lurking in the snow-packed gap between the empty brick shell on the other side of the road and the chainlink fence surrounding the adjacent lot, watching the 'Vette and, maybe, me as well. It could be she's just trying to work out if I'm a cop or not. Whatever her reasons, I'm curious. I use a break in the traffic to cross over and head towards her hiding place.

She lets out a little gasp and does a brief rabbit-in-the-headlights impression when I turn the corner to face her; apparently, she was just watching the car. I smile and take out a Marlboro. 'Hi. Have you got a light?'

'Who are you?' she says. Her eyes are wide, pale skin a little flushed. She's well dressed for the winter, so I guess the rosy blush means she's scared or surprised.

'You need ID to borrow a match in Vermont these days?' I say, raising my eyebrows and trying to keep my tone light. 'My name's Alex Rourke. Why?'

'Are you a cop or something?'

'I'm a private investigator. With cold feet and an unlit cigarette.'

'What do you want with –' she catches herself before she says a name – 'with that guy you're looking for?'

'Exactly what I told the manager of your apartment building. His mom back in Boston hasn't heard from him for a couple of months and she wants to get in touch. The company I work for does a lot of missing persons work, so she came to us.'

The woman sniffs and nods hesitantly. 'You got a card or anything like that?'

I return the cigarette to its pack and hunt around in my jacket for a business card. The woman takes it and reads it carefully. 'And you work for this Robin Garrett guy?'

'Call the office if you don't believe me.'

'Why are you looking around here?'

'I've been looking all sorts of places. I've covered the bars he might have gone to, now I'm checking out the places he might have lived while he was here.' I take out the Marlboro pack again and clamp one between my lips. This time I offer the woman one as well – she accepts – and light them myself. 'Do you want to tell me what all these questions are about?'

'Me and Adam were friends,' she says, taking a long, long drag on her cigarette.

Straight away, I pick up on the tense she uses. 'What do you mean "were"?'

She looks up at me, blinking, and tries to take another couple of lungfuls of smoke, then she seems to collapse inwardly as though all the air has been knocked out of her.

'He's dead,' she says, tears beginning to sparkle in the corners of her eyes. 'I think Mr Delaney killed him.'

I drive the woman to a steam-filled diner a couple of blocks down the street. Her name turns out to be Jessie Taylor, presumably the same Jessie mentioned by Adam's friend in

Boston when I spoke with him. Now she's the only way for Adam's mom to learn the fate of her son. She cries all the way to the diner, shuddering and sniffing, and keeps it up for a while inside, which draws a couple of odd looks from the waitress who serves us coffee. The place isn't busy, so I keep my voice down while I talk to her.

'Who's Mr Delaney?' I ask.

'He's the guy we worked for.' She runs her shaky fingers through her hair. 'Well, I don't know if we worked for him, but he was always the guy we spoke to.'

'And what did you do for him?' I take a mouthful of strong, gritty coffee, trying not to show any recognition of Delaney's name. At the same time, I'm thinking back to the notes found in the autopsy and to Reuben Wynne's visit to North Bleakwater.

Jessie looks up at me. 'You sure you're not with the cops?'

'Sure.'

'We used to carry stuff,' she says, leaning in closer. 'Y'know, over the border. We'd pick it up, usually near this place called Sutton in Quebec. Then we'd hike into the mountains like regular tourists, all the way down to the delivery point. Delaney told us it was always best to use a couple for that kind of thing, so we could pose as sweethearts or something if anyone asked. That way we wouldn't get so much hassle. But no one ever asked. Maybe they knew someone in the Border Patrol, or they paid off the cops.'

I can guess what 'stuff' Adam and Jessie were carrying over the border. I'm slightly surprised they'd take that route – if most dope in the state comes from the south – but I guess the old Vermont smuggler ethic dies hard. With the Delaney connection, I can also guess where their drop point was, although I don't voice my suspicions. I write the word 'heroin' on the back of my cigarette packet and show it to her; no sense having eavesdroppers picking up too much.

'Is this the kind of stuff you and Adam were carrying?'

She nods, looking away. 'Yeah. Not much usually, just a couple of bags.'

'Pure?'

'I guess. I never asked.'

'So how did Mr Delaney fit into all this? And why would he kill Adam?'

Jessie finishes the rest of her coffee in a string of gulps and motions for a refill from the waitress. She seems to be calming down now; her hand no longer trembles and her breathing is regular. Once her cup is swollen almost to the brim with dark liquid, she says, 'I don't know how Adam met him, but I heard about the job from a guy I was with in a bar. I needed money bad, so someone put me in touch with Delaney – I didn't know his name then. I guess Adam wound up working for him the same way. He explained everything to us, showed us where to go and such. I don't know if he checked us out to make sure we weren't cops or anything; I guess he must have done. The only time I ever saw Mr Delaney he was wearing a scarf, glasses and a hat so I couldn't see his face. He said that was what to call him, so I doubt it's his real name.' I nodded, encouraging her to continue.

'The way it worked, every now and then we'd both get a phone call telling us where to pick up. Then we'd get together, pack and cross into Canada. We'd collect the stuff, hike back – that usually took a couple of days, trail-camping – and call a number we got given. We'd let the phone ring three times, then hang up, to let them know we were done. There'd be cash waiting for us. And that was it.'

She pauses long enough to down half her coffee, breathes

out hard and then continues. 'The money's good, but once Adam saw how it all worked he wanted more than that.'

'Did he try skimming some off the top?'

'The packages were always sealed. They'd have known. And they were usually close by when we dropped the stuff off. One time we saw a car waiting.' She starts picking at one of her fingernails. 'But Adam figured he could switch a couple of bags of dope for a couple of bags of baking powder or something and they wouldn't find out until we'd gone.'

'You went along with his idea? You can't have known him long. You trusted him?'

The hand wringing increases. 'I didn't want to do it. But we'd kind of become friends from all that time alone together. He was a nice guy. Cute, funny. I could've done worse than end up with him. And he said he knew someone who'd want to buy such a large batch of dope and that we'd make a fortune out of it. I knew they'd kill us when they found out, but, well, my life was nothing much at the time and that money was real tempting.'

'That's understandable,' I say, nodding. 'Plenty of people would have done the same.' I don't tell her that in my experience there was only one way it was ever likely to end. Not that it's ever stopped anyone from getting greedy before, nor will it be any different in future.

'So one delivery, he had a plan. Before we went up, he left his car and some of our things in a rented garage in Newport. The plan was that he'd hike down and make the drop with the fake packages. I'd walk to Newport and pick up the car, and then we'd meet up at this place we passed through every trip we made. It's a patch of woods not far from Hazen's Notch. There's a couple of parking lots for summer tourists a little way down the slope, either side of trees. We were going to meet up in the woods, then head for New York State.'

'What went wrong?'

Jessie drains her cup and stares at the bottom of it as she answers. 'It was night. I got the car like we planned. I drove up to the woods; there's trees all over up there, our place was just an old-looking patch of forest. Nice, really.' She smiles briefly, then it's gone. 'I got out of the car and went up the hill, hoping Adam was already there so we could go straight away. Then I saw a light in the trees. When I got a little closer I could see shapes – people – moving. I heard a gunshot, and Adam shout out, but his voice was all garbled. The light stopped and stayed in one place for a while.'

'What did you do?' I ask softly.

'I ran, Mr Rourke. I didn't know what else to do. I couldn't call the cops and tell them what happened or they'd have arrested me. I couldn't speak to anyone I knew in case Delaney was looking for me as well, and I didn't have the money to run far. So I got the only shit apartment I could afford for more than a couple of months and I've been waiting ever since, either for Delaney to forget about me, or for someone to put a bullet in me too. You know what it's like when there's someone out there who wants you dead, Mr Rourke?'

I smile. 'Yeah, I do. Can you draw me a map so I can get to the site where Adam was killed?'

She nods and wipes her nose on the sleeve of her coat. 'Sure. Give me a pen.'

I watch as Jessie sketches a very rough plan of the area around the woods on a paper napkin. She looks tired and strung out. Maybe it's just living so long on her nerves, maybe she's been using a little of the stuff she once carried south to relieve some of the tension. I'd ask, but her problems aren't mine and it's not like there'd be anything I could do to help.

'Thanks,' I say when she's done. I check the map, then fold it and drop it into a pocket. 'Have you got a number where I can reach you if there's anything else I think of, or if Mr Delaney gets caught?'

'No. I ditched my cell after Adam died and my apartment doesn't have a landline. Drop me a note.'

'Okay.' I run over what I've learned in case there's anything more I should ask her now. 'Delaney – if you heard his voice again, you'd know it?'

She nods. 'Of course. He didn't sound local. West coast, maybe. California. Some place like that.'

I think of Randy Faber, one-time criminal from San Francisco, the guy who may have killed Gemma. Possibly involved in the drugs trade. 'Good,' I say. 'Did you ever see him or hear him with anyone else? Do you know anyone else working for him?'

'No. The time we saw the car near the drop point, there was a couple of people in it, but I don't know if either of them was him.'

'What kind of car was it?'

'I don't know. Dark colour. Might have been a station wagon.'

I guess that must have been the buyers, as it doesn't match any of my suspects. I continue. 'Whereabouts was the drop point? Did you use different ones each time or was it always the same place?'

'It was always the same,' Jessie says. 'In a room in this old abandoned hotel, someplace just off Route 100. We'd stash the packages under a bathtub.'

Bingo. If things had been different, Jessie's story about what happened to Adam would have been sad, sure, but commonplace. Small-time criminal gets greedy and tries to cheat his employers, gets whacked. I'd have checked out the site where he was killed, then called Mrs Webb and the State Police to report what happened. Some questions, some paperwork, and that would be the job taken care of.

Thankfully, I can do more than that. It's possible that Webb's body could hold evidence that could identify Delaney for certain, although if Randy wasn't someone grabbed at random out of a police book of crooks, he certainly fits the bill for me. There was nothing found on Gemma, but he knew he couldn't make her vanish the way he did the others, so he was careful at the murder scene.

Jessie has just left the diner, heading for home, and I'm about to follow suit when I get a call from Flint's office number. 'Alex, it's Karl Flint,' he says. 'I've got some bad news for you.'

'What's up?'

'I've decided to abandon the stakeout of the hotel. Apart from Wynne's visit we've seen jack, and when Detective Saric started her shift yesterday she found the dope had gone. They must've taken it while we were waiting for Randy Faber.'

'You haven't been there long,' I say.

'I know, I'm not stupid. But if they waited till we left to move the stuff and they sent Wynne out there – assuming the son of a bitch isn't directly involved, of course – then I guess they know we're watching. I'm not even sure you're right about it having a connection to Dr Larson's murder any more. I've passed the info on to the drugs taskforce, but I don't know whether they'll do anything with it. Priorities, you know how it is.'

'So get a patrol car down there to cover for you.'

'I already told you that wasn't going to happen. And now we have work to do tracing Randy Faber – especially now he's taken pot-shots at the police – and for that I can't afford to spend half my time watching the trees grow,' he says, sighing. Flint sounds like he's talking to a car crash victim, all syrup and reassurance. But he's out of practice, and it falls flat. 'Look, Alex, you've got to face the fact that what you found may be nothing to do with the murder. You did a good job checking the place out and you've sure put a lot of thought into the whole thing. But we can't follow your assumptions for ever. We have a firm suspect and now our job has to be to catch him. You might be better off going back to Boston. Take it easy for a while, relax and let us work the case. I can understand your interest, but it's not healthy. You're tired and stressed and that's not good for you or anyone else.'

A spark of anger runs through my reply. The mocking pity in his words just adds a little extra spice to mine. 'Maybe it's not good for me, *Karl*,' I say, practically sneering his name. 'But I'm only going back to Boston when I've got the guy who killed Gemma. I *will* hunt him down and I *will* find him, and when I do, I'm going to make damn sure justice gets done.'

He sighs again. 'Alex, this—'

I hang up, cutting him off in mid sentence. Rude, maybe, but I don't want to hear any more phoney concern for my well-being. I head out to the 'Vette for a cigarette and the chance to calm down. On impulse, perhaps to stop me dwelling on Flint's comments, I drive towards the corner of Stageway and South, and the place where Carita Jenner's battered body was found on a summer morning four years previously.

There's no longer any sign of what happened in the narrow gap running between a row of dusty stores and an old factory converted to office space. The urban fabric has reknit itself, closing over the brutal killing of a young woman, just as people forgot. I wonder how long it will be before Gemma's death is remembered only on her gravestone. The snow here is barely disturbed except where storekeepers have taken out their trash. At night I doubt there'd be any reliable witnesses living for at least a block in any direction. The walls lining the alley muffle the outside world, closing it out. I can imagine how alone Carita would have felt as the first blows rained down and her screams went unnoticed.

If she made a living working on the street, I guess there must be enough clients passing down South after dark. Those like Reuben Wynne might come just to pick up hookers, but I'd be surprised if there wasn't a lot of casual trade as well. I drive around the surrounding few blocks, trying to see where her customers might be coming from and going to.

After a few minutes of this, I pull up and phone Saric. 'Hi, Fiona,' I say when she picks up. 'It's Alex Rourke.'

'Hi. Did you hear about the stakeout?'

'Yeah, Flint told me. Someone picked up the dope while we were all waiting for Randy Faber to show up, so he cancelled it.'

'I don't like it. It's as though they were on to us right from the start, sending Reuben out there, then waiting until they knew we were gone to shift their delivery. Something's wrong with the whole thing.'

'Well, I certainly didn't tell anyone about it.'

'Yeah, and unless they keep a permanent watch on the old town I can only think of one other answer and it's one I'd rather wasn't true.'

'That someone inside the department supplied them with information?' I offer.

'That's right.'

'How many might have known about it?'

'In enough detail to know where we were going? Not

many. That could also explain Faber's actions, although I still think he might just have spotted us before he reached the farm.' She clicks her tongue against her teeth. 'His car was found abandoned this morning, by the way. We're checking for theft reports to see if he's grabbed himself another. The bullets he fired are with ballistics. Look like .22 long, maybe .223 calibre. Anyway, what can I help you with? Unless that's what you called about.'

'The Carita Jenner murder – the one Reuben Wynne was a suspect for. Elijah Charman told me some of what happened, but there's a few specifics I'm interested in. I was wondering if you could help me.'

I hear Saric's computer keyboard rattle as she types. 'Okay, Alex, shoot,' she says.

We talk a while longer and I ask a bunch of questions. When I'm through, I believe – I can't be certain, not without clear proof – that I know who murdered Carita Jenner.

But what implications has this for everything else that's happened? Maybe none. I sit for a while in the 'Vette, thinking hard.

23

Twilight is dwindling rapidly by the time I head for the site of Adam's murder. Jessie's scrawled map is easy enough to follow even in the dark. I have little problem finding the same gravel parking lot she pulled into on the night he died. Headlight beams bounce as the 'Vette's reinforced suspension negotiates the bumpy entrance, hinting at a sizeable copse of trees up the slope. I stop and kill the engine.

The overcast night sky is starless and I wait with the car door ajar for a couple of minutes, getting used to the chill air and letting my eyes acclimatize to the dark. The snow carpeting the slopes around Hazen's Notch glimmers faintly in the gloom.

'I could do this for ever,' Gemma says, nestling tighter into the crook of my arm. Lying on turf under a blanket, night air cooling towards chilly. Everywhere the flickering of insects drawn out by the darkness. Rocks off to our left, dull grey gleams. We're looking up at the stars, God's great join-the-dots puzzle.

'I'm warm, I've got you, and all that above me,' she continues softly. It's the end of one of the last days of summer. On the cusp of fall, nights already lengthening, warmth heading so far south it becomes a distant memory. We've spent it picnicking on the slopes between the bulwark of Mount Mansfield and White Face Mountain, in a little hollow out of the wind; I'm not sure where we are exactly and it doesn't seem to matter. Made love together as the sun went down, the sky a brilliant purple-orange. We haven't moved since. While Gemma talks, I'm wondering whether to suggest we get married.

It's not a simple matter, with our jobs and the distance between us, but it's the kind of thought that comes easy at times like this. As if it might be possible to fix and hold your feelings exactly as they were on a beautiful night in the middle of nowhere when nothing else mattered.

'Yeah, I'd like that,' I say. I don't know whether I'm replying to her or to my own thoughts.

Before I begin the climb I grab my flashlight and a snow scraper-cum-shovel folding tool from the trunk and, acutely aware of how alone I am, check my gun is loaded. Even standing by the car, instinct charges my veins with a hot line of adrenalin.

The trees here are primarily evergreens. I guess this is all plantation wood, not natural growth; I've seen plenty in my native Maine. On the edge of the copse the trees are still thick with needles but the interior is mostly bare brown trunks, with the only green parts high up in the canopy. The plentiful outer cover means that I don't have to go far inside to know I'm near the site of Adam's murder as Jessie couldn't have seen it otherwise. Under the high, heavy sheet of branches in leaf the snow is noticeably thinner than it is outside.

I start checking the ground, using the shovel to clear away the ice, looking for signs of the struggle that occurred here. The only sound I can hear is the white noise *swish* of the fir trees in the wind, like a hundred vengeful spirits from some Japanese folk tale pressing all around.

It takes maybe an hour to find the first sign that I'm on the right track. Two brass shell casings, from a 10 mm centrefire pistol. The earth nearby is disturbed, rumpled and crushed by what look like running feet. I drop both shells into a plastic bag and do my best to follow the mangled footprints in the dirt.

It looks as though Webb was chased and killed before the ground froze fully, when it was still wet enough to leave decent traces. Not long after, the cold set in and did a fair job of preserving what happened, albeit hidden beneath a few inches of snow. I'm able to follow the three, maybe four, sets of tracks back to the spot Webb waited for Jessie. There, one walks back and forth endlessly, with a good couple of dozen cigarette butts dropped in its path. The others – definitely now two of them – converge on this one from the direction of the second parking lot. By the time they've reached the camp they've spread maybe ten yards apart, the hunters fanning out as they closed on their prey. Once Adam started running they followed, trying to hem him in. There's no sign of other shell casings, so it looks as though they waited until they were certain of a killing shot before firing. They chased Adam to the point where I found the two cartridges, then to judge from the stride lengths, they slowed to a walk. Both hunters' tracks converge on one spot, the place where Adam's trail ends. Here and there I catch signs of what could be a third set, coming from the same direction as me. The tracks are frozen into the ground, so they're not mine. Smaller, maybe a woman's. Jessie's, perhaps. With all the movement, it's hard to tell. The prints become confused, milling about.

On the edge of this well-trodden patch, my shovel clears away the snow to reveal the beginnings of chopped and broken earth, still with a couple of thin, mangled and shattered tree roots protruding from the surface.

I clear away more snow. Six feet long, maybe just over. A

couple of feet wide. All frozen soil that was turned over and broken up not long before winter set in.

Here lies Adam Webb. I start digging.

The grave turns out to be fairly shallow. I'm a little surprised the killers chose to bury him here, but then they had no way of knowing anyone would look for him in this place. A couple of feet down I uncover the fingers of his right hand, blackened and distorted, but unmistakable even in the dark. Further down his arm, the remains of a wolf tattoo are still visible. If there's any smell beyond the moist, slightly acidic scent of the soil, I can't detect it through my numb nose.

I carefully scrape away the rest of the dirt packed around his corpse. He's still dressed in the same kind of hiking gear that Jessie wore when I spoke to her. The winter has held back the decomposition process enough for me to instantly recognize the face as Adam's, even discoloured and smeared with powdered dirt. His eyes are open, but the orbs are cloudy and have a cracked look, fixed and half-shattered where the fluid inside has frozen. There's a ragged, slowly rotting bullet wound at the base of his throat, slightly off centre, and another in his left-centre rib cage. Lung level. The first wound is so similar to Gemma's that for a split second I can't stop myself imagining what she must look like in her own grave near Bangor and I almost lose it. Breathe out, focus, get it under control.

I look at the clouded icy eyes of the corpse. I know I should leave it alone for the forensic technicians, but I'm also aware that I need as much information as possible. I tighten my winter gloves and kneel down to check his pockets, clothes, and the ground underneath his corpse.

The pockets yield a fair amount. There's his wallet: ATM cards, Blockbuster membership and other crap, all in the name of Adam Webb, as well as his driver's licence. Just over a hundred bucks in cash, a couple of business cards from the kind of small-time places he might once have applied for work, and a scrap of paper with what looks like a cell phone number on it. In his jacket there's a decent quality map of the Green Mountains, on both the US and Canadian sides of the border, as well as an unused-looking guidebook entitled '101 Secluded Walks In Northern Vermont' – part of his cover story, I figure – and a half-finished pack of Starburst. A pocketknife, some keys, loose change and a couple of tissues complete the ensemble.

Rolling the body on its side so I can check the floor of the grave is awkward, but I manage. The effort doesn't look like it was worth it; it's empty, just blank dirt, cut here and there by the blade of a shovel.

I lower Adam back and go over what I found in his pockets. In particular, I check the scrap of paper with the phone number on it again. It's not one I recognize. My first impulse is to call it, but I don't want to do it on my own cell since that would give the owner my number in return. I'll have to find a payphone.

Which only leaves the question of what to do with Adam Webb's body. This isn't easy; for a while, I even consider reburying him and then revealing his location later when I've worked out who killed him. What to do with a corpse no one knows about and which I'm not supposed to have disturbed isn't a question I've ever faced. In the end, I decide to leave the shell casings on top of the body and then call the Orleans County Sheriff's Department with an anonymous tip. Not perfect, but it'll do. At least then Mrs Webb will be able to bury her son properly.

I drive to the nearest town and find a payphone. First, I let the Sheriff's Department know that there's a body in the woods. I give fairly good directions, but don't say who I am or how I found it. Then I dial the number on Webb's scrap of paper. Delaney's, or so I assume. The one they'd call when they'd made a drop.

One ring.

Two rings.

Three rings.

Four rings.

Five.

'Hello? Who is this? What do you want?' says a voice at the other end of the line.

The voice is that of Karl Flint.

24

I let the phone drop back into its cradle and stand by the booth. I know this is no accident. I just can't believe the son of a bitch could have spent so long leading me on. I think back to the conversation I had earlier with Saric about Carita Jenner, parked in the 'Vette in Burlington.

I asked her when the murder happened. She replied, 'Four and a half years ago, as I recall.' I could hear her still using her computer, accessing files. Information. 'Let's see. She was found on the morning of July eighteenth by a Mr Jack Sorensen. He ran a liquor store that backs on to the alley where the murder took place.'

'The forensics people were certain it happened at the scene, she wasn't dumped?'

'According to this, they were certain. Hair, blood spatters, a couple of her teeth, all at the scene. Weapon was never found. Estimated time of death was somewhere between eleven-thirty p.m. on the seventeenth and one-thirty the following morning.'

'No witnesses?'

'None,' Saric said.

'How about DNA?'

'Nothing on fingernail scrapings. No semen traces; Carita made sure her clients used protection, I guess. Forensics found three different sources of pubic hair mixed in with her own, most likely from her last three customers, one of whom may or may not have been her killer. None of them was ever identified. Wynne wasn't a match for any of them. Neither was her regular dope dealer; he was eliminated early on.'

'You never managed to trace her last few clients? They wouldn't even come forward to take themselves off the suspect list?'

'It's hard enough for most guys to admit using a hooker, but tell them they might have been the last person to see her alive and thus a potential suspect and suddenly everyone's an amnesiac.'

I nodded, unsurprised. 'Elijah told me there were rumours she'd been seeing a cop. Either she was feeding him information or he was shaking her down every once in a while.'

'We all heard that one. Burlington PD said it wasn't any of their guys, and no one here in the BCI owned up to it. There's plenty of cops live in Burlington, and not all of them had alibis. But no proof of that rumour was ever found, so it never went very far.'

'And the murder happened some time during the night of July seventeenth–eighteenth?'

'That's right.'

'Thanks, Fiona.'

'Don't mention it,' she said, but now I wonder what and how much I should tell her, or whether I should somehow get proof to support my thinking.

After I hung up the phone I thought for a while, looking up at the unlit neon sign on the drab brick building next to the 'Vette. I thought about the one question I couldn't ask Fiona, not without revealing my reason for calling about Carita.

The neon sign read: 'Bar None'. Four and a half years ago, a couple of weeks after Fourth of July, Karl Flint was thrown out of there for getting in a fight. Saric had to drag him away from a couple of regulars. Apparently, he was in a real mean mood. I couldn't ask Fiona the exact date she went for a drink with Flint.

The bar is three blocks from the spot Carita Jenner, a prostitute who may have been involved with a cop, was beaten to death.

When I reach Gemma's house I call Rob at home, hoping he's in. 'Hello?' a woman's voice answers.

'Teresa, it's Alex. Is Rob there?'

'He's coming. How are you holding up? Rob told me you were taking some time off out of town. I hope it's helping. I can't say how sorry I am you're having to go through all this.'

'Thanks, Teresa. I appreciate that. I'm okay. I just have one or two more things to do and then I'll be back in Boston.'

'That's good. I'll talk to you soon.'

There are some muffled noises as the phone changes hands and Rob comes on the line. 'Hi, Alex. What's up?'

'I've found Adam Webb.'

'That was quick,' he says, sounding surprised.

'I told you he'd either turn up in a day or two, or he wouldn't turn up at all. I had a lucky break and ran into someone who used to work with him. She gave me what I needed to know.'

'That's great. Where is he?'

'At the moment, buried in a shallow grave near Hazen's Notch, shot twice. Give it a few hours and the crime scene techs will probably have moved him.' I anticipate Rob's next question and continue. 'When he said he was working as a tour guide, that wasn't true. He was involved in smuggling heroin over the border from Canada with the woman I met; they posed as hiking newlyweds. Adam tried ripping off the people who ran the delivery service and they found him and killed him. The cops will probably be calling Mrs Webb before long to tell her what they found; I told them where the body is anonymously. It might be good to let her know before they get in touch.'

'I'll call her in a minute. What about you, what are you going to do now?'

'The guy Webb worked for, the guy who had him killed, was the same "Mr Delaney" whose name cropped up before. He was using North Bleakwater as a drop point. I think he could be a cop, or more likely someone working for a cop, the same Detective Flint investigating Gemma's murder. "Delaney" could be a hired thug from San Francisco called Faber, but I don't know. I need to find some way of tying them both to Gemma, Webb and the three people who disappeared, and figuring out what the hell's been happening here. Then I'll come home.'

Rob stays silent for a moment. 'A cop, huh? You'd better be sure before you try anything, Alex.'

'I will be.'

'Okay. Take what time you need. Thanks for finding Webb for me, I know it must have been tough having to drop everything like that.'

'No problem. I'll see you in a few days.'

I lie on the couch in the silent dark, occasionally rolling from one side to another in a bid to get comfortable. It's cold, far colder in here than usual, but it doesn't stop me drifting for a couple of hours, more or less asleep. In my dreams I've lost something, someone, and I'm wandering through the woods trying to find it. I feel as though I'm following a trail, an invisible set of tracks that I can sense even though I can't see them. But it's confused and patchy, faded. Eventually I come to the edge of the twisted trees to see an expanse of calm water stretching out in front of me. Somehow, I'm able to walk across its flat, motionless surface, still searching. I've gone some way out when I begin to realize I'm in the wrong place, that this lake is too small and the one I need is larger and deeper. The one where I'll find what I'm looking for. Cold seeps through my clothes, making it hard to hold on to unconsciousness. I try to ignore it and keep up my search, to stay inside my dream, but eventually it's too much and I snap rudely awake.

There's no couch.

No living room.

No roof.

I'm lying on a flat sheet of white beneath a dark sky. The edge of the ice is just visible as a line of shadows deeper than the night, surrounding me on all sides like the rim of a bowl. My head rests on my arm, which is wedged in the snow covering the ice. My clothes are slowly becoming soaked with snowmelt, failing body heat doing what it can. I stand, wide-eyed, and look around at my surroundings. A line of scuffed footprints leads towards me from the edge, beyond which some faint lights are studded against the black. I'm in the middle of Silverdale Lake's frozen surface.

I don't bother to wonder how I got here because I know. I don't bother to wonder why because there's no logical answer. All I do know is that my fucked-up sleep patterns need sorting out, and soon. Weird dreams and falling out of bed are one thing, this is totally different. I've got an emergency supply of pills for insomnia in the car – don't trust them much, not these days, but they should knock me out enough to stop any kind of somnambulism or fugue or whatever the *fuck* this is. Tomorrow night, I promise. I'm through with this.

Gingerly I make my way home, shivering with the cold. Shuffle through the snow, wrap my arms around my chest to ward off the worst of the night, as I follow my own tracks towards the trees.

I finish my morning coffee and cigarette, then call Elijah Charman. I've more or less rationalized last night's walk on the ice. Insomnia has always been much more my thing, but I have had a couple of episodes of sleepwalking in the past, though never quite like this. Always when work was at its toughest and I was under the most stress. As far as I know it's a symptom rather than a problem in itself. Nothing to do with the dream either, although I doubt that helped. In the short term the cure is the same as for the insomnia – those emergency pills, Benzodiazepenes, hand-picked and fresh from the farm. Long-term, I wonder how much I'm pushing my limits without realizing. The case, my grief over Gemma's death, the fact that someone tried to kill me a couple of days ago. I've got nothing outside the job right now and maybe it's starting to show. Maybe what I saw at night in North Bleakwater wasn't concussion but the same problem again. It wouldn't be the first time.

Of course, worrying about it only makes it worse. I remember *that* from my days in therapy. Clear my head, try to chill.

Elijah's in work early, early for a journalist anyway, trying to hammer out a story for tomorrow's front page. 'Nice juicy murder,' he says. 'Don't know much so far, but it should be fun. I don't often get the chance to work these.'

'Sounds exciting. How's the flu?'

'It looks like I'm over the worst of it, so it's probably just a bad cold, thanks for asking. Anyway, what can I do for you, Mr Rourke? I had a quick check for what we had on Carita Jenner.'

'You're going to hate me for this, but I need to ask another favour.'

'Sounds ominous,' he says, then sneezes loudly down the phone. The sound is like a gun going off. 'Sorry about that. Go on.'

'Could you do some more research for me? I'm interested in the case history of one of the detectives who worked the Stephanie Markham disappearance. Anything going back the past six or seven years. His name's Karl Flint.'

There's a long, low exhale from the other end of the line. Eventually, Elijah says, 'That's going to be a pile of work. Is it urgent?'

'Yeah, it could be.'

'I don't know if I've got time to do it myself, not quickly.' His voice brightens suddenly. 'There's Neal, our intern, though. He's there to make himself useful. Is there a story involved? Is this going to result in something I can print?'

'Hopefully. And if it does, you'll be in an exclusive position, as far as the story goes.'

'Really? Something good?'

I keep my answer vague. 'I hope so.'

'Okay,' Elijah says with only a second or two's hesitation. 'You're on, Alex. I don't get much chance for this kind of cloak-and-dagger shit. Sounds interesting.'

'Thanks, I owe you.'

'You'll have to come by the office, though. I doubt we'll be able to read it all over the phone. How soon do you need it?'

'If I leave now I should be in Burlington in less than an hour.'

'Then I'd best get Neal working.'

'I can't thank you enough for this, Elijah. If we come up with what I'm looking for, I'll take you both out for a steak dinner. My treat.'

'In that case,' he says, a smile in his voice, 'I'll make sure he works real fast.'

*

The *Burlington Free Press* has its home in a large red-brick box on College Street. I park a block away and walk through the slushy snow; by the time I reach the foyer my shoes are half-soaked with ice-cold water. A young guy wearing a shirt and tie underneath a thick grey sweater guides me through the open-plan office towards the paper-covered desk where Elijah waits. Combed brown hair and narrow-framed glasses. He introduces himself as Neal Skipworth, the intern Elijah referred to.

'You've given me a pretty busy morning, Mr Rourke,' he says. 'I wasn't told what it was for, though. Anything interesting?'

I smile despite the sensitivity of the subject and shake my head. 'Would you be satisfied if I told you it was a matter of life and death?'

'Whose?'

'I'll have the answer for you in a day or two.'

'You'll have to read everything off my screen,' Neal says, peeling away as we reach Elijah's desk. 'I didn't have time to print it out. Whenever you're ready.'

I take a quick glance at the story in front of Elijah. 'Murder victim found near State Park', the headline reads. There's a lengthy wad of text underneath.

He follows my eyes and says, 'Happened late last night, too late for me to get anything before the deadline, so local TV and radio put it out before we could. We're just going to have to beat them for detail.'

'It looks like you won't have any problems there.'

'Don't be fooled. Most of what I've got is nothing to do with the dead guy, it's just "police went there, did that". But it looks good. I'll fill it out when they release more.'

'What have they said so far? I don't listen to the radio.'

Elijah shrugs. 'Just that Orleans County Sheriff's

Department got an anonymous call that there was a body in some woods near Hazen's Notch State Park, a patrol car was sent to confirm it, and when they did, the State Police took over the scene. Oh, and they're certain it was murder. They haven't released the name of the victim and nothing about how he was killed, stuff like that. With a bit of luck, I'll be able to get hold of it before anyone else. I've got a couple of friends in the VSP.'

For a moment I consider giving him a morsel or two of information, just to repay all the help he's given me. But since that would inevitably be an admission that I dug up Adam's body in the first place, I just nod and say, 'Well, good luck.'

'Thanks. Anyway, we've got the things you wanted.' He hands me a couple of news clippings. 'There's the stuff on Carita Jenner. Not much to add to what I said over the phone, but there may be something. Neal has what he found on Detective Flint in the archives. I don't suppose you'd reconsider telling me what you wanted them for? At a guess I'd say both requests were connected.'

'No, I'm afraid I can't right now,' I tell him.

Neal has dug up an impressive collection of files containing references to Flint, covering almost his entire career.

'I trimmed out some that repeated earlier stories,' he says. 'And some little ones you wouldn't be interested in. Enjoy.'

Flint's case history looks reasonably solid on the surface. His earliest mention in the archives is as a young detective nearly ten years ago, before his promotion to sergeant. He worked a couple of relatively high-profile cases, or what passes for them in a low-crime state like Vermont. He made sergeant five years ago, after his investigation into a serious assault uncovered a ring stealing cars from Montreal and bringing them over the border for sale. The Damien Ackroyd case was his first at his new rank, and one that receives considerable coverage here. The collapse of the original charges against Ackroyd was followed by widespread criticism of the police, with specific accusations levelled at Flint as he was the guy who arrested and then apparently beat the hell out of Isaac Fairley. While some parties went on about police brutality, others made allegations – later retracted, presumably under threat of litigation – about corruption, violence and drug abuse by certain members of the State Police BCI.

Flint's suspension lasted for just over three months. No charges were made against him and no further action was taken. He returned to work four weeks after Carita Jenner was killed.

After that he dropped off the press radar for a while. His superiors probably made sure he missed out on anything too big until things had cooled down. His subsequent case history is much patchier than before the Ackroyd case. Over the four and a half years since reinstatement, he successfully worked a couple of murders – both domestic killings by one family member on another – several robberies and violent offences and a couple of child abuse cases. However, he was also responsible for several failed investigations, predominantly violent crimes and disappearances. From the information in front of me, and the things he is sometimes quoted as saying at the time, his performance seems rather erratic. I remember what Saric told me about him being out on the ragged edge during his suspension; I guess he's never quite come back.

At times this scattered approach could almost seem deliberate. Stephanie Markham is the first example that jumps to mind, but also a couple of serious assaults and hit-and-runs on file. Maybe Gemma's murder too. If Flint is posing as or working with Mr Delaney, then there's enough here to suggest he could have helped bury a few crimes that may have been connected to the drug operation. Maybe more, if, like Adam Webb, the victims simply disappear and no one kicks up a fuss. Or if he's able to find a convenient person to fit the frame, as he tried with Reuben and possibly Randy Faber.

I finish reading. Neal has vanished, so I wander over to Elijah's desk and thank him for his efforts.

'No problem, Alex. On a different subject, have you heard anything new about the guy the police want for the murder of your girlfriend?'

'No, I haven't. Have they said much about him?'

'Only that there's a male suspect they want to question. No name, no description, nothing. I thought maybe you might have heard more about him.'

No name. Flint wants to make sure that he'll be in at the kill when Randy is caught. He doesn't want to risk an eagle-eyed sheriff's deputy or patrolman making the arrest. Either he's real eager to look good, or he's covering up. I could leak the name, but I don't; I may have my own score to settle.

I shake my head again. 'I'm afraid not. You know how it is when cops don't want to spook the guy they're looking for.'

'I suppose so.'

'Well, I guess that's everything for now. Thanks again, Elijah.' We shake hands.

'Just make sure you tell me what all this was about,' he says, smiling. 'I want my story, you know. And don't forget that steak dinner.'

My phone rings as I walk back across the lobby of the *Press* building. I recognize the number, but I can't remember from where.

'Hello?'

'Hello, Alex.' It's Murray Larson, Gemma's dad. His voice is flat, clipped. 'I've been trying to reach you at home, but I guess you're away at the moment.'

'That's right,' I say. I don't want to sound rude, but remembering how angry he was with me at the funeral, I'm also not about to try and launch into a full-on conversation.

'Where are you?'

'Does it matter?'

'Maybe. Under the terms of Gemma's will, her possessions pass to her family and her property is to be sold. Her lawyer is handling those matters. Do you have anything that belonged to her at your apartment?' Murray sounds as though he's forcing the words.

'No.'

'Are you sure? If you're going to be home any time soon I can have Mr Chalmers call round just to see if there's anything you've forgotten.'

My tone is starting to mirror his. 'I loved your daughter, Mr Larson. I don't like the suggestion that I'd steal from her or her family.'

'If you loved her, you wouldn't have asked her to make the sacrifices she did. She did everything for you.'

'Goodbye, Mr Larson,' I say. I don't want to be drawn into an argument, so I cut the connection.

The call puts me in a dark mood and I spend the drive home remembering Flint sitting in his office, calmly telling me that he had no real leads in the investigation into Gemma's death, that sometimes shit just happened for no good reason. I think of him trying to tell me it might have been a hunting accident.

Crack.

Flint telling me I should go back to Boston and relax, let the police handle the investigation. Staking out the hotel where Delaney's organization arranged the delivery of heroin smuggled in from Canada.

Crack.

Flint storming out of a bar on a July night. Beating a young woman to death because he was angry and she wouldn't do what he wanted.

Crack.

With every image I hear Gemma's windshield smashing as the bullet punches through it, killing her over and over again.

For a long time, I sit in the 'Vette, parked in the driveway with its engine dead, and try to calm down. When I finally leave it and head for Gemma's living room, Randy Faber is sitting in one of the armchairs facing me.

25

Slam my fist into my jacket, fingers clawing for my Colt. Randy jumps out of the chair with his empty hands outstretched. If he's armed, he's not going for his weapon. Not that I care.

'Whoa, whoa!' he says. His words aren't loud enough to carry outside the house. I recognize his West Coast accent from the recording of Gemma's death. Randy Faber. Mr Delaney. 'Easy now, man.'

I drop the coat and snap up my gun two-handed, flicking the safety off and drawing the hammer back as I sight down the barrel at his face. It takes a supreme effort of will not to pull the trigger. Every microsecond that passes, I think of Gemma's windshield going, of her slumping against the wheel with blood pouring from her throat, of this son of a bitch lowering his gun and going to fix the scene. Every regret for every lost opportunity I've ever had, every shameful memory of every fuck-up I've ever made, every moment I've spent living out the results of a bad decision, all of it coalesces into a single voice screaming for me to get it right this time and shoot, to kill the guy in front of me and avenge everything Gemma and I had together and everything we'll never experience because of him.

Two things stop me. Even with the blinding fury thundering through my head, there's still a part of me that suspects, proof or no proof, that Flint is involved in the whole thing and Faber could be the key to finding out how and why. Number two, he no longer looks like the cold professional I picture pulling the trigger to kill Gemma, or shooting his way out of a drugs bust in California. His eyes are red and puffy, his skin is pale and his hair and clothes are a mess. He looks like he hasn't slept in a couple of days. And he's scared, and not of me. On the table is a police scanner, quietly squawking radio chatter into the air.

'What the fuck?' I murmur hoarsely, blinking hard once or twice and trying to regain my composure. I want to say more, but the roiling sea of emotion inside won't let the words out. The gun stays trained on his forehead.

'Easy, easy,' he repeats. 'We need to talk. I'm not going to cause trouble.'

I laugh openly a couple of times, no real humour in it, at the irony of his statement. 'You've already—' I try, but my throat clamps shut again. I have to blink and it feels as though I'm close to tears. 'What the fuck do we need to talk about after what you did?'

'Steady,' Randy says, still keeping his hands out. 'Look, I can help you.'

'Help *me*?' This time I keep my jaw clenched as another laugh threatens to break free.

'I can give you the guy who told me to shoot the doctor. I swear. You know who I'm talking about, right? I mean, you must be getting close.'

'Flint?'

'That's right.' Randy drops, very slowly, back into the armchair. 'He must be shitting bricks about you by now.'

I don't shift the Colt at all, but I slowly manoeuvre on to the couch opposite Randy. 'You mean you can get evidence that'll see him arrested, convicted, all that? Or do you mean you can just set him up to go someplace I can kill him?'

'Whatever you want, man. They're both as good as each

other. You want to take police along, or you want to do it yourself. I can do that, yeah.'

'Why?'

Randy sighs and slumps a little in his seat. He seems to know I'm not about to kill him. 'Look, I'm fucked right now. The cops are looking for me, they'll know I've stolen a car and probably have its licence number, and I can't touch my credit cards or my cell phone in case they trace them. The only friends I've got here are all people I've met through him. If I go to them for help, he's going to find out, and I can't ask people I knew before.'

I frown. 'Why not?'

'There's a guy in San Francisco I worked for a few years ago. He's big. I mean, Karl Flint's operation is nothing to what this guy has going. I had to leave, and he's wanted me dead ever since.'

'Curtis Marshall. The way I heard it, you shot his nephew so you could escape from the cops.'

Randy scowls and runs a hand through his hair. 'Whatever. Point is, I can't ask anyone I know from California to help me get out of the state, and I can't ask anyone here either. Except you. If I help you get Flint, you can get me away. Give me a ticket to Miami – I've got a cousin who lives down there – and a ride to an airport outside Vermont and I'll repay the favour. I've got my own reason for wanting to see that fucker Flint get what's coming to him, now he's sold me out.'

He seems to be telling the truth. The fact he's even here at all, talking to me, suggests he really doesn't have anywhere else to go. I'd like nothing more than to kill him, but he's correct when he says he could be useful to me.

'Okay,' I say, keeping the pistol pointed at him. 'First, before I decide whether or not I'll help you, I want to know a few things. I want to know how your operation works, who else you've killed to keep it covered up and what you did with them afterwards, and I want to know why the fuck Gemma died. Then we'll see about whether or not we can do a deal. And I want to know how you came to be here in the first place.'

Randy pinches the bridge of his nose. 'You must know most of that already.'

'You run dope over the border.'

'Flint does. I just work for him, man. He's a delivery service, kinda like UPS.'

'The two of you bring heroin down from Canada,' I continue. 'There's people who ship it that way rather than through the Caribbean or the East Coast. Either they or the buyers pay for your people to smuggle it safely across the border. They work as couples, hiking down to North Bleakwater where they stash their deliveries under the tub on the top floor. They pick up their cash and they leave before the buyer comes to collect. I guess you use a dead-drop system and no one ever sees each other, just to keep it all secure. Every so often, someone sees something or hears something and you have to silence them. What I don't know is why anyone pays you for the delivery when they could do it themselves.'

'Stuff that comes south is purer than what gets up here from New York,' Randy says. 'It's been through fewer hands. Buyers make more of a profit on it, but they can't afford to lose any shipments. Flint's a cop and he says he's got a friend in the Border Patrol, so he can pretty much guarantee it makes it.' He sniffs. 'Plus his system's solid. Even I've never met him, face to face, and I'm the one does most of the work.'

'And this has been going on, what, a few years? How come you never met?'

Randy shrugs. 'He's careful, I guess. Sometimes we talk over the phone. Urgent stuff mostly. Other times we use email. Anonymized and all that shit. No way anyone could trace it to us even if they did manage to get a look at it. It's a tight system.'

I lean forward. 'So what about when someone finds out what's happening despite all that? What do you do with them? Who were they? My guess is there was a couple called the Haleys, a girl called Stephanie Markham and then Gemma. You also shot one of your couriers, a guy called Adam Webb, because he tried stealing from you.'

Randy can't maintain eye contact and looks down at his feet. For a pro he doesn't seem particularly proud of his work. I guess he was used to killing other people in the business when he started out, not just those who walked into the wrong place at the wrong time. When he answers, he doesn't hold back.

'The first time, just over three years ago, it was this husband and wife who must have been here for hiking in the fall – what do they call it, foliage season?' I nod and Randy continues, 'I got a call from two of our couriers saying there was a couple joined up with them, heading in the same direction. The couriers were shitting themselves in case they were undercover cops or something. I would have let it lie – it seemed harmless – but Flint said no. So I had to go and intercept everyone on the trail. I told the two delivery people they should just clear out and I'd deal with the people tagging along with them. And I did: I killed them, stabbed them right there, and hid the bodies. The guy was dead before he knew what was happening and his wife, she just stood there looking like she couldn't believe what the fuck she was seeing. Blood all over the place, man. I called Flint and he said to get their corpses away from there. Stick them in the trunk and take them to Lake Champlain. He'd have a boat ready. So I ditched them.'

'That would be the Haleys,' I say.

'Fuck knows.' He shrugs. 'I just killed them, I didn't get introductions.'

I frown. 'Who was next?'

'The summer after we were expecting a delivery. I went inside the old hotel in that ghost town across the lake to arrange the cash for the pair carrying the dope. I was just on my way upstairs when I turned the corner and there was a girl wandering down the hallway towards me. She fucking saw me, and she saw I had a gun. So I told her I was a cop and she should clear the building. Nothing to see here. She walked away a little, but must've known that was bullshit because she ran. Didn't make a sound. Just ran. And I took off after her.'

'Red shirt, dark hair, early twenties?' I ask.

Randy nods and keeps looking at the floor. 'She was quick – I didn't think I could keep up with her – but I caught her eventually. Smashed her in the jaw as she ran. I did the same to her as I did to them other two, with my knife.'

'Why didn't you just shoot her?'

'The noise, man. I didn't know if there was anyone else nearby. It was broad daylight in the middle of summer, for Christ's sake. Flint told me to do the same with her body as he'd done with the first two – wrap it up in tarp and chickenwire to weigh it down and stop it ever surfacing again, and drop it into the lake but to leave the knife and the shirt I was wearing for him to deal with.'

'Flint doesn't help you dispose of anyone?'

'No. Guess he don't like to get his hands dirty. Plus this girl was mostly my fault and he was pissed off at me.'

'But he makes sure there's no proper investigation, right?'

'Sure. He says he's untouchable. He says this is his kingdom and he can get away with anything he wants. He told me about this time he killed some hooker in Burlington, said no one even thought to touch him for it. I reckon he enjoys it. Until you showed up.'

'You broke into this house a few nights back, right?' He nods. 'So why didn't you kill me then?'

'Flint hadn't told me to. I was just supposed to make sure she hadn't left behind anything that could tie back to us, and to maybe scare you away. You hadn't been enough trouble to kill you by then.'

'If it hadn't been me, someone would have investigated him sooner or later. He's not well liked. What about at the farm the other day?'

'I knew he must've set me up when I saw the tyre tracks – I don't often have to meet with anyone and when I do, I make sure I'm there ahead of time. No fucking way they could've beaten me to the farm. So it wasn't a big surprise when I came through the woods and saw you and a bunch of cops. I figured I'd take a little revenge before I split.'

'So why shoot at me and not Flint?'

'Like I said, we've never met. There was only one guy who looked like a detective, but I didn't know if Flint would have had the guts to show up himself. And if you shoot a cop they *really* fucking hunt you down. So you seemed easier, and I knew you were the one who'd turned everything to shit in the first place, so you had it coming. I would've had you but you moved just when I fired.'

'Lucky, I guess.' I get Randy's confession back on track. 'Who next?'

'Then things were quiet for ages. But a couple of months ago, that courier got greedy and tried to steal a shipment. We found out as soon as the buyer collected their dope that he'd switched it for powder. He might have got away, but the seller had a transmitter in the packages – like a LoJack – and the buyer knew what to look for. We knew where that kid was before he did.'

'So you went up there with someone, shot him and buried him.'

'Some guy called Wallace, worked for the buyer. We caught up with the kid in some woods about ten miles north of here. No boat this time, so we had to bury the guy where he was. Wallace took a couple of photos to show them we'd done it. Then it was the doctor.' He paused, studied the floor. 'I guess you know about that.'

I lean forward again, a fresh spike of anger-fuelled adrenalin burning through me, and say, 'Explain it to me, you son of a bitch. Why and how.'

Randy's voice sinks even lower than before and he doesn't dare look me in the eyes. His words come almost as a continuous stream as though he's afraid I'll kill him when I think he's reached the end.

'I got up in the rocks looking down on the road. I've got a hunting rifle with a starlight scope. The rifle's not very powerful, but it was all I could afford. I waited until I saw the car Flint said I should look for. She was driving slowly, trying to stay safe on the ice, I guess. I aimed just above the steering column where I figured she'd be sitting, and fired. The car carried on a little way and I thought I might have missed, but then it coasted off the road and into the trees. I went down there to check she was dead and to find the bullet. Flint said I should make it look like it had passed all the way through and out the back, so that's what I did. The slug was lodged in the seat. Then I made sure I hadn't left anything behind and got the fuck out of there, covering my tracks as well as I could.'

'Where did you leave your car?' I ask the question in a flat, dead tone of voice.

'On the dirt track leading to the old town.'

'Did you use a silencer, anything like that? There didn't seem to be much noise when you fired.' I smile at him with intense distaste. 'She was on the phone when you killed her. I listened to the whole thing.'

'Shit, man, I'm sorry. I never wanted to get—'

'Who gives a fuck what you wanted? Did you use a silencer?'

'No. The rifle's quiet because it's low calibre, not very powerful. I don't have any kind of silencer.'

'I had you pegged for some kind of ex-military hired killer type,' I say, shaking my head. 'All the best equipment, proper training. Shows how wrong you can be.'

'I didn't plan to end up doing this kind of thing,' he says. Self-pity shading into sorrow. A kid who got sucked into violence and killing, just because that's the way it happens. A guy bullied into doing other people's dirty work because he's too scared to say no and finds he's stuck with it. Not much different from Adam Webb. 'It just happened that way. Even working for Flint, I was hoping I wouldn't have to do shit like that, I thought maybe I'd left that all behind in California. Most of the time, all I did was pretend to be "Mr Delaney" to recruit new couriers and make sure the dope turned up smoothly. Shit.'

'Why did Flint want Gemma killed?'

'A few days before, Flint had someone whack a dealer who'd told him to go fuck himself. Made it look like a hit and run. When Flint called me, he said the doctor was doing the autopsy. Apparently, whoever killed the guy didn't check the body too well because the doctor found out the dealer had a note with "Delaney" on it. Flint had sent him the note with a photo of the courier we killed – with his face blanked out, of course. The photo was missing and Flint thought the doctor had taken it because she'd already been asking questions about the guy we buried in the woods, sending out pictures and stuff. Flint was fucking furious. He hates problems, and now he thought she'd recognized the kid's body and knew everything. He said that was enough and he'd kill me if we didn't silence her.'

I rest my forehead on top of the pistol in my hands and close my eyes, once more struggling to hold back tears. Gemma's dad was right when he said I got her killed. If I hadn't asked her to help with the Webb case, she'd still be alive.

'So he called me straight away,' Randy says, oblivious to me. 'When she left, he followed her car a little way back and phoned every few minutes to say how far away they were, so I knew when she was going to reach the road in front of me. Then afterwards he just carried straight on past while I cleared up. I checked but she didn't have the photo. Flint found out the dealer had just left it at his house.'

For a long time neither of us speaks. The only sound in the room is the faint chatter of the police scanner on the table, crackling and indistinct. Eventually, I lean back on the couch and drop the gun next to me. Randy hasn't moved since he stopped talking.

'If you don't like being in this kind of business, why the hell haven't you quit before now?' My voice is strained through a tight throat.

He smiles ruefully. 'I wanted to when I got out of California, but I never finished high school and there's not much else I'm good at. By the time I reached here, I needed cash, so a guy in Burlington put me in touch, just when Flint was starting out. But once you're involved in all this, you can't just walk away. The people you work for are paranoid, and if they're serious they'll usually kill rather than risk being betrayed. Curtis Marshall was serious enough, even if I hadn't fucked up and panicked in that drug bust, shot through every fucker between me and freedom. Flint is serious enough that I couldn't say no to him the first time he asked. You do it once and you can't refuse to do it a second time because they can turn you in if you do. Flint was even worse. He kept shit on me, I know it.'

'What do you mean?' I say.

'When I stabbed the husband and wife, he told me to leave the knife and the shirt I was wearing on the boat, not to dump them. He said he was going to ditch them properly so they'd never come back, but I doubt it. After that, I had to do pretty much anything he said.' Randy suddenly smirks. 'But now I've got my own insurance.'

'Yeah?'

'A few days ago, I guess after you showed up, he called and said he needed me to pick something up for him, and that at the same time I should leave our contact cell phone with him, the one we used for talking to our couriers. I think he was worried about someone tracing it or something. Anyway, this package he left for me was all wrapped up, hidden in a parking lot in Burlington. I didn't see him, but he must have been watching, else he couldn't have collected the phone after I'd gone. It was this piece of steel pipe he said he'd killed that hooker with. He said he'd been hanging on to it in case he ever needed to fit someone with the crime, but with you here he was worried it wouldn't be safe with him. Like maybe you'd see it at his place or something. He figured I'd keep it safe for him for a week or two until you went away. Funny thing is, he told me he'd wiped his prints off it – no sense framing someone with it if he hadn't – but

I saw there was still a couple in the blood on the end. Prints, blood, hair. Dumb fuck had even bagged it to keep it clean so they're real nicely preserved.'

I raise my eyebrows. 'That was careless of him. Didn't he check it before he gave it to you?'

'Flint must have had it a few years, kept it wrapped up all that time,' Randy says, shaking his head. 'He probably doesn't even think about looking at it now. Why bother after all that time? For me, it was something new. And like I said, he thinks he's the king of northern Vermont. He thought he'd wiped it, so he didn't worry. Same as he didn't worry about anyone seeing the doctor getting shot, or finding out about how we use the hotel. The way he sees it, he's invincible and if anyone causes trouble, he can just kill them too. Except you, because you've already talked to too many people.'

'And it's that steel pipe you're offering to help me with?'

'That, and more. He leaves some of his cash under the floorboards at the old hotel in the room next to the bathroom – that's where I always take my cut from and get the cash to pay the couriers. He probably cleans it out regular, but there's still plenty there. He's probably got shit at his house if you can get a warrant. I dunno if he'd have any dope there, though. He always told me he'd kill me if he found I'd been using. He said someone in his family got fucked up on drugs, so I couldn't touch it because he didn't want any more screw-ups. If you don't want the cops involved, I can just call him and tell him I gave that pipe to you, so he'll have to come and get you himself. It's up to you.'

'And all I have to do in return is buy you a ticket to Miami and make sure you get to an airport out of state?'

'That's right. I want out of here, away from Flint and all the shit that comes with him. Maybe this time I *will* be able to stay out of trouble.'

'Why'd you come and see me? Why not just steal another car, or hitch a ride out of state? You could even walk the same route into Canada your couriers do.'

'A stolen car isn't safe for long. Once it's reported, they've got the plates and it'll only draw cops to it. Anyhow, they'll be checking the roads for me, and if they know about me, they probably know to watch for hikers over the border. When your guy drives me away, I can hide, way down in the back. And without you, I can't buy a plane ticket. Besides, I know I've got something you want – Flint – so I know we can work something out.'

'You've not thought about testifying against him, cutting a deal for immunity, that sort of thing?' I ask. I can guess the answer.

'No way,' Randy replies, shaking his head violently. 'Flint's friends, people from San Francisco, everyone who's ever been pissed off at me, they'd all come for me. I'd probably be dead before the trial even started. No, fuck that idea. I just want out.'

I think for a while, running my mind through possible ways of handing in the weapon that killed Carita Jenner without it seeming strange or leading to a lot of awkward questions. Eventually, I say to Randy, 'I'll help you out like you wanted. But here's what I want you to do. You leave the pipe in its bag and write a note to go with it like: "Mr Rourke, here's the weapon that killed Carita Jenner. I've been holding on to this for Detective Karl Flint. I was working for him, but now he's turned on me so here you are." I can take it to the police and tell them it was left on my doorstep. They'll check it and hopefully haul Flint in for questioning.

'I want to make sure they've got more on him than that, though. So I want him caught in the most incriminating way possible. I'll make sure the cops are willing and ready to question him. When they are, I want you to call him and say you've cleaned out his cash from the hotel and you're going to send the pipe to the cops. With any luck, he'll head straight to North Bleakwater to see if you were lying or not. I'll get you your tickets.'

'Why go through all that?' Randy asks, voice pitching upwards with worry. The change in tone sounds strange coming from someone who, moments before, was coldly recounting the murders of five people. 'Just give them the weapon. That'll be enough.'

'Even with his prints on it, matching the blood on it to Carita's DNA is going to take days at least, giving Flint time to hear about what's going on and get out of the state. I don't want him getting away. That's my deal, Randy. Take it or leave it.'

26

'Are you serious?' Sylvia Ehrlich asks. I'm sitting in front of her desk in the squad room of the LCSD headquarters in Hyde Park, a few miles south of Bleakwater Ridge. She's leaning back in her chair, temporarily ignoring the report she'd been writing on the glowing computer monitor next to her. The package containing Randy's note sits on the desk next to a small, neat stack of paperwork and a couple of framed photos of her with her husband. Her superior, Sergeant Ken Radford, an old guy whose permanently scowling features make him look like a bulldog chewing a particularly sour lemon, is standing next to her, alternately looking down at the package, then at me.

'Absolutely,' I say. I've just finished giving them a complete run-through of everything I know, leaving out only Randy's appearance at the house – I told them he called me to explain what he knew – and my voice is a touch hoarse. 'I've suspected it for a while. Now I've started to get the proof to back it up.'

'And you want us to arrest a detective sergeant in the State Police?'

'That's right. I'd take this to the VSP, but I don't know how many friends Flint has there.'

She raises an eyebrow. 'And do you think Faber is reliable?'

'Talking to me was a long shot for him. You can't have many friends left if you're willing to confide in a guy whose girlfriend you killed. If he's giving me the weapon from the Jenner murder, why lie about everything else?'

'You said it'd be best if we spoke to him quick, and searched his house and everything,' Ken Radford speaks up. 'Getting a DNA match on that blood is going to take days or weeks, depending on lab workloads. And without it, we won't get a search warrant. You might have to wait. In any event, Carita Jenner's murder is a state case, not ours.'

'And when you've got a DNA match or whatever you need, it can be. But until then, the more people in the VSP hear about it and the more time that passes, the more likely it is the news will get back to him and he'll destroy any evidence and then either vanish or come up with a story to explain the pipe.'

Sylvia shakes her head. 'Even so, Ken's right. We can't get a search warrant until then, and there'll be questions asked why we didn't go straight to the VSP with this. What you heard from Randy Faber isn't evidence, not unless he testifies himself, so we can only take Flint on the Jenner murder and that needs confirmed proof.'

'How about if you had a confession?' I say.

She looks surprised. 'What do you mean?'

'If you had a recording of him talking about the murder, maybe admitting it or his involvement in the heroin operation.'

Radford nods. 'That would do it. How do you plan to get it?'

'I can get him out on his own, where he's not likely to worry about anyone hearing him. He knows I'm getting close, so if I confront him, I might be able to get him talking. If you're close by, you can listen in and get the whole thing on tape.'

'You want to wear a wire,' Sylvia says. 'D'you realize if it's true, he might just kill you to shut you up?'

'Yeah, I get that a lot,' I reply, smiling wryly. 'Seriously, I think that could work.'

'Where are you planning on doing this?'

'North Bleakwater. I can get him out there. Are we due for snow tonight? I haven't seen the forecast.'

'Yeah,' says Radford. 'Supposed to be.'

'Then if you get out there tonight, the snow should have covered your tracks by tomorrow. I'll bring Flint out there in the morning. Just make sure you wrap up warm.'

The two cops look at each other, then Sergeant Radford shrugs and nods. 'If you want to do this, I'll agree on one condition. I want the steel pipe checked for prints first; that won't take long. If Flint's ever been involved with crime scene work, he should have been printed, just to eliminate any of his from others they find. The blood can wait. We'll need a proper, official statement from you as well, saying what you've found out. We might need another one, afterwards, just to be sure. You do understand we're not going to be able to give you much backup? One car, two people there, maybe another car or two able to respond if they're called for.'

'Yeah, I know. I'll take the risk.'

It takes a while for one of the department's deputies to deliver the pipe to the State Forensics Lab. Sergeant Radford makes a call to ensure it gets processed as quickly as possible and that the results of the checks won't go any further than they need to. Then the office falls more or less silent. The cops talk a little amongst themselves – work, family, small stuff.

I say nothing. Tomorrow, I'm going to catch the guy responsible for Gemma's murder, and it feels strange. Relief, sure, but also uncertainty. Has Randy been telling me the truth? Have we missed anything? At the back of my mind is the nagging sense of guilt from my earlier conversation with

Randy – the knowledge that Gemma died because I asked her to help with the Webb case. I share some of the responsibility for her death and it sits in the pit of my stomach like a brick. I hope catching Flint will put paid to it for good.

Eventually, we get the call we're waiting for. Radford listens to the receiver for a minute or so, occasionally murmuring, 'Uh-huh.' Then he puts the phone down, looks at Sylvia and me and says, 'Three prints plus another partial. One of them very good quality, all three a positive match for Karl Flint. They'll start DNA tests on the blood tomorrow. I guess we're on, Mr Rourke.'

Sylvia, Ben Paladino, the other half of my backup, Sergeant Radford and I head out to North Bleakwater so the three cops can have a look at the ground. I drop the 'Vette at Gemma's house and transfer to the cramped police red-and-white for the rest of the journey.

When we emerge from the trees on to the old town's main street, Sylvia slows the car to a crawl. The three cops take a good look at the crumbling buildings they're passing, the decaying dreams of a previous age.

'This place gives me the creeps,' Paladino says quietly.

I smile. 'Wait till you see it at night. That's the hotel,' I add, pointing at North Bleakwater's most prominent landmark. 'The back entrance, the only one that's not locked, is on this side. Front doors on the other side have been shut tight for years. The rooms used for Flint's operation are at the top of that five-storey tower-like section.'

'Where do we park?' Sylvia asks. 'We need somewhere we can hide the car.'

'I know one,' I reply. I grin inwardly, thinking back to the person who showed it to me. 'Pull into that gap between buildings there. Then I'll take you inside.'

*

'Is this place safe?' Sylvia is the first to voice everyone's misgivings when the four of us step through the hotel doors. I show the cops the route upstairs, making sure we disturb as little as possible. The top suite is much the same as last time I was here, although the heroin bundles beneath the tub are gone. I wonder if Flint took them himself during his shift on 'stakeout'. Radford and Sylvia look over the suite and the view from the windows, checking sight lines and making sure their car is still hidden even from up here. Paladino keeps one wary eye on the hole in the floor. On the way back down, I see Sylvia nodding whenever she hits a creaky floorboard, making a note of its position.

Back at the car, we split up. Sylvia and Paladino get comfortable and prepare to wait through the night while Sergeant Radford accompanies me back to Bleakwater Ridge so I can drive him home.

'Remember,' he tells Sylvia, 'stay off the radio. Use your cell phone if you need to get in touch; I'll call you when Mr Rourke is ready to go. And don't wander out in the open, either of you. When the time comes to take a leak, do it in the woods by the lakeside.'

The walk back through the twisted brown trees bordering Silverdale Lake is a quiet one. Radford asks a couple of questions, mostly about my time in the Bureau, and I give him a couple of answers. Neither of us is a great conversationalist though, so we mostly keep our thoughts to ourselves. I can't read anything in the sergeant's face. I'm thinking about Flint, Randy, tomorrow and about Gemma.

Walking through the trees on the other side of the lake, we're heading back towards the parking lot at the foot of the ridge and West Road. All I can hear is our feet crunching through the leaf litter. No talking. We've had an argument. Brief, like the few others I can remember, and we're now in the period of silence that should, hopefully, lead to making up. I'm not sure what I said wrong; maybe it was the way I said it. Gemma hasn't lived here long and I think, hope, the stress from that is the main cause. She asked if I'd ever consider moving closer to Vermont. I didn't think it was anything serious, so I said that with my job, living outside Boston would be a real pain. And here we are, trudging in silence.

We hit the parking lot. The lake a sheet of blue-grey through the thin screen of trees to the left, a couple of families with young kids leading them towards the water's edge. Gemma's shoulders drop a little and she shortens her stride, dropping back and linking her arm in mine. She rests her head on my shoulder and says, 'I'm sorry, Alex. I guess I haven't quite settled in yet.'

'That's okay, I know.'

'I didn't mean to take it out on you.' She looks up at me, eyes wide. 'Promise.'

I lean down and kiss her. 'Like I said, it's okay.'

She smiles. 'You know I can't stay mad at you. I don't have the willpower.'

'You're only human,' I say, smiling back at her.

When we reach the 'Vette and I unlock the doors, Sergeant Radford glances up and says, 'Was that your girlfriend's house?'

'Yeah.'

'It's nice. Are you sure you're up to what you've got planned for tomorrow?'

I nod. 'Sure.'

'Good, because I don't want you screwing up and risking two of my officers. I also don't want you losing it and shooting the guy. I've never had a dead suspect on my hands before and I don't plan on starting now.'

I'm not sure if he's happy with our plans and we don't talk further in the car. But when I drop him off outside the department's office he claps me on the shoulder and says, 'I'll see you tomorrow to get you fitted with a wire. Best to be here bright and early, that way we can get all this done before Sylvia and Ben miss their breakfast.'

Route 100 is almost busy as I drive home, with people returning from visits to the larger towns north and south, or heading towards those towns for a Saturday night out. Bleakwater Ridge looks cheery from a distance, but up close the high glowing windows and old buildings start to loom alarmingly, staring down at me from the heights of the ridge. I keep my eyes on the road.

Randy is in the kitchen when I come through the front door. He's been smart enough to dim the lights in the living room and close the drapes and blinds in the kitchen, to keep as low a profile as possible. He looks up from rooting through the fridge as I come in.

'There's not much to eat here. What are we doing for dinner?'

'Sorry. I guess my girlfriend hasn't been keeping up with the shopping lately.'

He shuts up pretty quick and makes do with a sachet of instant soup. I have a coffee, but I decide after half an hour's awkward silence that spending much time in Randy's company is either going to drive me nuts or end with me killing him. So after booking him into a hotel in New York for tomorrow night and then on a flight to Miami the following day, I make for the Owl's Head.

Ed and Charlie have just moved into their regular table as I walk through the door to the bar. I get myself a beer and order a burger and fries, then go to join them.

'You look like you've got something on your mind, Alex,' Ed says once we've exchanged greetings.

Charlie nods. 'He's right.'

I shrug and take a mouthful of Bud. 'One or two things, maybe. How about you? I haven't seen you in here the last couple of nights.'

'I'm okay. I've just been doing some thinking and I didn't feel like doing it here.'

I decide not to pry. 'Do you feel better for doing it?'

'Yeah, I suppose. It was mostly trying to remember. I looked at some old photos, things like that, thought back to things I'd forgotten a long time ago.'

I nod and thank Bella as she brings my dinner to the table. 'It's a strange thing, memory. I look at this burger and I know I'm hungry, but I can't remember when I last ate.'

And I really can't when I try to think back. Every detail of the case is pin-sharp, everything I've learned or guessed about Gemma's murder and the events connected to it. I can remember everything about Carita Jenner, Adam Webb, the various suspects. But everything else is a grey haze, memories no more tangible than thick smoke. I don't know if I've eaten at all today. I can't remember if I ate yesterday or shaved this morning. I can't remember whether it snowed or not. I can't remember what I was listening to in the car on the way home from Burlington. It's as though I only fully exist when I'm concentrating on something, and the rest of the time I just ghost through the world.

I try a smile. 'My system must be fed up with the all-coffee diet by now, but I guess I haven't felt much like food.'

Ed raises an eyebrow. 'But tonight you do.'

'Yeah, tonight I do. You ever heard the expression, "eat, drink and be merry"?'

'"For tomorrow, we die",' he finishes, nodding, and says nothing more.

After a couple of moments' silence, Charlie decides to steer us on to firmer ground. He contemplates his beer, then finishes half of what's left in one swallow. 'Have you heard about that body they found near Hazen's Notch?' he says.

'Yeah, I heard about it,' I tell him.

'I can't remember the last time we had so much of this sort of thing happening around here.'

Think about the murderer sitting in Gemma's front room right now, probably watching her TV.

'Do you reckon we've got one of those psychopaths living here?' Charlie continues. 'That could explain it.'

'No, I don't think so,' I tell him. Flint's face surfaces in my mind.

'Where's your girlfriend buried?' Ed says, out of the blue.

'Maine. Why?'

'When everything's over, if you catch the guy who killed her and Steph, I think I might like to go and see her sometime, if you don't mind. It seems a bit crazy, but it'd feel like the right thing to do.'

'That's fine with me.'

Charlie seems to sense that his friend isn't his old self and that I've got even more on my mind than usual. He leaves after a couple of drinks, saying something about a TV show he wants to catch. Ed and I sit there for another three hours or so, not talking much. I switch to Coke after the first two beers, figuring I'll need as clear a head as possible tonight and tomorrow. I just hope the caffeine won't be a problem because despite last night's sleepwalking, there's absolutely no way I'm taking sleeping pills with Randy in the house.

It's just gone ten when I leave. I say nothing to Ed about what could happen tomorrow; I figure he'll find out soon enough when it's all over. Snow is falling heavily outside, so it looks like there won't be any tyre tracks for Flint to spot by morning. The wind is picking up as well, and clumps of ice whip against my eyes. The breeze blows the sound of my footfalls back past me, echoing with every step I take. It must be the wind because when I check behind me, there's no one there.

Randy is indeed watching TV when I walk in. I was half-expecting to find him slumped on the couch, but he's perched on the only chair in the living room from which you can see both the door and the windows. I take off my jacket and sit down.

'Where am I going to sleep tonight?' he asks. He sounds slightly nervous again, as though the hours alone have given him time to remember how much trouble he's in. 'On the couch?'

'No, I'm on the couch. You'll have to make do with the kitchen floor. I'll sling some blankets down or something. It won't be too comfortable, but it'll have to do.'

'What about –' he pauses and scratches his ear, dropping his gaze – 'upstairs. Aren't you sleeping in the bedroom?'

'No, and neither are you. You even set foot in it and I'll kick your ass out and let you deal with Flint, the cops and everyone else by yourself.'

'Easy,' he says, holding up his hands. 'I was just asking. I'll be fine on the floor. In fact, if you get those blankets, I think I'll turn in now.'

With Randy out of the way, I try to get some sleep myself. But the thing that stops me now is his presence in the house. For all that he seems to need me, and appears too scared to risk trying anything here, Randy's still a killer. I'm also uncomfortably aware of the fact that he's *Gemma*'s killer. Even the house seems to be reacting, creaking and groaning louder and more violently than I can remember before. The stairs and landing have joined in this unrest, the shrill squeal of their worn boards occasionally adding to the commotion. At first I think it might be Randy moving around, but when I go to check there's no one there and the kitchen door is firmly closed.

Some time in the small hours of the morning – I can't tell when exactly without hunting for my watch because the clock on the mantel needs replacement batteries – I get an impulse to stretch my legs and maybe get some fresh air outside, born perhaps of the frustration of the near-sleepless. I cling to the hope that a minute's movement might bring enough fatigue to drop me into unconsciousness, that a blast of the cold might make me appreciate the couch more.

I open the front door and step out on the thin icy crust blanketing the porch. The flecks of snow settling out of the sky seem to be falling *upwards*, carried by an updraft I can't feel, as though the night is somehow rewinding, time flowing backwards, a chance to unmake all the mistakes for which I can't forgive myself.

From the snow-scattered, TV static blackness I hear footsteps crunching through the ice, a figure approaching. Long dark coat, hood pulled up and over the face, hands scrunched in the pockets. A single lock of hair, pale in the night-time monochrome, drops down from the dark-shrouded face. My throat clenches and I catch myself nearly saying 'Gemma'.

Two, three steps forward to the bottom of the porch steps, lifts her face. Flash of the eyes, reflecting some distant light, from another time, maybe, another world. I try to work out when and where I am – whether this is a memory dredged up from a lost backwater of my mind, a hallucination or a genuine visitation, a temporary crossing of the ephemeral boundary that forever separates us. Gemma and me.

She smiles, quick and pure, the way she used to. I catch a faint scent, metallic like rain or damp steel. Then she's gone. The snow steadies, seeming to hang on the air, then begins to flutter downwards again. Sluggishly, time returns. I go back indoors and close the door behind me.

If I sleep in the hours before dawn, I don't notice it.

27

Crouched by the cracked panes of a rot-laced window as an approaching engine gets louder in the still morning air. My knees feel cramped and the microphone rig on my chest and belt feel uncomfortably out of place, but I keep my concentration on the car. It seems to take an eternity for the vehicle to crawl out of the snow-covered trees and emerge into the open ground by the hotel.

Flint's Taurus glitters in winter sunlight that weakly takes its chance to shine after the night's heavy snowfall. I watch through as little of the window as possible, hoping I can't be seen, as the car stops at the side of the building's former lawn and Flint climbs warily out. He's alone.

I'm lurking in one of the abandoned rooms on the first floor, one of those that leads off the north–south corridor connecting the main stairs with the smaller, narrower flight running up through the tower. The bed is still intact, though in danger of imminent collapse, but the rest of the furniture is nothing more than a pile of shattered timber turned to damp matchwood. It shouldn't be long before Flint passes by, following the route to the top suite. All I have to do then is follow as quietly as possible.

I slip behind the door, briefly running my eyes over the mildewed carpet, trying to see if I've left any trace of my presence. When Flint's muffled footsteps pass by, I wait for the sound to fade and then sneak out in his wake, trying to remember where the loose boards were. Flint heads as expected for the uppermost chamber. I pause outside the door and listen for a moment to the sound of wood scraping over wood, a muffled grunt, then the creak of floorboards followed by a couple of hollow thuds like a coconut being dropped on the floor.

I turn the corner to see that the door leading into the suite's second bedroom is open. Inside, the dresser has been pushed out of place. Squatting next to it on his haunches, his gun and a couple of prised-up floorboards by his right hand, his left delving feverishly into the narrow void beneath, is Flint.

'Good morning, Detective,' I say, stepping as far into the suite as I can without getting too close to the hole in its centre.

Flint whirls around at the sound, snatching up his pistol and whipping it towards me in the time it takes to blink, finger practically squeezing the trigger. There's a faint sheen of sweat on his forehead and his eyes are dark pits. When he sees that it's me, he stops himself from firing and partially lowers the gun. Its barrel is shaking a little.

'Alex,' he says, exhaling heavily. 'What the hell are you doing here?'

'I came to see you. Everything there that should be?' I nod at the exposed floor joists where, I presume, his cash is hidden.

'It was you that called me?'

I shake my head slowly, keeping one eye on the gun. 'No, but I might know who did.'

'So, what do you want?'

'I want to know why you killed Carita Jenner, for one.'

'What?' His face looks blank. Something in the eyes, though. A flicker of betrayed thought.

'Drop the pretence, Flint. It's over. The State Crime Lab has got the steel pipe you beat her to death with. They've got your prints on it, now they're just matching the DNA in the remaining bloodstains.' I don't smile; watching this son of a bitch living and breathing in front of me without going for my Colt is about all I can manage.

Flint stands up slowly. His pistol is still lowered, but I notice his arm isn't entirely relaxed. 'What are you talking about, Alex? Why does some hooker who died years ago matter to you, now?'

'Because she should've mattered at the time. Because she was the start of something. Unless beating a confession out of Isaac Fairley was the true start, in which case she was just your first murder.'

At the mention of Isaac, Flint shakes his head and runs a hand through his hair. His skin is pale, drawn. 'Lawyers,' he says. 'You've been talking to someone about me, I guess. Who?'

I ignore him. 'So you knocked Fairley around to get the statement you wanted. Why'd you kill Carita?'

'I don't—'

'You enjoyed it, right? It felt good. You were a couple of months into suspension, everyone on your back, pissed off at the world. She didn't want to give you any favours, not that night. She should've known better, right?'

'I don't know what you're talking about, Alex.'

'I should've got photos for you. A length of steel pipe like they make handrails out of, about three feet long. A little rusted but nothing too bad. A bunch of old blood at one end. Some hair from where you cracked that pipe against her head in an alleyway behind a liquor store. And fingerprints. Not many, after you wiped it down, but enough.'

Flint blinks. 'Where did you get it from?'

'A mutual acquaintance. Why'd you kill her?'

'It doesn't matter now. Shit just happens, and that night

it happened to her. She was a nobody. I don't deserve all this, not now. One mistake shouldn't fuck up an entire life like this. She'd have been dead before long anyway. What difference did it make?'

I switch tack. Now I've got the confession on tape, I have the questions *I* need answers to. 'What about the others?'

'What?' His face goes blank again. I get the impression Flint would make a decent poker player.

'The Haleys, Stephanie Markham, Adam Webb –' blood begins to pound in my ears – 'and Gemma. What about them?'

'What about them? I didn't kill them.' His eyes are wider, darker. 'I *worked* three of those cases. Alex, what the hell is going on? What are you doing?'

'I want to know what's so goddamn important that you had to kill Gemma for. I want to know what great secret Stephanie Markham saw that meant she had to die. I've looked into your sordid little business, Flint, and I don't see anything I'd take a shit to protect. So explain it to me.'

Fear sparks in his eyes as he raises the gun again. Panicky, aiming high – head rather than heart like he was trained. 'Hold things the fuck there, Alex. I don't know what's up with you or why you're here. Truth be told, I don't care. But I'm taking my money and I'm leaving. I didn't kill your woman. Don't go doing anything stupid.'

I try to estimate the distance between my feet and the hole in the floor, the most tempting escape route. Failing that, I wonder whether I might be able to get *over* the hole, out of his line of fire, and draw my gun before he got through the bedroom door. I flex my legs slightly.

'You aren't going anywhere,' I say.

Flint rolls his eyes, twitching like Woody Allen on speed. '*What?*' he yells. 'You're on your own and there's a cop pointing a gun at you, Alex. Tell me, who's in charge of the situation? What's your grand plan?'

I stay quiet.

'Look at you. You're not thinking straight.' He shakes his head and takes a step forward. 'I'm going to leave now, Alex. Just back up into the far corner, out of the way. Try anything and I *will* shoot you – I'm on kind of a tight schedule here thanks to whoever gave you that pipe.'

'Tighter than you know,' I say, and make the jump.

Flint must think I'm diving for him because I see his index finger whiten, clench. But I'm moving sideways, out over empty air in an arc, aiming for the far side of the hole in the floor. I'm hoping it'll give me enough time out of his line of fire to draw my gun. Looking at Flint's pistol, I know I could be dead by the time I hit the ground again, but it doesn't seem important. Behind me, I feel, rather than see, movement and hear someone shout.

Flint's finger squeezes and the hammer falls. A sharp *crack* like a distant thunderclap or snapping glass. Before my elbow hits the floorboards on the far side of the hole, there's a second gunshot from behind me.

I manage clumsily to roll into a semi-crouch and draw my gun before I take stock of the situation. There's a bullet hole in the wall behind and to my left, right in line with where my head would have been. Sylvia and Ben Paladino are clustered in the doorway, both in firing stances. Smoke is rising from the barrel of her pistol.

Flint yells, 'Fuck!'

'Drop the gun, Detective,' Sylvia yells back. 'It's over. You're under arrest.'

I risk a brief glance towards Flint, leaning out over the hole again so I can see into the bedroom. He's still standing, clutching his right shoulder with his free hand. Blood is already soaking through his suit and running down his sleeve from the ragged hole left by Sylvia's round. It doesn't look like a life-threatening outpouring, but it's serious nonetheless. Good shooting on her part. His pistol hangs limply in his right hand. He lifts it, maybe trying to aim up, maybe trying to switch to his good hand. All that happens is that the blood flows even faster.

The detective glances all around him. I can see his eyes glazing as shock kicks in, along with the realization that his carefully built life has collapsed for good. His gaze flickers across each of us, then back at the walls.

And he drops the gun.

'He'll survive,' Sylvia says as we stand in the snow outside. Flint is being loaded into an ambulance under heavy police escort. Between the LCSD and the State Police, the old town has become busy again. I find myself hoping Ed Markham can see the commotion from Bleakwater Ridge and knows that his granddaughter can finally rest. The old man deserves some peace. Flint's blood has left a trail of dirty red-brown ice leading from the back of the hotel. Sylvia doesn't look flustered by having to shoot her suspect, cool despite the gunfire. I've seen people handle it worse.

'If he doesn't, sometimes shit just happens,' I tell her, smiling to myself.

Sylvia looks away from the ambulance. 'Maybe. You seemed pretty calm, even with what was going on up there.'

'I didn't have much to lose. It helps give you perspective.'

'Good work, Alex,' Sergeant Radford calls out behind us. 'Everyone might still be able to make breakfast.'

I turn as he climbs out of his cruiser and comes to join us. 'No problem,' I say. 'Besides, Sylvia made the collar, not me.'

'Yeah, well, let's put it down as a team effort.' A smile

threatens to break out on his perma-scowl features. 'I thought you might like to hear in person. A State Police search team has already started tossing Detective Flint's house. They won't have detailed results for maybe a day or two, but they've already found a couple of bags of dope – possibly the ones that you found here at the hotel – as well as cash, needles, you name it. It seems as if he was using on the quiet. Half his possessions were in his car, too, so it looks like he was planning on running.'

'I'm surprised no one found out about his habit before.'

'I hear models and such inject between their toes – no needle tracks that way. Maybe he did the same. Probably just an occasional user, too, not a junkie.'

'What about blood tests?'

Radford shrugs. 'You'd have to ask him. I don't know if you have to take them unless you work narcotics. Plenty of ways around it, if you have friends in the right place. I guess you never can be sure about the things people keep hidden.'

The next few hours are filled with making full statements detailing my involvement in the events at the hotel as well as going over my previous work again, just to make sure everything's covered. If the State Police are unhappy about being left out of the loop until the very end by the Sheriff's Department, the fact that it was one of their own under investigation means they keep their mouths shut. Elijah Charman shows up and I keep up my side of the bargain, filling him in on everything I can.

Once my part in proceedings is done, Sylvia gives me a ride home. She smiles as I get out of the car. 'It's been a pleasure to work with you, Alex,' she says. 'I guess I did right by not arresting you for being a nuisance when you first got here.'

'Yeah, thanks for that,' I reply, returning the smile. 'And thanks for everything else, Sylvia. I wouldn't have managed to get as far as I did without you. If I'm ever up here again, I'll expect to see sergeant's stripes at the very least. You'd better have a good explanation if there aren't.'

'You got it. I'll let you know how it all works out. Stay in touch.'

'Sure.' I wave as she drives back up the street towards the intersection. Then I let myself into the old house, now silent and still in the daylight.

Randy has already left, picked up by the driver I hired to take him to New York and his ticket to a new life in the south. If things had worked out differently, I know it could have been Gemma and me on that plane, heading for a vacation in warmer climes. Sitting on a beach, hand in hand. Basking in the warmth of the sun, and each other. We won't have that opportunity, not until some other life. Flint wasn't the only one who took that from me.

I call Rob. Ask him to search the net for me, looking for a particular name and that of any business attached to it.

'Here we go,' he says after a minute or so. 'Bluewave Financial.'

'Is there a number?'

He reads it off while I scribble it on the back of my hand. 'What's this about?' he asks. 'Something to do with the case?'

'In a way. I should be back at work tomorrow. I'll tell you everything then.' I know I won't, even as I say goodbye, hang up on Rob and make the call.

'This is Bluewave Financial Services, Michelle speaking, how may I help you today?' a perky Californian voice says.

'Curtis Marshall, please.'

Vivaldi plays briefly before a second woman's voice says, 'Curtis Marshall's office. How can I help you?'

'I'd like to speak to Mr Marshall,' I say.

'I'm afraid he's in a meeting right now, can I take a message?'

'This is extremely urgent and it's a call Mr Marshall has been waiting for,' I tell her. Picture Randy in the car, listening to the radio as it takes him south. Relaxing, maybe thinking about hooking up with his cousin in Miami. 'It concerns his nephew Joel. If you could put me through, I know he'll be grateful for the interruption. It won't take long.'

'Who should I tell him is calling?'

'You shouldn't.'

More Vivaldi, this time for a minute or so. 'Who is this?' A man's voice, deep, a little hoarse.

'Mr Marshall?'

'Yeah. Who is this?'

'We've never met, Mr Marshall, but I guess right now I'm a friend.'

'What do you want?'

I smile a little, thinking of Randy's look of panic when I pulled my gun on him. 'Same thing you want, Mr Marshall. A guy called Randy Faber stole someone close to you once.'

'What do you know about Joel?' Marshall's voice cracks a little as he says the name. Anger, hope. Same thing.

'Not much. Randy has also taken someone close to me. But he's run out of friends, and I know where he's going to be twenty-four hours from now. If you're interested.'

No hesitation. 'Go on.'

'He's getting on a flight from New York to Miami at ten-thirty tomorrow morning, touching down at thirteen-forty-five. I won't go into details over the phone, but let's say I'd very much like it if Randy got everything he deserved down in Florida. Maybe he'd like to see some familiar faces, being in a strange town and all. I know how eager you've been to catch up on old times.'

'What is this information costing me?'

'Nothing. All I want is peace of mind. You can give me that by making sure Randy doesn't take any more lives.'

There's a slight pause at the other end, then Marshall breathes out and says, 'I'll be more than happy to make arrangements for you. I'll see to it the little shit gets the welcome he deserves and I guarantee you'll have your peace of mind.'

'Thank you very, very much, Mr Marshall,' I say, and mean every word of it.

I pack my meagre things, take out the trash, and make sure I've left the place as tidy as Gemma would have wanted. Before I leave, I take one final look around, breathe in the faint traces of Gemma's scent for the last time.

I've just dropped my bag in the 'Vette's passenger seat when a new-looking maroon sedan pulls up by the curbside. Two middle-aged men get out, both wearing suits. One carries a clipboard, his eyes wandering over the building, and the other has a briefcase. They see me and walk over, careful to keep their footing on the icy driveway.

'Good morning,' says the older and better dressed of the two. He checks his watch. 'Well, just about, anyway. Lindsay Chalmers.'

I give him a little wave but don't shake his hand. 'Alex Rourke.'

A light goes off in his head. 'Ah, you have my deepest condolences for your tragic loss. I'm the attorney handling Dr Larson's estate and this is—'

'Jerry Rendina,' says the second guy.

'He is valuing the house as part of the handling of the will.'

'A realtor and a lawyer. I'm sure there's a joke in there somewhere. Well, do what you have to. I'm going home.'

His eyes stray briefly towards the bag on the 'Vette's seat. Then he sees me watching him and guesses from the distaste colouring my face that I'm not the sort to go stealing my loved one's possessions. He tries an awkward smile. I don't return it. 'Have you been here long?' he says. 'If you have anything to attend to here, please, feel free to stay. I wouldn't dream of intruding.'

'A few days. I had to pick up some of my stuff and deal with a couple of things, but they're taken care of now.' A pair of police cruisers cross the intersection up the road. Chalmers doesn't notice. 'If you need me for anything, here's my card. It's got the number of my cell on it.'

As I reverse the 'Vette on to the road, aiming to drive away from the two men, away from Gemma's empty house and away from Bleakwater Ridge, I think about what I've done to Randy. I think about Flint and how he ordered Randy around, giving him the power to kill people with a single phone call. To me, it does feel good, but not because of the sense of control it gives me. That doesn't appeal. I just feel I owe it to Gemma, and I hope she understands why I've done what I've done.

Then I think some more about Flint's orders to Randy and something clicks. With a cold, sick feeling, I realize what's happened. What I missed.

Grab the phone and call Sylvia. As soon as she picks up I say, 'We got the wrong man.'

28

Screaming down the interstate towards Burlington, the strobes on Sylvia's Impala glaring from the sparse Sunday lunchtime traffic as we pass. There's another cruiser, this time from the State Police, up ahead. Burlington PD will beat us all to Fiona Saric's house, but we won't be far behind.

'I knew there had to be a cop involved in the operation,' I say to Sylvia, raising my voice over the siren. 'I just thought it was Flint. But Fiona knew everything that he knew. It was Carita Jenner that threw me off, and it was Saric's fault I started suspecting Flint for her murder. She had Randy Faber send Reuben Wynne out to North Bleakwater while we were on stakeout so I might make the connection. She told me about Flint being in a violent mood that night and that he had a reputation for being a dirty cop. Randy Faber thought he was working for a guy called Flint, but it was just Saric putting on a low voice over the phone and using his identity in emails to Randy. That's why they never met in person. All along she was setting Flint up to take the blame if it all went wrong. She was smart in the way Damien Ackroyd wasn't – never making it obvious what she was involved with.'

'What gave it away?' Sylvia asks.

'When I spoke to Randy he said "Flint" had a big thing about not taking drugs. Randy was told he'd be killed if "Flint" ever found he'd been doing them. "Flint" told him one of his family was ruined by using drugs. Fiona said her older brother Dan OD'd. I just didn't put the two together until now.'

Sylvia whips the Impala into the right-hand lane as the Burlington off-ramp draws nearer. 'And the real Karl Flint was a junkie himself,' she says.

'Right. He killed Carita Jenner, sure, but that was it. Saric must've followed him after they left the Bar None and seen the whole thing, then picked up the steel pipe from wherever Flint tried to ditch it. She was planning to use him, even then. I guess she gave it to Randy a few days ago because she knew the whole thing was over anyway and had already decided to let Randy and Flint take the heat. Might as well make sure the wrong guy goes down for it. She was probably the "informant" who tipped Flint off about Randy's meeting at the farm. I guess it didn't make any difference to her whether he was killed and we assumed it was over or if he survived to land Flint in it, so long as no one suspected her.'

Ahead of us, the State Police cruiser makes a sharp right. 'Nice of the VSP to let everyone in on this,' I say.

'Damage limitation,' Sylvia replies. 'This is a nasty scandal for them, so they come out looking best if they're co-operative. That's why they were so quick about checking her phone records.'

When Sylvia phoned them earlier, a check on Saric's office line found two calls from a week or so ago to the same cell number used by 'Mr Delaney' – the number that I, and later the VSP, found on Adam Webb's body. The cell phone she asked Randy to leave with her, and which I guess she then planted in Flint's car during one of the changeovers for the stakeout. No wonder he sounded surprised when I called; he didn't even know he had it. This connection to a previous murder, along with natural suspicions over her association with Flint and the VSP's need to crack down visibly on any corruption within its ranks, was enough to bring us all out to look for Saric; they found she hadn't returned to her office after visiting North Bleakwater. Her domestic and cellular phone records would take longer to check. People were already trying to figure out where else she might have gone.

We pull up in front of a pleasant-looking old brick house. Tidy front yard, nice street. Two Burlington PD cruisers are already here, along with a second State Police vehicle. A couple of uniformed cops are standing by the open front door to Saric's house. One of them shakes his head as Sylvia climbs out.

'She's gone,' he calls out.

Sylvia and I don't stick around. As a civilian, my presence is definitely an unwelcome breach of procedure, and besides, with Saric escaped there's nothing more to do here. Sylvia drives us down to the lakeside and buys us both a hot dog and some coffee. We sit there for an hour or so, sporadically talking. All I can think about is how I'm not going to avenge Gemma's murder. I signed Randy's death warrant with a phone call, but Saric is beyond me. Beyond justice. It hurts, almost as much as losing Gemma.

Local radio stations are already running the story of Flint's arrest, and no doubt will cover Saric's disappearance as well. Sylvia walks over to Burlington PD headquarters, a couple of hundred yards away, and persuades them to fill her in on how the search for the fugitive detective, as well as that of her house, are going.

'They've already found a knife and a shirt covered in blood and they're going to have it DNA tested to find out whose it is,' she tells me when she returns.

'It's Stephanie Markham's. Saric told Randy to leave them at the scene so she could dispose of them properly.'

'They also found a bunch of business records on her

computer, all to do with the smuggling operation. I can't understand why she didn't delete them, or get rid of everything else. Apparently, they're expecting to find a whole load of stuff from that house.'

I shrug moodily. 'Why delete them? They don't do her any harm. What does she care if the people she used to work with end up facing the consequences? The same with the knife – that implicates Randy. She's already in trouble. She might as well keep the cops busy following up what she left behind. All this means is that she's not planning on coming back.'

Sylvia nods. 'They've informed the airport, the docks here in Burlington and the Border Patrol that she's on the run, and they're watching the roads. But she'll be long gone, won't she? Probably driven all the way to Montreal by now.'

'That's right.'

'You want me to take you back so you can pick up your car?'

I think for a moment, then shake my head. 'Let's give it a little while yet. I could use some fresh air. How about I go get us both another coffee, then we can head back?'

'Sure.'

I step out into the cold and walk along the periphery of Battery Park. Five minutes, ten, fifteen, I'm not sure. Arrow-straight lines of snowbound trees, bare for the most part, mirrored by paths and the low stone walls of the old fortifications. Beyond it, the lake and the last, unmarked resting place of Stephanie Markham and the Haleys. The wind blows briskly across the top of the bluff and I keep my hands in my pockets. There's a few people out, but only a few and I'm left alone with my thoughts, an array of flat grey feelings that mirror my surroundings perfectly.

*

I reach the Starbucks-variant coffee shop I'm aiming for, and buy two cups, one caff, one decaff. I'm on the way out the door when my phone rings. I figure Syvlia wants to know when I'll be returning so she can go back to work. Fumble both coffees into one hand, then pick up.

'Hello again, Alex,' Fiona Saric says. The door swings shut behind me. 'I hear all hell's broken loose back home.'

'Yeah. What do you want? Unless you're calling to tell me where you are, I doubt I'm interested in what you're going to say.'

'I thought I'd apologize. I overreacted with Dr Larson – I thought she was on to something when she wasn't. That was probably the only mistake I've made in all the time I've been doing this. I shouldn't have killed her; I'd still be in business if I hadn't.'

'Business? Is that what you call it?'

'Just words, really. A question of semantics. Listen, Alex, I still have something that belongs to you. Well, sort of. I thought you might like it back.'

I pause. Somewhere, muffled in the background at the far end of the line, I hear a man's voice calling something in French. The high-pitched tones of a child answer a second later. 'What?' I say eventually.

'You don't know?' She sounds curious.

'No. Don't know, don't know if I care.'

'I thought Randy told you. I've still got some of your girlfriend's jewellery. He took it from her body.'

I frown. 'What?'

'Oh, I suppose her family were given her personal effects, not you, and they wouldn't have known. It's a silver necklace with a flower-bird-thing hanging from it. Very nice, although I'm afraid it's in two pieces now. The bullet went through the chain, cutting it in half.'

I think of Gemma, holding the necklace up to the light when I gave it to her. The last time I saw her. The last time we were together.

'I forgot I had it,' Saric continues. 'If you want it back, you can have it.'

It sticks in my throat, but I ask anyway. 'Where are you?'

There's a slight roar of the wind as she turns or moves. 'You might want to move the phone away from your ear for a moment.'

I do so as a deep, thunderous boom erupts from the earpiece. 'Who did you kill this time?' I ask once the noise has subsided.

She laughs. 'Not me, Alex. Cannon. I don't understand it myself, but I'm told it's a tradition. They fire the cannon out over the river this time every year. A little cold, but everyone's enjoying themselves.'

'Name the place.'

'Figure it out. There aren't too many spots this side of the border that will fit the bill. I'll be waiting.'

Click back to the dial tone as she disconnects.

I make the return journey to Sylvia's cruiser in quick time. She's hunched in the front seat and looks bored as hell, glancing up only when I open the passenger door.

I place the coffee on the dash. 'I don't suppose you know much about tourist attractions in Quebec, do you?' I ask, climbing in beside her.

'What'd you mean?'

'I had a call from Saric a few minutes ago. She was somewhere with a cannon or two by a river. I guess that must be an old fort or something, but I don't know where. I heard people talking French so I assume she was in Quebec.'

Sylvia thinks for a while. 'There's Fort Lennox, not far

from the border. But that's mostly open during the summer. I don't know if they'd be firing off any cannon this time of year.'

'Is that on the road to Montreal?'

'Not quite, but it's close. I don't know anyone from the area, though, so I'm not the best person to ask.'

It's my turn to think a little. And maybe I *do* know someone who'd know the area. I last saw her, shivering and all in black, at Gemma's funeral. I hunt around for the number and call Bethany.

'Yes, I might be able to help,' she says when I've explained the situation. 'I've been to visit Mike quite a few times since he started working in Montreal.'

'I'm looking for a place, probably an old fort, near a river or lake.'

'There's several along the Richelieu River. They're tourist attractions now.'

I cross my fingers. 'How about one where it's traditional to fire a cannon at –' I check my watch – 'two o'clock. I don't know if it's just today or every day.'

'Fort St Marc,' she says straight away. 'I can't remember why they do it, but I know it's the anniversary of something that happened in the war with the British. They have a fête, fireworks, everything. It's a pretty well-known festival. Second-to-last weekend in November. Mike was planning on taking me there this year, but we couldn't sort it out.'

'Whereabouts is it?'

An hour and a half later, I turn the 'Vette into the visitors' parking lot next to the hulking stone bulwark of Fort St Marc. The place looks busy enough. Carnival atmosphere, almost, with everyone wrapped up warm. Stepping out of the car and hauling my coat around me, I feel isolated, cut off from the people milling to and fro. Exposed. My gun's back in the US with Sylvia – I don't have a permit to carry one in Canada and don't fancy getting caught with it – and there's no backup from the RCMP. I haven't even told them. For a start, Saric is likely to be long gone. If she's not, no way she'd be stupid enough not to watch for the authorities and vanish at the first sign of trouble. Besides, I'm not entirely certain this *is* the right place.

I join the weekend visitors to the old fort, heading through the gates and up on the flat-topped ramparts. The central courtyard is alive with food stalls – most of which are adopting a pretence of simple period stuff – as well as entertainers of all sorts. The sun is going down and I guess it won't be long before the fireworks start. From where I am on the western bastion I've got a great view of a sweeping bend in Richelieu River, everything for at least a mile in almost every direction.

My gaze turns inwards, though, as I scan the faces of the people ambling around below me, looking for Saric. Not easy, not with so many scarves, hoods, big coats. Plenty of ways to hide. She could be down there, but I don't get the feeling she is. I've switched to the visitors on the ramparts when my cell rings.

'I was beginning to think you weren't coming,' Saric says. 'I thought I'd got it wrong again and you couldn't work out where I was.'

I twist and turn, flicking my eyes over everyone in the fort, looking for anyone holding a phone.

'I nearly couldn't. Nearly didn't bother, either.'

One, two. Deep in conversation over their cells. Both men.

'What, can't see me?' she says.

No point hiding it. 'Not yet.'

'You're looking in the wrong place. Turn around.'

The rampart behind me is empty all the way to the edge. Beyond, though, on the far side of the river, a figure is leaning against a dark car parked by the side of the track that runs above the bank. The figure waves.

'Hi, Alex,' Saric says in my ear.

'I thought you might have had the guts for a face-to-face.'

'Don't be stupid. I thought it might be fun to see you one last time, but I'm happy doing that through binoculars. And don't even think about trying to get round here in time to catch me. The nearest bridge is three miles away and I'm gone as soon as I see you leave.'

'Where's Gemma's necklace?'

'The people organizing that shindig have a property collection point. There's a package addressed to you, but no postage on it. I told them someone must have forgotten it on the way to the post office.' Her tone changes. Nasty, controlling. 'Go fetch, boy.'

Before I turn away, I ask, 'At what point did you stop being a cop, turn your back on everything you should have stood for?'

'I saw that big old house that Damien Ackroyd had, all the things he owned, and I thought about my idiot junkie brother.' She sighs. 'He must have known the dope was killing him, but he still had to keep buying it. Dealing didn't appeal to me, but that kind of customer demand was real tempting, as was the money, so I decided to go into delivery. Karl was an easy fall-guy if I ever needed one. I was already giving it serious thought when he killed that hooker. When he made a half-assed attempt to wipe that pipe down and hide it in a dumpster a couple of blocks away, he became my "get out of jail free" card. It's all been roses ever since.'

'Well, I sure am sorry to ruin everything for you.' Looking

at her, everything tastes bitter. Only a few hundred yards away, but it might as well be a million miles. And I know she's enjoying herself.

'Don't sweat it, Alex. It had to happen eventually. I'd already made up my mind to fold the operation, that's why I let the pipe go. When Randy called me this morning, I knew it was all over for good. I phoned Karl pretending to be a mob guy who was grateful he'd whacked Carita, that the cops were coming for him but that I'd seen to it there was enough money waiting for him that he could go on the run safely. He's so easy to control, once you know what buttons to push.'

'You were in it for the cash, huh? Was it worth killing for?'

'Alex, do you have any idea how it feels to be top of the heap? Do you think someone with my talent should spend thirty years investigating burglaries and auto theft and then retire on a police pension? Really?'

'No. I'd never have let someone like you join the force in the first place. I'd have let you rot under the rock where you were living.' I wish I had a gun, Randy's rifle, anything. Grab that cannon they were firing earlier, put it to use. Anything at all, if it could only reach her. Hit her with the full fury I have balled up inside. Give her what she deserves. But I can't.

'Do you know how much *fun* it is to know you can have someone killed just because you want it to happen? And when I've done it, they vanish and I still get invited to all the department's parties. I only wish it was possible to drop it into conversation. "How was my day? Well, I did a couple of hours at the office, then I had a couple of tourists stabbed to death, then I did lunch. How was yours?" Too bad it doesn't work that way.'

The line goes quiet, although I can hear her breathing. When she speaks again, her tone is lighter, almost playful. 'You'll never bring her back. You know that, don't you? You can't get back what I took from you.'

I hang up. Try to forget her words, the truth of them, the lines of bitter, stinging ice they leave all the way through me. I go to collect Gemma's shattered necklace and face the drive south knowing Fiona Saric is well and truly beyond my reach.

Sylvia meets me back in Burlington and returns my Colt to me. She doesn't ask what happened over the border, and I don't tell. I don't show her the split links of silver stained black with Gemma's blood. I don't share the conflicting things they mean to me – at once a reminder of the woman taken from me, and of the fact that the woman responsible for taking her got away.

In the evening I take Elijah and Neal out for the steak dinner I promised them. I stay quiet, not talking much. After a return overnight visit to the E-Z-Rest, I say my goodbyes and leave Vermont, but I don't head for Boston. I take US-2 east, all the way to Bangor, Maine. The cemetery there is covered in a fresh coat of thick snow and more falls in slow, heavy flocks from the charcoal-grey sky above. From the top of the low hill where Gemma lies buried, I can no longer see my car, the wall that lines the cemetery, nothing but snow falling against the blanket of white beyond, cutting this place off from the world outside. I look down at the new, clean stone marker, cold tears studding the corners of my eyes like shards of glass. Then I think back and remember her face, the way she moved, the warmth of her body. Her eyes, shining in the light. Her voice, her laugh. I feel her moving against me, feel her hand brushing against my cheek, her hair on my shoulder.

I stand there in the snow with my eyes shut, holding Gemma long and tightly for the last time, the touch of ghosts upon my skin.

WINTER'S END

John Rickards

(Penguin, £6.99)

They have the body of a slaughtered woman.
They have a half-naked man standing over her.
They have no idea how to make him talk.

And so they call in ex-FBI interrogator Alex Rourke to the traumatized Maine town of Winter's End. The Boston Private Investigator knows the place well - it's where he grew up. But as Rourke probes the mind of the enigmatic 'Nicholas', he is forced to re-examine his hometown and his own past – and what he finds is a place built on secrets.

Strange things have been happening in Winter's End. The question is why. And if the man in custody does hold the answers to crimes both present and past, then Alex will have to get to them – and quickly. Because it soon becomes clear that what Nicholas has been waiting for from the beginning – is Alex Rourke.

'A clever, gripping and original thriller' *Time Out*
'Very spooky, very good' *Daily Mirror*
'A chilling puzzle with a devastating outcome' *Scotsman*